WAER

Meg Caddy was the 2013 Young Writer-in-Residence at the Katharine Susannah Prichard Writers' Centre, and has been mentored by fantasy author Juliet Marillier. In 2013, *Waer* was shortlisted for the Text Prize.

WAER

MEG CADDY

TEXT PUBLISHING MELBOURNE AUSTRALIA

textpublishing.com.au

The Text Publishing Company
Swann House
22 William Street
Melbourne Victoria 3000
Australia

First published in 2016 by The Text Publishing Company

Typeset in Bembo Book 11.75/15.75 by J & M Typesetting
Cover and page design by Imogen Stubbs
Map by Simon Barnard

Printed in Australia by Griffin Press, an Accredited ISO AS/NZS 14001:2004 Environmental Management System printer

National Library of Australia Cataloguing-in-Publication entry :
Creator: Caddy, Meg, author.
Title: Waer / by Meg Caddy.
ISBN: 9781922182210 (paperback)
9781925095210 (ebook)
Target Audience: For young adults.
Subjects: Historical fiction.
Fantasy fiction.
Dewey Number: A823.4

This book is printed on paper certified against the Forest Stewardship Council® Standards. Griffin Press holds FSC chain-of-custody certification SGS-COC-005088. FSC promotes environmentally responsible, socially beneficial and economically viable management of the world's forests.

To my mother and brothers.
Dad can be in the next one,
if he behaves himself.

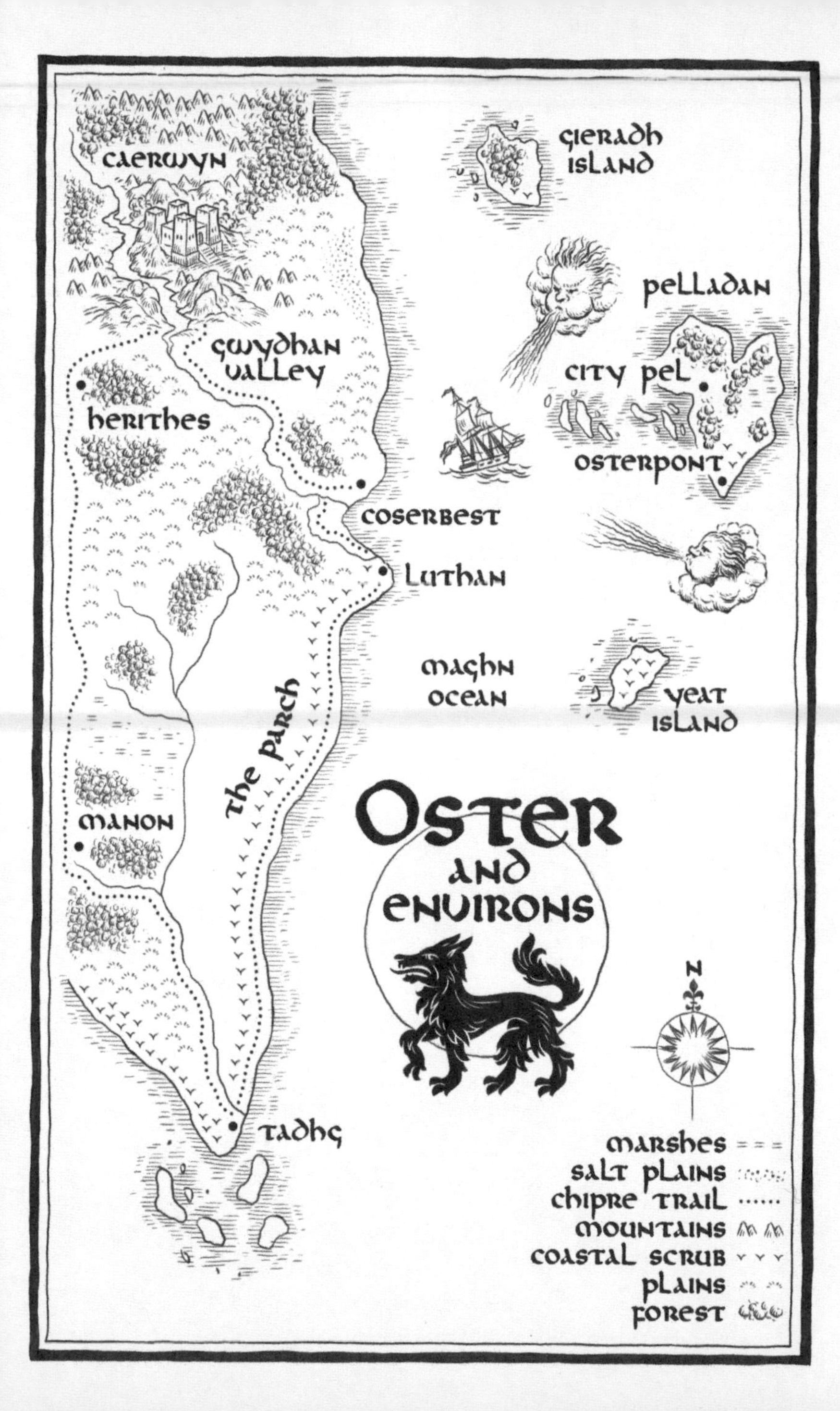
Caerwyn
Gieradh Island
Pelladan
Gwydhan Valley
City Pel
Herithes
Osterpont
Coserbest
Luthan
Maghn Ocean
Yeat Island
The Parch
Oster and Environs
Manon
N
Tadhg
marshes
salt plains
chipre trail
mountains
coastal scrub
plains
forest

Kaebha

Winter was on its way. Cold, hard winds hit the fortress of Caerwyn, perched upon a sheer cliff face and framed by craggy peaks. Narrow strips of flora fringed the river that gnawed at the gorge below Caerwyn. The river flowed fast through the ranges, then opened and slowed as it travelled south-east through the Gwydhan Valley and on to the eastern coast of Oster.

As night fell, something stirred the darkness. Birds shrieked, rising into the air. The peace cracked and fell apart. Flashes of crimson uniform cut the smothering black of the woods. The smell of smoke lifted through the boughs and choked the leaves. A drum beat out a steady pulse as soldiers tore over dead leaf matter, hacking their way through the web of forest.

The prisoner ran.

Branches ripped at her face and clothes. Scratches latticed

her pale limbs, and the moon illuminated her in spite of her attempts to keep to the shadows. Behind her, soldiers pounded their way through the mountain forests. Her legs burned. Sweat poured down her face. Her chest was knotted with snarls and whimpers, sounds she could not choke down.

The river surged below her. She reached the ledge; stood there, leaning out over the water. A steep drop. If she jumped here, the river might be deep enough – she might survive the fall, but not what came after. Rapids, waterfalls, rocks.

She looked over her shoulder. Torches glowed through the trees. Her limbs shook, sweat beaded on her brow and stained her clothing. Her skin cooled and became clammy. She edged towards the open space that gaped before her and stood frozen. Torn.

As a branch snapped behind her, she stepped forward, wobbling as her bare, bloodied toes curled over the ledge. A voice halted her. Cold. Familiar.

'Stop,' ordered Kaebha.

The prisoner refused to look around. Kaebha's lip curled. It would be a waste if the wretch jumped. She could still be salvaged.

'Stop,' Kaebha said again. 'Come here. Come back.'

'I don't need you,' she spat.

'Oh, you do,' Kaebha replied. 'You need me, and you need our master.'

'Your master. Not mine. He was never mine.'

'And you believe that?'

The river. The shouts of the pursuing soldiers.

'You would do better to turn yourself in.' Kaebha's voice was almost kind.

The prisoner flinched. She shook her head, teetering towards the edge. Kaebha snarled; her quarry bled and swayed. Daeman Leldh had left his marks on her.

Kaebha took a breath, tried again to reason with her. 'The longer you run, the worse it will be.' Her mouth twisted like the edge of a knife, hard and lethal. 'He will break you.'

'He already has.' She did not look away from the river. 'Go, Kaebha. I want nothing more to do with you.'

'You would never have survived if not for me!' A spark of anger kindled in Kaebha's eyes.

The prisoner looked over her shoulder, eyeing the flames nearing her; Leldh's men were coming, hunting her down.

'I should have died, then,' she said.

'Do not be a fool.' The anger was gone. Kaebha could control herself. She softened her voice once more, a coaxing note rolling off her tongue like warmed honey. She stretched out a hand. 'Do not throw your life away. Stay with me.'

The fugitive wavered. If she lingered, Kaebha would win her over. They both knew it.

The prisoner stepped forward, let herself drop through the air, her body twisting into the still night. Kaebha let out a loud curse, jerked away and disappeared into the darkness.

When the young woman hit the water, she barely made a splash.

Lowell

I stood at the top of the hill, and let the smells of the Gwydhan Valley wash over me. The rain of the night before. The grass, long enough to brush my knees. Sheep. The faint traces of waerwolves who had passed through recently. The familiar scent of our family earth. Then, stronger, the smell of soap, and clean clothes, and honey. It was unmistakably a *young* smell; not that of an infant, but not so many years from it.

My brother.

Kemp stood a few paces behind me. He struggled to keep still. I knew the wolf inside him – the *pup* inside him – was desperate to get out. Kemp had only Shifted a few times in his young life, and it was still a question of instinct at this point. Later, he would learn to Shift at will, and would be able to control the wolf when it emerged. Our mother and father would be glad when he stopped chewing table legs and harrying the sheep.

'Now?' he demanded. He hopped from one foot to the other.

'Not yet.'

'*Lowww* –' He drew my name into a whine. He scratched at his skin, already feeling the prickle of stiff black fur, impatient to break through.

While Kemp was so young, it was important that someone was always with him when he Shifted. Otherwise he might go wild. Forget to Shift back to his human shape. Attack our sheep or our neighbours' livestock. There were always accidents in the Valley, but fortunately the community had enough experience to take them in stride. One savvy man named Brom had made quite a business breeding rabbits and selling them to local families so we could release them into the wild and let our young chase them down. He was branching out now into pheasants and hopping-mice for the older children.

Someone from our family tried to take Kemp hunting at least twice a week. On this occasion, my father was occupied with the flock, and my mother was at the worship-house honouring the last month of autumn with homage to the deities. So I was left with the pup.

'*Now,* Lowell?'

I turned to face Kemp. He favoured our father; short and tubby, with a mop of dark curls and a stubborn chin. He had inherited our father's restlessness and impatience, also. Particularly his impatience with me.

'What must you learn?' I asked, as I asked every time we went on these outings.

His shoulders slumped. 'Patience. Are you *ever* going to let me Shift?'

The childish despair made me smile. I put a hand on his shoulder and steered him around. I pointed at the creatures drifting across the grass in front of us, pathetic bundles of rain-sodden wool. White at birth, now they were older they had achieved a filthy brown. They were the ugliest of creatures in winter. When summer came, we would shear the ugliness away, turn it to honest use, and reveal the good creatures underneath. They smelled of oil, and grass, and thick mud.

'Do you see the sheep?'

'Yes.'

'Then as a wolf, you will also be able to see them. I doubt you could kill one, little brother, but our parents do not want us injuring any, either.'

'I will not chase them.'

'Considering the chickens you managed to kill last time, forgive me if I doubt your self-control.' Kemp, staying with friends down the Valley, had Shifted out of turn and run wild in their poultry. Our parents had paid for the damage with a bale of fine wool – and considerable embarrassment.

I steered Kemp down the hill. 'We are to go to the river, and you can hunt rabbits.'

'Did you hunt rabbits?'

'Of course. Well, I was supposed to. The first time I was taken out I snapped at a donkey's heels and got a kick in the head. I had to be stitched, even after Shifting back into this shape.' Shifting would heal most open wounds, unless they were inflicted by silver. 'When I teach you, Kemp, it is because I know from experience what *not* to do.'

The story of my failure cheered him up, and we walked towards the forest and the river. It was a pleasant walk, for ours was the nicest land-plot in the Valley. Our house stood at the top of a hill near the north end, close to the mountain-pass and the river-mouth, so any mountain traders came past our home first and we saw the best of their goods before they were sold.

Most importantly, it was quiet. Our Valley was not what one would call a crowded den. There were barely four hundred inhabitants in the village itself, and only a handful of families like ours on the outskirts. To my shame, even these few people overwhelmed me when I visited the village market. I preferred the rolling hills and the hushed glades.

The trees closed over our heads. I breathed in the dark aroma of oak and pine. Kemp's face turned upwards, his nose twitching. I knew he could smell the rabbits, the squirrels, the river running along the muddy bank ahead of us. I released his shoulders and crouched close to the ground. I could smell his excitement. He dropped beside me, quivering, his small hands sinking into the dirt and wet leaves.

'*Now?*' There was a kind of agony in his voice.

'Now, little brother.'

Kemp shed his clothes and flung his body forward. I heard a crunch of bone, his whimpers as his limbs contorted. There was nothing I could do to help his transition. The first few Shifts were always hard. Kemp dropped to his side, half-Shifted, panting as thick black fur pushed through his skin. The winter coat was a challenge for the younger ones. Kemp's jaw grew long, hands twisted and shaking. His small, pink fingernails had stiffened, blackened, and were slowly pushing outwards. I reached over and stroked a hand across his soft head. He whined and squirmed on the ground.

'A little further, Kemp.'

A strangled noise, and then – it always seemed sudden – he was a wolf. His black fur was glossy, his ears alert, and his tail thumping in the mud. He rolled to his feet and bounded, almost bursting from his new skin with the elation of being wild and new. It was always this way. I smiled and removed my own clothes. Over the years, I had been taught to control the animal aspect of my nature, but control did not lessen the joy. For me, the Shift was easier. My muscles laced themselves into their new position. My bones clicked smoothly until they were secure. I felt air rush into me, and life surge through my body. The dirt at my feet moved. Each Shift expelled energy, pushed it into the world. It was why we rarely Shifted indoors. I had tried it as a child and knocked over chairs and tables, breaking several of my mother's ornaments.

As soon as I was a wolf, I lifted my head and ran to Kemp. He gave a cracked, puppy-voiced howl. He felt it as much as I did, the mad delight of being wolf, being part of a pack. He chased me, tried to catch my tail in his teeth. I knocked him over and roughed with him. He rolled, fell clumsily, and leapt to his paws again to dance around me. I had a distant memory of doing the same thing to my father, and receiving a good nip on the ear for it.

Kemp stopped, mid-leap. He crashed to the ground in a heap and his tail went stiff, fur rising as he caught the scent of rabbit. He launched away from me and darted through the trees. I raced after him, faster as a wolf than I could hope to be as a man. The forest was alive with scents and sounds. Wet branches slapped our faces and shoulders. Kemp, his legs an ungainly length, scrabbled through the undergrowth and crashed into trees and bushes as he went. I cleared logs, loving the rush of cool air. I caught a glimpse of a rabbit and it was all I could do not to chase it down and take it. Instinct warred with intellect, but this was for Kemp. Kemp had to learn how to hunt away from the farms. I whined, but held myself back.

Kemp spotted the rabbit. He howled again and pounced after it as I circled around to drive it towards him. The rabbit was frantic, ducking back and forth under logs and behind bushes. Kemp harried it, not fast enough to make the catch and not canny enough yet to trap it. I slunk, low and slow as I pushed the rabbit towards him. Kemp did not notice. All his senses were directed at the small creature. I knew from experience, that every inch of his furred body would be screaming *Food!* He was too young and untried to ignore it.

Kemp burst from a bush, spraying leaves, twigs, and dirt through the air. The rabbit screamed and leapt towards me. I started forwards, and…

The smell of blood.

Waer blood.

The rabbit darted away unharmed.

Kemp went through the slow process of a Shift in order to berate me.

'We almost had it!' he complained. 'Why did you let it go?'

I changed shape as well, needing all of my human mind to work through this. 'Hush,' I told him. 'Concentrate, Kemp. What do you smell?'

He frowned, and lifted his nose. 'Rabbit?'

'Concentrate.'

He stilled. 'Blood.'

'What kind of blood?'

His voice dropped. 'Blood like ours?'

'Go and get our clothes.'

Kemp ran. I tried to focus on the source of the blood. Strong; close. It was easy to tell waer blood: I felt an uncomfortable connection to it. A deep familiarity. When Kemp returned with our clothes, I pulled mine on without saying a word. He looked pale now, and frightened. I put my hand on his shoulder, holding him steady as I followed the scent toward the river.

The river was flowing fast, driven by nights of rain. I stopped Kemp a few yards back and held up a hand. If someone was dead, I did not want him to see. *I* did not want to see, but this was Sencha family land. If someone was injured here, it was our responsibility to help them.

The stench of blood nearly overwhelmed me. I bent and braced my hands on my knees. I did not want to lose my stomach in front of Kemp. It would frighten him even more.

'Lowell?'

'Stay where you are, Kemp.'

'*Lowell.*'

I turned and saw where he was pointing. My stomach dropped, clenched in a cold fist.

'Look away,' I said. Kemp turned away, but I saw his face crumpling. I tried to put aside my horror. Our land, our responsibility. I forced my legs to move. They were heavy and shaking. It seems strange to fear the dead, but I could not throw off revulsion.

The body slumped on the bank. Sodden, legs still hanging in the water where the river had widened and slowed. I approached and crouched. I forced my hands to touch the person's head. I felt blood there at once, sticky and thick. My stomach turned over. I lowered my eyes to offer silent prayers. *O Hollow, lord of the dark night, scourge and hunter, we implore thee; rest the wandering spirit. O Freybug, our lady of healing, spirit of the dawn, we implore thee…*

The person stirred.

I jumped back. It took me a moment to calm my mind. Not dead, thank Freybug, not yet dead.

'Kemp!' I turned to him. 'Go and get Father. Mother too, if she is back from worship. Quick!'

Kemp scrambled through the trees. I neared the body by the water again. There was a lot of blood, but on closer inspection it seemed the damage was not as bad as I had thought. The head wound and the water, the cold, were my biggest concerns, though I suspected a dislocated shoulder as well.

I pushed damp hair away from the face, and realised the person on the bank was a woman – and not a woman from the Valley. She was too fair to be one of our people. I took a thin reed and held it by her face. The slight movement told me she was, at least, able to breathe. I removed my coat and settled it over her. I did not want to move her in case I worsened some unseen damage.

I knelt in the mud, ignoring the wet that seeped through my clothes. We often had traders and chipre-folk come through the Valley with their wares, but this was different. What was she doing in the river? How far had she travelled, and for what purpose? I looked over my shoulder, towards the mountains. They towered over us, dark and distant. Beyond them, Caerwyn, the stronghold of the northern mountains. The traders whispered of chipre-folk going missing in the area, and had started taking longer routes to avoid it. Once, during the summer, I had even seen soldiers from a distance as they marched along a path in the mountains framing the Valley. I shivered, wondering if the stranger had come from Caerwyn.

A cold hand gripped my elbow and I yelped. I stared at the stranger, read the fear in her pale eyes as she met my gaze, or – no, looked through it. It did not seem she really saw me.

'Kee vah,' she hissed.

'What?' I tried to pry my arm away, but her grip was surprisingly strong. She lifted her head, shuddered, and spoke again.

'Kee vah.'

I took her hand and uncurled the fingers from my elbow. She dropped back, but did not lose consciousness. Her eyes remained wide and staring, not taking anything in. I feared she was mad.

'Lowell.' Our father ran down the hill and knelt by me in the mud and I edged away to give him space. He searched for the stranger's pulse. She gave no indication of noticing. Her eyes were closed again.

'Is she badly injured?' my father asked.

'Her head wound looks serious. There is a lot of blood. She is half-drowned. She roused herself and spoke to me, but I...' I shook my head, uneasy. 'I could not understand what she said. Kee vah.'

'Perhaps she does not speak the Trading Tongue.' *Gwen, help me.* The last remark was a soul-whisper to my mother, still out of earshot as she slid along the bank to join us. I could barely hear it.

Mother must have been on her way home from the worship-house, to get here so swiftly. She arrived out of breath and paused for a moment to collect herself. Then she too knelt, ran a hand gently along the stranger's back, checking for damage. Once she was assured there were no breaks there she nodded at my father and together they lifted the stranger.

I heard a sniff and looked over at Kemp. He was holding tears back valiantly, but they stood in his eyes. His nose was swelling and his chin wrinkled. Our father shot him a disapproving glance. Ioan Sencha had no time for tears.

I went to Kemp and wrapped my arms about him.

'Well done,' I said. 'You were brave. You did exactly as I asked you to.'

He was aware of Father's gaze. He squared his shoulders, tried to fit an adult's stance into a child's body. 'Who is she, Lowell?' he asked. 'How did she get here?'

I had no answers for him.

Lowell

I sat with the stranger. By all rights she should have been dead; I could not fathom how she had not drowned in the river, with such a severe head-wound. I thanked Freybug for delivering her safe to us. I thanked our capricious lady of luck, Felen, for washing her onto the bank. I thanked the fearsome Hollow for turning a blind eye and sparing her from the grey earth.

I prayed, most of all, she would wake and recover. We were responsible for her now. Her life had been put into our hands. It was our duty to ensure we treated it like the treasure it was.

Mother checked the stranger for injuries. She was reluctant to disclose the information to me, but I pressed her until she did and regretted it almost instantly. Burns, long scars, brand marks. A sprained ankle. Places where the bones had broken and never fully reset. Some missing teeth. The fresh wound on her head, and older scars parting her hair. A dislocated shoulder.

The day after we found her, she stirred again. Her eyes opened. Glazed, green, unseeing. I tried to speak to her. Faltered when it became clear she did not hear me. She convulsed, thrashed, called out without words, and I backed to the door. I had no knowledge of healing. I shouted for my mother, but by the time she arrived the stranger had slipped back into a deep sleep.

For the next week, the stranger woke often. She lay like the dead, or shook like a ripple on water. Eating was an effort. Often, she vomited. My mother bound her head and tended to her other wounds, but there was no swift recovery, and it seemed the injuries were beyond our capabilities. In those days, I missed almost every Dawn Worship. Mother was troubled, of course, to have me miss the services, but I was secretly relieved. It always troubled me that in that place of reflection and healing I felt hemmed in, short of breath. Unsettled by the good folk.

Each morning, I performed a humble imitation of the Dawn Worship rituals at home with the stranger – quietly, for fear my father would think it disrespectful. I lit a candle and set it upright in the water-bowl, the flame a bare inch from the shimmering surface. I burned a sprig of rosemary in the candle, and let the ashes fall into the water in homage to Freybug, born from a rosemary bush. Finally, I blew out the candle, sipped from the bowl and trickled some of the water over the stranger's brow. It was a bitter brew, but all elements of life joined in the water. Drinking it was a giving of thanks. I did not force the stranger to drink; I did not know what faith she kept or whether, as I had heard was the case with people from Luthan, she had no faith at all. Nevertheless, she needed all the protection she could get.

I saw something more than the ordeal of the river in the stranger's eyes, but I could not explain that to my parents. With no cooperation from the woman, not even her name, it was impossible to tell what traumas she had suffered. My father dismissed her as simple. My mother was tempted to do the same, but I convinced her to consult the village healer. The healer said the head wound had addled the stranger's brain, and believed we should petition the landlord to transport her from the Valley to an asylum of sorts.

The thought horrified me. No madhouse could be more healing than our green Valley.

'Moth Derry,' I finally suggested. Mother looked over her shoulder at me, calm brown eyes thoughtful in her long, weathered face.

My father, shining his shoes at the table, snorted.

'What about her?' Mother asked.

'Moth and Dodge are usually in Herithes at this time of year. It is not so far from here, and the mountain trails from the south are still passable.'

Mother went back to washing the dishes, but I could see she was thinking it over. I glanced at Father. He thought Moth Derry's husband was a frivolous vagrant and that Moth was a fool for marrying him. But he was busy rubbing at a spot the polish had left on the table, probably hoping Mother did not see.

'It will take days for a bird to reach them,' Mother said. 'Longer still for them to get here. I do not know if we can care for this young woman until then, Lowell.'

'Let me care for her.'

She lifted an eyebrow. 'Do you think it appropriate?' she asked, in a tone strongly suggesting it was not.

My father's expression suggested it even more strongly.

I spoke before he could, struggling to keep my voice level. 'She is injured and she needs help. Sending her out of the Valley, too weak for the journey, *that* would be inappropriate. She is not a lunatic, Mother. She is just hurt, and frightened.'

Mother folded her arms. Almost as tall as me. I had been blessed with her height, but not with her grace. Mother was all angles and worn hands, but her eyes were gentle.

'And if Madam Derry recommends she be taken away?' Father demanded, breaking the silence.

'She is a healer of renown. I would defer to her expertise.'

'Hm.' Mother leaned against the kitchen table. 'Go outside and wash the bandages in the basket, then,' she sighed. 'The wound is healing, in an ugly sort of way. We need to keep it clean.'

I called Kemp along with me, and we went outside to do as Mother asked. When I closed the door, I could hear Mother and Father beginning to argue on the other side.

It was a sunny day; I thought it might be the last bright day of the season. I did not make Kemp handle the bandages, but it was good for him to be playing in the sunlight before the weather turned dark and bleak. The last week and a half had been tense and busy, and he had been craving company.

'Lowell?' he said as I soaked the cloths. 'Is she from the Valley?' There was no need to ask who he was talking about.

'No, I think not.'

'Then why is she a waer?'

'Not all waer come from the Valley, Kemp.'

He had a carved set of soldiers whittled by our father, but they stood unattended on the grass. His brown eyes were fixed on me. 'I thought we were the only ones.'

'No. There are waer in the southern desert, near where Dodge Derry comes from. But they are...different from us.'

'How?'

'Much bigger, and more savage. They do not cook their kills, they take meat raw. And some others are not...born waer.'

'*How?*'

It was difficult to explain to him. I had only a basic grasp of the idea myself. 'Waer blood is stronger than human blood. If the two are mixed, waer blood takes over, and so the human becomes waer.' It had caused rumour and superstition outside the Valley, my mother had told me. Stories of maddened waer with rotting teeth biting humans. *Turning* them. Many from towns such as Herithes, to our south-west, believed just a single bite from a waer could do it. We avoided such places, but Mother had once told a story of newly turned waer coming to the Valley for help with Shifting. There had been none in my lifetime. Now I wondered briefly whether this was the stranger's story. Had she intended to seek our aid in the Valley, and simply fallen into the river? Or had she been carried there by chance?

'If Madam Derry comes,' Kemp's mind had skittered ahead, 'will Mister Derry come too?'

'I imagine so. I have never seen one without the other.'

Kemp whooped and ran off; Dodge Derry was coming, and that meant stories. I finished washing the cloths and pegged them out to dry. Dodge would entrance Kemp with tales of the golden Kudhienn, who had once enslaved all of Oster. If we were lucky, he might even slip in the Watchers when our father was not listening. Father thought the Watcher stories inappropriate for children, but in my mind the gods were gods and the Watcher fables were mere stories, told to entertain. And instruct – they were about duty, and cooperation, and defending the innocent. About balance, which was so important to us. Of course when Dodge launched into the deeds of the Assassin, the Healer and the Dealer, the instruction tended to take second place to the entertainment, but I couldn't see the harm in it.

The washing completed, I went to our vegetable garden to gather food for lunch. Father had taken Kemp fishing early that morning and brought in several fat trout that I hoped we could coax the stranger into eating. She could sit and hold cutlery, but her hands shook too much to guide the implements, and sometimes the food would not reach her mouth at all. I stooped to pull some carrots and leeks, and as I straightened, I caught the smell of horse.

I peered down the hill, hastily wiping my hands on my tunic. Horses meant wealth or worldliness in the Valley. The waer scent made most horses nervous; to find a young one with a gentle breeding line and train it was expensive. As this one, a fine-boned grey, stepped up the hill, I recognised the straight back and simple black cloak of Lord Alwyn. Our liege, technically a nobleman of Herithes, did not affect the extravagant clothes of his peers. Nor did he look at us, as they did on their infrequent journeys through the Valley, as if we were sheep-ticks. Alwyn treated us with courtesy and respect. More importantly, as Father always said, he taxed us fairly, and was there with his coat off and his sleeves rolled up if there was a storm or a landslip.

I set the vegetables down and went to the fence to meet him.

'My lord.'

'Young Master Sencha.' I doubted he remembered my first name, but he knew my family. 'We are having fine weather today.'

'Yes, my lord. Are you having a pleasant ride?'

'Indeed. Thank you.' He seemed less direct than usual, his eyes roaming the garden.

'Can I offer you some vegetables, my lord? Our garden is doing well this year.' He had no need of vegetables from us, of course, but it was a mark of respect.

'Thank you, no.' And it was a equally polite of him to refuse. We were not starving, but we had more need of the food than he did. Alwyn hesitated, then swung himself off his horse. Holding the reins in a slender hand, he approached me. 'I hear you had something of an adventure down by the river, Master Sencha. Your father reported it to my steward four days ago, as was proper.'

'Yes, my lord.'

'And you now have a. . .visitor staying with you.'

'Yes, my lord.' I frowned. I had never seen him so anxious before. Lord Alwyn exuded calm most days, even when we battled the elements or stood in the face of a crop failure; even when he was furious, like the day the old blacksmith went on trial for beating his wife and children. I had watched Alwyn's pleasant face closely that day, as the blacksmith's wife described how she had been abused. His expression did not change, but his eyes were black with rage.

'I have received a concerning missive, Master Sencha. From a keep in the mountains. You know of Caerwyn.'

The military stronghold to the north-west of the Valley. A few years ago there had been some issues between the soldiers and the traders trying to use the mountain-pass. For a while, there had been talk of Caerwyn using the Valley as a training-ground for the new recruits. Alwyn had petitioned Herithes, and after some months our worries had been assuaged. We had heard little from Caerwyn since. Until now.

'I do, my lord, but not intimately.'

'I received the message from that location this morning.' He pulled a letter from his coat, but did not unfold it. He paused, uncertain, weighing his words. 'It is the first contact I have had from Caerwyn. The tone, Master Sencha, was discourteous.'

Threatening. I did not know why the word sprang to my mind, but once it was there, I could not dismiss it.

'The lord of Caerwyn is a man named Leldh,' Alwyn said. 'He is searching for a young woman, a criminal it seems, who evaded his forces a week and a half since. She was last seen jumping into the river.'

My lungs contracted and turned to lead. Alwyn studied my features. The letter wavered in his hand for a moment, and then he pressed it into my grasp.

'I would not send a flea-bearing rat to the hands of a man who writes such a letter as this, much less an injured young woman. I suggest some accident befalls this letter. A fire. A good soaking in a bucket of water.' He cleared his throat. 'And perhaps you should keep any news about your visitor discreet.'

I took the letter and stepped back.

'Yes, my lord. I understand.' My voice sounded oddly flat, even to myself. 'Was...did they name her? Understand, we do not even know our visitor's name.'

'No name was given. Perhaps it is a good thing. The less you know, Master Sencha, the less you can tell.' He stood motionless, as if trying to decide whether he had done the right thing. Then he gave me an uncomfortable nod and returned to his horse. I grasped the letter tight enough to crumple it.

'Freybug bless you, Master Sencha. And may Hollow stay far from your door.' Alwyn pulled himself into the saddle and clicked his tongue, steering the horse away and riding him hard down the hill.

My lungs slowly regained their function. I unfolded the letter to read the contents.

The words sickened me.

I went to the stranger's room and knocked. It was a futile thing to do; she did not respond. I pushed the door open slowly, giving her time to cast me out if she wanted, and stepped into the room when I heard no protest.

She was asleep. I did not know whether to be relieved or disappointed. I desperately wanted to confront her with the contents of the letter, but I questioned my right to do so. If she was the escaped prisoner – and there was no reasonable doubt in my mind as to that – I was still unconvinced that she was a criminal. The vitriolic letter made it clear this man Leldh had no love for waer. It was possible she had been wrongly accused of some crime, or sentenced harshly for a misdemeanour. Regardless, we could hold her accountable for nothing until she could speak for herself. Even then, if she was truly a criminal, it would be better to send her south to Herithes than north to Caerwyn. The Valley was not owned by any one of the cities to the north or the south of the mountains, but for serious matters we deferred to Herithes. They, also, had little love for the waer people, but no conflict arose so long as we kept ourselves to ourselves.

The words of the letter jumbled and turned in my head. *Half-breed dog.* I had never heard such a phrase. *Vile criminal. Not to be given sanctuary or sanction. Swift and just retribution.* My stomach turned. The man had no jurisdiction over our Valley, but his words filled me with dread. We were a peaceful settlement. For generations, my family had worked the land of the same hill, and we had never seen a war.

I kept a respectful distance from the sleeping woman, but my eyes drew back to her. Her face was narrow and pinched, her pallor shocking. It made her look small beneath the swathes of bandages and poultices. Her fair hair, what I could see of it, was cropped short. It was uneven, growing in ragged patches, and standing on her head like tufts of dry grass. She smelled of sweat, salt, blood, and the thick poultices Mother had applied to her head.

If she was a...my eyes strayed back to the words of the letter. *Vile criminal.* If that was the case, she would be able to do no damage in such a state. She was no threat to us. So long as we kept her presence quiet, we could wait until Moth and Dodge Derry arrived.

'Kee vah.'

I startled. She stared, unseeing, at the ceiling. *Kee vah.*

Kee vah. Was it a name? A place? Some phrase in a foreign language? I shivered. It was something important, to weigh on her mind so.

Vile criminal.

I left the room and took the letter to my mother.

The smell of flour, salt and woundwort washed over me as my mother and I greeted Moth Derry at the door. She smelled as she had smelled for as long as I could remember, of baking, herbs and strong, sweet tea. Of comfort and security. Moth Derry was one of life's constants. She had been there to deliver Kemp when he was born. She had cared for me during my first difficult months of Shifting.

As usual, I could not prevent myself from staring at her. Her fairness was such a strong contrast to the dark hair and eyes of a Valley inhabitant that it always turned me about. She was a neat woman, bright spectacles perched on a sweet face. She wore colourful dresses and spoke with the gentlest voice I had ever heard. Beneath her mildness, though, was steel. Her grey eyes were sharp, and she could command a room with a few clipped words. As a child, I had been fascinated by her; I had followed her into the forest to gather herbs, and sat in the kitchen for hours while she cooked and talked with my mother. The last time she had stayed in our house, she and I were the same height. Now I stooped to greet her.

'Madam Derry,' Mother greeted. 'Freybug bless you. Did you travel well?'

'Our journey was well enough. We were fortunate to miss the worst of the weather, though the pass was difficult. We just managed to get through, and we had to leave the horses behind.'

'Aye. It was close. Luckily, we took up with the chipre-people on the trail, and they took in our horses. It's thanks to them we got here so fast.' Dodge Derry stepped into view, smiling and filling the air with the reminder of desert sand and ale-soaked taverns. He was lanky and dark, with bright black eyes and a smile that split his beard. Dodge came from the bardic city of Tadhg in Oster's far south. Further south even than Luthan, which was as far as any Valley waer had ever travelled, so far as we knew. Moth and Dodge Derry were constant sources of fascination to me. They were not waer and could not have a soul-bond; were not able to whisper soul to soul as waer couples did. But they were as close and loving as any waer couple I had seen. I wondered how that worked, when they were unable to know one another's thoughts.

'Thank Felen you did get here so quickly,' my mother said. 'We have scraped by, but it has not been easy. Do come in, please. Rest yourselves, set your things down, wash, and eat.'

'Washing, resting, and eating can wait,' Moth said. 'I would like to see this patient of yours.'

I took her bag, and we went through the house to Kemp's room. While Moth and Dodge stayed with us, he and I would sleep in the family room, as my room was already occupied with the stranger. Kemp did not mind. He was delighted to be of service to the Derrys.

'Mister Dodge!' He flew out of his room and flung himself at the lanky storyteller. Dodge laughed and scooped Kemp into his arms.

'Look how big you are!' he exclaimed. The Derrys had

no young ones of their own, and Moth was of an age that meant they never would. It seemed a shame; they both loved children.

'Dodge, my love,' Moth interrupted. 'Keep your voice down. They have an invalid here, remember.'

'Sorry,' Dodge whispered, smiling like a guilty child.

'Hm. Perhaps you should take Kemp outside and throw him around a bit,' Moth said. 'But please shave first, my love. Your beard is taking on a life of its own, and I fear it may colonise if left untended.' She turned to me, brisk. 'And you, Master Lowell, should show me where your patient is.'

Brisk, yes, but there was something else in her tone I did not recognise.

'This way.' I led her through to my room, where the stranger lay. As usual, I knocked, and as usual, there was no reply. I pushed the door open quietly and stepped aside for Moth to walk in. 'She was half-drowned when we found her. She sits up sometimes, but she…' I trailed off.

Moth was not listening to me. She had eyes only for the stranger. She reached for a chair and pulled it to her, sitting down heavily. Her cheeks flushed, and I became aware that she was holding back tears. I had never seen the healer cry, not even on the rare occasion when she lost a patient.

'Madam Derry?'

'Lycaea.' It did not take long for Moth to regain her composure. She sat straight, her voice calm and level, though she could not tear her eyes from the woman lying on the bed. 'Her name is Lycaea.'

'You know her?'

'I have known her since she was a child. Her mother was…

like a sister to me, once.' She cleared her throat. 'Lycaea disappeared. We thought her dead, but with the missing you never quite stop hoping. When your mother told us you had recovered a young woman from the river…'

'Who is she? Where did she come from?' The questions tumbled from my lips. 'What is "kee vah"? Why will she not speak to us? What happened to her?'

'I wish I could answer all those questions,' she said. 'What I can say is this: she is dear to us. She lives in Luthan, or she used to. She disappeared in Caerwyn. It was three years ago, Lowell.' She reached over and took Lycaea's hand. 'We thought she was dead.'

There was no doubt in my mind, now, about the woman in our care and the message Lord Alwyn had received from Caerwyn. With difficulty, I reined in my questions. I could see Moth was in no mood to answer them. She sat without speaking, her fingers laced with Lycaea's. When I felt Moth had recovered somewhat, I reached into my pocket and took out the message Alwyn had passed on to me. I had not burnt it. It seemed like an answer, though I did not know to which question.

'This came a week and a half after we found her,' I told Moth. She took the note and read it. Her eyes narrowed to slits, and her lips pressed into a tight line.

'I see.' She folded it and thrust it back to me. 'Filth, Lowell Sencha. Lies and filth. You would do better to burn foulness like this.' She saw my expression and softened her voice. 'But I am glad you showed me, dear. It confirms what I suspected. Once Lycaea is well, we will take her south, back to Luthan. She will be safe there, and she will be able to fully recover.'

'Do you think she *can* recover?'

'She has no choice in the matter,' Moth said, and went to work. Dodge joined us a short while later. His reaction was lightning-charged. He caught Moth in a tight hug, swung her around. He asked endless questions. Finally, when the elation wore down, he sat in the chair by Lycaea's side and took her hand. Kissed her brow, fatherly and loving.

Moth removed the bandages from Lycaea's head. 'Healing tolerably,' she commented to me. 'You have cared for her well.'

'Sometimes she wakes, but she does not seem to see us.'

'Head wounds are strange things,' Moth said. 'And I have no doubt the assault on her mind is playing a part in delaying her recovery. She is too thin for my liking, and it is clear she has been subject to much cruelty.' She passed Dodge on her way to heat some water, and she kissed the top of his head. 'Tell her a story, love.'

Dodge rubbed his chin, then sat forwards. 'Once,' he said, and his voice changed; it deepened and softened, richer and clearer somehow. His words were simple, but he was a master of tone and pace. 'Once, when stories had legs and walked the earth,' he began, as he always did, 'there were three children...'

Moth grimaced. 'You know I don't like this one, love.' She leaned over Lycaea and started to clean the wound. 'Is it really necessary to tell Watcher stories *every* time? You have plenty of others.'

'...there were three children,' Dodge repeated, speaking over her last sentence, 'who were destined to change the fate of the world.'

Moth rolled her eyes, but lapsed into silence and let him continue as he told the old tale I had heard so often. The nobleman's daughter, kind-hearted, but spoilt. The daughter of a poor farm-woman, uneducated but sweet-natured. The city-bred lad, tall, strong and quick with his fists.

'As different as could be, but called together by a common duty,' said Dodge.

'Hold this,' Moth said, passing him the bowl of hot water.

'Stolen from their lives by the three Watchers,' he continued as he put the bowl aside, 'who knew their own time was drawing to a close, and chose these children as their heirs.'

I knew how this went. The children rebelled at first, but in time they accepted their roles and became the new Watchers. The Healer, gifted with power over hurt and sickness but powerless to inflict harm. The Assassin, who wielded darkness like a sword. The Dealer, who brokered bargains with power.

'Roles of servitude, not domination.' Moth looked at me over her glasses, as though no one had ever stressed the lesson before. 'To be a Watcher was to be a slave to the Balance.'

'Who's telling this story?' Dodge's voice broke from its resonant tone. 'You do your job, bonny, and let me do mine.'

Moth smiled and went to sit by the window for better light as she crushed some herbs.

'To be a Watcher,' Dodge went on, slipping back into his tale-spinner's cadence, 'was to be a slave to the Balance. Compelled by an unseen force to go where they were called. Punished with agony, even blindness, should they disobey.'

Dodge went on then to tell of the battles, one great conflict after another, all across the world. A ceaseless struggle to maintain order over chaos, until the greatest conflict of all. The war with the golden-eyed Kudhienn who had taken over Oster and made all the people of Oster slaves.

'All but the half-breeds,' whispered Dodge. 'Them, they hated and feared. Them, they killed out of hand.' This was the part that made little waer children shiver and reach for their mothers, and most storytellers moved on quickly, like Dodge, to the climax of the story. Watchers and waer standing together against the Kudhienn. Fighting shoulder to shoulder until the rest of Oster fell in with them and a momentous victory was won.

The room was quiet when he stopped speaking.

Then I said, 'But what happened afterwards?' The story never went on any further, and I had never thought to ask.

'After the Kudhienn surrendered?' Dodge said in his normal voice. 'Well, the Watchers retreated, and set about mending the land, and their own hurts.' His voice grew sad. 'While they were gone, the newly freed people of Oster rose up. They slaughtered the Kudhienn, every last man and woman of them. It was a senseless slaughter, born of the suffering the people had endured.' He sat back, and I saw him look around for Moth. She met his gaze. Dodge cleared his throat. 'Oster lost its innocence then.'

'And what happened to the Watchers?'

Dodge thought for a moment. 'They drifted,' he said at last. 'Bound by terrible oaths and laws, burdened by power and still, at their core, human. Never to love, never to have a family.'

Moth had paused in her work. I was aware of the small lines at the corners of her eyes and lips. Her mouth was folded into a flat line, and I remembered she had not wanted to hear this story in the first place.

'The Assassin knew nowt but fear and death, and the Healer

couldna lift a hand against anyone, even to defend herself. Each broke the oaths in some way. Some fallible, unforgivably human way.' He sounded almost bitter. Not like the Dodge I knew. 'The Balance cracked, and so did their powers.'

'Enough, love.' Moth came back to Lycaea's bedside, putting a gentle hand on Dodge's shoulder. 'This tale has no happy ending.'

He took her hand and kissed it.

She smiled. 'Go on with you,' she said. 'Both of you, please. I need to see the rest of the damage and I would prefer some privacy for it.'

I did not ask Dodge to finish the story as we left the room. Moth was right. It was a good tale, and he told it well, but it left an uncomfortable weight in my heart, which I could not dislodge. That night I dreamed of soldiers with golden eyes. Of the Watchers, with their endless and unhappy duties.

Lycaea

I awoke.

The room smelt like Leldh's chambers, thick with burning plants and incense. I felt sick. Forced myself not to think about Caerwyn, to remember the river instead. Running, trees, Kaebha, and the river. The water. The river-bank. Mud. Slime. Grasping at reeds and pulling myself onto land. Lungs burning. Limbs water-logged. Strangers and their hands. A swamp of pain and fear.

It meant I was not in Caerwyn. I was *out*. Free.

My head was heavy. Bandages, I realised. I could smell the poultice. The thickness of the herbs choked me. I tried to take stock of my injuries. I did not remember hitting my head, but it could have happened on the rocks in the river. My ankle was bound, but it did not feel broken. Dislocated shoulder? Healing. There was little discomfort. Ribs were sore. Cracked, but also healing. I almost laughed. I had dived into a river and almost drowned, but the worst of the damage was a sore head and some angry bones. For a brief moment, I felt the wild elation of escape; elation I had not allowed myself to feel when first I fled Caerwyn.

It flickered and faded. I had no idea where I was, or how long I had been there. Leldh would be scouring the mountains for me, dredging the river, sending out messages. He could be close. He could be anywhere.

The floors were wooden, but there was a rug and a mat to the side of the pallet that had been set aside for me. There were rough blankets. There was a window, but the curtains were drawn, and the room was warm. I could smell something cooking on the other side of the door, and the faintest traces of people. I could smell burning wood. A fire smoked and crackled in the wall opposite.

'Hold her. The metal still warms.' Gold eyes. Cold cuffs. Hot brand.

I rolled over and retched. Vomit burned my throat.

'Easy. Breathe, Lycaea.'

Confusion. Horror. Anger. I raised my eyes.

Moth Derry. She did not speak again, but she handed me a wooden cup of water. I wanted to throw it at her. Instead, I drank. How long since the river? Was I home? I sat up. It hurt. The room rocked.

I hated her. That, at least, I remembered.

'You are safe,' she said. *Safe.* I wanted to scream at her, call her a liar. I just stared. She tried to ignore it. 'You are in the Gwydhan Valley.' Not Luthan. Relief warred with sour disappointment. 'One of the families here took you in. The Sencha family. They sent for me when you did not recover.'

'Go away.'

'Lycaea, look at me. Please.'

Look at me, dog.

'Lycaea.' Her voice quivered. 'I know... I know what we did. I know we let you down. But you are safe now.'

Too tired to find a reply for her words. She was a liar. She and the other two. They had sent me into the spider's web. Abandoned me. Left me in the dark, with golden eyes and torturers.

'I sent a message to Hemanlok.'

Hemanlok.

'Why would you do that?' I made no attempt to keep accusation from my voice. I grabbed her arm. Held it tight enough to bruise. My body rejected the sudden movements. The room rocked. 'Why would you do that, Derry?'

'Why does it anger you?' she whispered back. She freed her arm, with difficulty. '*Lycaea*. I sent a message to Hemanlok. If the bird is true, he should receive it soon. And we have another carrier yet if you wish to contact the rest of your family.'

'I have no family.' No one had come for me. Three years.

'The Own, the people you love. They can help you heal.' She took advantage of my breathlessness and went on. 'I'm doing what I can for your wounds. I have to be careful, though, or the family will suspect. You should be able to get onto your ankle in a few days. Your head wound will take longer to settle.'

I folded silence around me, made it a fortress. I lay back on the bed and closed my eyes. My body unknotted with relief as I stilled. Moth did not try to speak to me again. I could smell her in the room for many minutes longer before the floorboards creaked, and the edge of the door rasped along the floor, and the door clicked shut.

I opened my eyes and watched shadows chase one another over the wall.

Kaebha.

I knew I was living with waerwolves. Their smell was like my own. Before Caerwyn, I was not like them. I was human. Leldh ended that. Ten months ago he opened a wound in my arm and splashed waer blood into it. The blood took over my body until I became one with it. At the time, Leldh was fascinated by the waer as much as he hated them. The change was a punishment and a means of control, but more than anything it satisfied the deep need he had to keep his old wounds close, to pick at them like scabs. The waer had fought against his people, all those years ago, and they had won.

Now, with heightened senses and an increasing urge to change forms, I had never felt less like the person I was before. I could still feel enemy blood in my veins. The scar in my arm was little more than a pale, raised streak now, but it was a constant reminder. I hated it. I hated *them*. Animals.

From what I could tell, there were two siblings in the house with the parents. One was a child; I could hear him playing with Dodge and shouting through the house when he grew overexcited. The other was perhaps my age. He was quiet and tall. The man who had found me, I reminded myself. Whenever he was in the room, he watched me with steady eyes.

In the evenings, I heard the family praying in the next room. I heard the young man praying to Freybug in the morning when the rest of the family left the house. He offered that I join, once, but I ignored him. The family prayed together at dusk, to a goddess named Felen. They mentioned Hollow, a third god, but they did not pray to him. They prayed for protection *from* him. I didn't know these deities; I knew the Bonny Gods from down south, in Tadhg, and something of Pelladan's goddess, but not these homely rustic daemons.

Moth's presence, as much as I resented it, spurred the healing process. I was able to leave the bed, then to walk around the room, albeit shakily, my ankle stiff and painful. My bruises turned yellow and faint, and the head wound stopped oozing although it still left me disoriented and sick if I moved too suddenly. Moth assured me that would fade. I had to hope she was right; I was no good to anyone in such a state.

The nights left me weak and frightened. It was hard to tell reality from the nightmares. Sometimes I thought Leldh came for me. Sometimes it was Kaebha who stalked through my dreams. Fear and disgust bled into my days. I knew it would be impossible for me to stay in the waerwolf household but I could not bring myself to leave the house. Not until I knew for sure where I was going, what my plans were. Fight or hide. The first seemed impossible; the second contemptible.

I stood by the fireplace and weighed my options. I could go south-east, to the whaling town of Coserbest. Further south to Luthan. All the way to Tadhg, at the very south of Oster, if I survived the trek through the desert. Or I could cross the eastern ocean, to Pelladan. It was a miserable little island, and I had not been there since childhood, but it was my birth-place. I could surely find somewhere to hide. If I made it that far.

A knock startled me from my thoughts. I looked towards the door and said nothing. My muscles were tensed. There was a poker I could use if anyone attacked. I reached across slowly and curled my hand about the metal rod. Somewhere inside me, the beast growled and stirred, hackles rising, ready to split my skin and make me savage.

The young man entered the room. He saw me with the poker and stepped back, both hands raised to show he was unarmed.

'My name is Lowell.' He was tall, but he did not carry it well. He was awkward, lanky, with it. He tried for a smile but just looked uncomfortable.

'What do you want?'

He did not reply. The beast within me quietened. The man's stillness was calming. I lowered the poker. He was a stark relief after Moth's ceaseless fussing and Dodge's wild energy.

'What is...' He paused, framing the syllables with some clumsiness. 'Kee vah?'

The calm evaporated. My chest hurt. My muscles wrenched, almost dragged me into a Shift. I held back. My breath turned harsh and painful.

Kaebha.

'How do you know that name?' I hissed. His reply was slow and measured.

'You have said it often,' he said. 'When I first found you by the river, you said it twice. And once again the day we sent for the Derrys. I wondered whether it was another language, or the name of a place.'

'No.' I forced the fear down. Kaebha was far away. I was

beyond her reach. 'Kaebha is a woman.'

'From Caerwyn?'

'Yes.'

'She is an enemy to you.'

'Yes.'

He turned and pulled across a chair, sitting in it. I gingerly lowered myself onto the bed.

'Who are you?' The question was abrupt and rude on my lips, but I made no attempt to soften it.

'My name is Lowell Sencha.' He reached out a hand. 'Madam Derry told us your name. Lycaea.'

I did not take his hand. 'How do you know about Caerwyn?'

He hesitated. 'Madam Derry said you disappeared in Caerwyn,' he said at last. There was a lie there, or something withheld.

'And?'

He sat without moving or speaking for a while. I waited.

'People are searching for you,' Lowell said at last. 'A missive was sent to Alwyn, the lord of the Valley. He gave it to me and told me to be discreet about your presence. That was some weeks ago now. The message came from Caerwyn,' he added, as if I had not guessed. 'I imagine we are not the only ones to have received something like it.' His face hardened. 'It was hateful.'

'He has no love for your people.'

Lowell cocked his head, quizzical. '*Our* people,' he corrected. Disgust contracted my gut.

'Your people,' I maintained. Lowell furrowed his brow, but he did not argue. Again, he deliberated on his words.

I wondered if he always took so long to phrase an idea, or whether it was due to what, for him, must have been an unusual circumstance.

'A "vile criminal", you were called,' he said. 'Is it accurate?'

I had the irrational urge to laugh. After all his consideration, it was the bluntest question he could have asked. I wondered, for a moment, if he was in jest. A glance at his expression told me he was serious.

'How should I answer?' I demanded. 'If I say "yes" you send me to Caerwyn. If I deny it, I doubt you will believe me.'

'A fair answer,' he conceded. The man unnerved me. Did anything surprise him? I could not read his expression. I doubted I could trust him. Or the landlord who had supposedly opted to conceal me rather than assure the safety of the Valley. Or Moth, who had allowed me to be sent me into Leldh's hands in the first place.

The things I had suffered for her mistakes.

'I'm tired,' I told Lowell. 'Let me sleep.'

'Tomorrow, come walking with us,' he said. 'It will be good for you.'

'Let me sleep,' I said again. I had no intention of going anywhere with any of them.

'After you disappeared, we searched for a year.'

Moth dropped a coat about my shoulders and leaned forward to wind a scarf about my neck. I swatted her hand away and laced the toggles of the coat. My fingers shook. The thought of leaving the house made my head reel, my vision blur. I could bear it if she just stopped talking.

'We sent people to Caerwyn. They died. We waited in the

mountains, hoping to catch a trace of you. There was nothing. We tried to get in ourselves, but Leldh has ways of blocking us. Perhaps we could have managed it, with your mother helping us, but she refused. There was no way for us to get to you.'

'I know.'

'It's why we sent you in the first place.'

'I *know.*'

'We tried everything, Lycaea. We could find nothing. Not even with our particular resources.' Ridiculous, that she still labelled them 'particular resources'. She and I both knew what she could do. 'And then so much time passed. We thought you were dead.'

'I imagine it makes you feel much better.' I pulled to my feet, gripped her shoulder for balance. 'I may as well have been, but I'm not. And I don't have the information Hemanlok wanted, if that's what you're concerned about. Three years later, I doubt it could be of much use in any case.'

'I'm concerned about *you.*'

'Well, that's a nice change.' Where was their concern when I was fifteen? What good had it ever done me?

Moth swallowed. I could see her hesitate. She did not know whether to ask me the question I knew she had come to ask. The question she had been waiting for three years to hear the answer to.

'Lycaea,' she said. 'Daeman Leldh. Were our suspicions correct? Is he what we think?'

And this was the real reason she had brought me back from the brink. To her, I was just another resource. I was tempted to make her wait. I was tempted to give her nothing. Instead, I inclined my head, and looked away so I did not have to see the fear and deep weariness flash over her face.

Lowell stuck his head through the door. He gave a slow smile when he saw me.

'Better every day,' he said. 'Are you ready?'

'No.'

'She's ready,' Moth said. 'I think we could all do with a walk. Is Kemp coming?'

'No. He was sent to his room for tracking mud through the house. He will help to prepare the evening meal as penance.' Lowell came forward and offered me his arm. 'We will not walk far,' he promised. 'I need to be home for the Grey Worship, when dusk falls. The fresh air will do you good, though.'

Pride and revulsion warred with necessity. Necessity won out. I took his arm. By the time we reached the front door, I was glad of it. It was difficult to focus, to keep my balance. Each step was steadier, though, and the open door blew fresh air into my lungs. It was a cold day but it was dry. I stepped onto the grass, felt it brush my shins.

'One in front of the other, lass.' Dodge took my other arm and guided me out. I forced myself to accept his help. I needed to regain my strength. I had not escaped Caerwyn to just lie down and die. Leaning on Dodge and Lowell, I went out onto the hill.

I could see the whole Valley from there. It stretched down towards the south-east, away from Caerwyn. The Sencha house was the first residence of the settlement, a good way from the village. It stood at the crest of the hill, squat and stone and swamped by trees. In front of us was a small field, and then a cluster of trees before the river at the foot of the hill. Sheep bedded down in the field, bleating as we drew near.

'Sheep.' It was a poor jest, if it was one. 'Kept by wolves.'

'The irony hasna been lost on any of us, lass,' Dodge chuckled.

'We raise the sheep for the wool, and for trading with the chipre-folk,' Lowell explained. 'Sometimes the local lads stray this way when they hunt, but for the most part they have enough control to leave our flock alone. We have had some troubles teaching Kemp to do the same.'

I wished he had not mentioned hunting. The wolf stirred in my gut, scented out the sheep. I shuddered. *Control.* I focused on the Valley instead. The grass was the deep green of a land blessed with frequent rain. The skies were grey, but I could see the sun shining through faintly, and it was enough to throw the emerald of the trees and grass in sharp contrast. I was never much one to dwell on aesthetics, but after weeks inside I had to appreciate my surroundings.

'This way,' Lowell said. He took us around the hill, where the slope was gentler. He was more comfortable outside; I could see it in the way he walked, hear it in the warmth of his voice. It was the wolf in him, I suspected. I followed Lowell Sencha, but at every turn I reminded myself what he was.

What I was.

Lowell

Every afternoon before the Grey Worship, we walked Lycaea down the gentle slope of the hill. The winter air was cold, but it was preferable to the risk of her capture if she was seen in the bright of day. Sometimes Kemp came with us. Sometimes Dodge stayed behind with him. Moth always walked with us, in spite of the clear tension between her and Lycaea. Even as they clearly repelled one another, there was something binding them together. I did not ask.

Lycaea herself was cool and dour. The vulnerability I had seen in the early days of healing was gone. Her face was all sharp lines and caution, and she moved with quick jerks and starts. Her voice was flat and hard, like a piece of slate. Beyond our first conversation, she told me nothing about Caerwyn, or about Kaebha. Even more forbidding was the matter of waer. It was clear to me from the beginning she had her own distaste for our people, complicated by the fact she was one of us.

Once or twice, her body seemed as if it wanted to Shift. Her muscles would contract and she would lean forwards, her face pale and tight with restraint. It was particularly bad around the sheep, or the other animals. I found myself wondering if she ever Shifted at all. I could not imagine being confined to the one shape.

Our three gods were all shape-shifters. Felen could take the form of a large cat. Hollow changed into a wolf: black like us, but bigger. As large as the souther-waer, my mother said. Freybug was the only one who took more than one shape. Sometimes, lore had it, she was a black dog who shadowed Hollow and repaired what he destroyed. At other times she was an insect, or an otter, or even a little brown wren. She was quiet and subtle, and went where she was needed most. All three maintained a balance between their shapes. As children, we were told stories of when Felen decided to shun her cat form and became maddened and sick from it. A tale designed to teach us the dangers of staying in the one shape for too long.

Lycaea, though, curled her lip whenever she saw Kemp in his Form, or heard me speaking of Shifting. I let the matter be. She could not have been a waer for long; I had never known anyone to resist Shifting for longer than eight or nine months, and that was only expectant mothers who had been advised to refrain. Perhaps when she returned to her home in Luthan she would be able to work through it.

I enjoyed the evening walks. Each day, we went further. I steered us away from the river; I thought it best to avoid as many memories of trauma as we could. Instead, I took them the back way, around the hill and behind the house, where the meadow stretched out between home and the mountains.

'It is a sight in the spring,' I told Lycaea. She was walking on her own now, though I sensed her frustration at her slow pace. 'And sometimes we get deer, though usually our scent unsettles them. The sheep are used to it by now, but not the deer. Lots of rabbits, though. You should see Kemp go after them.' I glanced at her out of the corner of my eye. 'We were hunting rabbits the day we met you.'

'The day you found me.' She would not let me be obscure with my words.

'Yes.'

'Mind your footing here,' Moth said to Lycaea. Dodge was at home, regaling Kemp with stories before the hours grew late and my brother was sent to sleep. I was a buffer between the two women, intercepting the rising tensions between them. I offered Lycaea my arm, but she was strong enough now to do without it, and she stepped across the rabbit-hole.

'Rabbits,' I apologised. 'Everywhere.'

'Just as well you work so hard to reduce their population, isn't it?' I could not tell if she was being humorous or unkind.

'Control and balance,' I told her. 'It is better to have rabbits for food than to have waer stealing livestock from one another, or attacking humans.'

'So who goes hungry?'

I frowned. 'What?'

'Who goes hungry? In every community, someone loses out. There is always someone who goes hungry, unloved, unwanted. Who goes hungry here?'

I could not frame my thoughts around such an idea.

'No one,' I said. 'No one goes hungry here.'

'Liar.'

'The Valley is an unusual phenomenon in Oster,' Moth said. 'Lowell is correct. They care for one another here.'

I turned to face Lycaea, but she was not looking at me. Her eyes were on the mountains. There was movement. I squinted, tried to make out what she was seeing.

'Get to the trees,' Lycaea snapped, and strode ahead of us. She seemed unsteady, but she did not falter.

'What is it?' I could smell something, something strange. It distracted me, pulled my attention from Lycaea. I glanced around, then looked towards the mountains. I could see nothing amiss. 'Lycaea?'

'Lowell.' Moth grabbed my arm. Her face was ashen. 'Run. *Run!*'

I stumbled into a run. I would have sprinted across the green, but Moth was so slow. I could not leave her alone. By the time we joined Lycaea at the treeline, I was soaked with sweat, and we were both breathless. I removed my clothes and Shifted. I was better as a wolf. I did not panic, as a wolf.

'Soldiers.' Her voice was bleak. 'Leldh's soldiers. They've found me.'

'Not yet, they haven't. Keep in the trees. We must get back to the house.' Moth gathered my clothes and tucked them under her arm. Her face was grey. Her voice shook.

'They will search the house.' Lycaea made an effort not to look at me. 'They will kill anyone in there.'

The words rattled through my head, but I could not understand them. Kill. *Kill?*

'No one is going to kill my husband,' Moth said. She reached down and touched my back. I barely felt it. 'We are going to the house, Lycaea. You may stay here if you wish, but we are going back for the others. They need to be warned.'

'Are you *addled?*' Lycaea spat. 'What can you hope to do about it? It's the first house they'll come to! We have to *hide,* Derry!'

Moth, in her yellow frock and her round spectacles, squared her shoulders and started moving through the trees. My thoughts clicked into function and I ran. My paws skimmed the earth. *Kemp. Mother. Father. Kill.* Anger and fear pulled my mouth into a snarl. Growls ripped through my chest. I could smell them now: metal and sweat, oil and smoke. They were close. They spoke above the wind, and I could hear them. I caught Lycaea's scent as she joined us. She was drenched in sweat and fear. We started towards the open, but Moth gave a whimper and pulled back, hauled Lycaea along with her.

We waited in the growing shadows as men dressed in red and black streamed past. They clattered and shouted. I heard one cackling. Another clapped him on the shoulder. They carried torches, weapons. Our Valley had never seen such weapons. It was hard to remain silent. I shook, suppressing growls. I could hear Moth's breath by my ear as we crouched in the shadow of a large oak. The sounds of the soldiers faded and Lycaea pushed Moth forwards. Again, we ran. All I could hear was air rasping through my lungs, and the sound of my paws hitting the earth. Someone burst through the trees. Another Valley wolf, from down the way. Running in the wrong direction. He collided with Moth, then bounded away. Howls sprang through the Valley. A demented chorus. I saw a break in the trees, saw a flicker of light, knew my home was close. I pressed forwards.

'Stop. Stop, stop! Stop here.' Lycaea grabbed my scruff and dragged me to a halt. 'Fool. You'll be seen. Derry, stop here.'

We were surrounded by trees. Dusk was upon us, and the light of the sun faded swiftly. I pressed against the ground, straining to hear. Lycaea crouched. Her eyes were animal. The smell of smoke drowned my senses. It was everywhere. I could not pinpoint the origin.

'We cannot be seen,' Lycaea whispered.

'There are no trees between here and the house,' Moth said. 'Can you move fast enough, Lycaea?'

Lycaea said nothing. She rolled back her shoulders, sprang to her feet, and moved for the edge of the trees. I was a step behind her when she swore and stumbled back. She tumbled over me, fell heavily. I choked back a yelp, smothered it into a growl. Lycaea, breath ragged, scrambled to her feet.

'Fire!' she hissed.

I was deaf and blind, and animal. I ran. The fire, bright in the night, blinded me. Someone was screaming. The wood snapped, roared as it fell and sent flame howling into the night. I made a sound. Something neither a bark nor a howl, but a scream that left my throat sore and my lungs empty. I ran for the door, but the wall of flame knocked me back. I had never felt such heat. I tried the window, but it belched smoke and fire at me. I yelped and fell back. I scrabbled in the dirt. I was neither wolf nor man. I was made of pain. *Kemp. Mother. Father.*

Moth ran past me.

'Dodge!' she screamed. '*Dodge!*'

I imagined Kemp, choking on black smoke. My mother and father, crushed beneath the wood. Hollow taking each one of them.

Lycaea grabbed Moth about the shoulders and held her back from the flame.

Kemp, crying out for me. Burning. My mother and father, holding one another. Unable to escape. Wondering where I was. Needing me. *Needing me.*

'Sencha. Sencha!' Lycaea. Angry, or frightened. Both. I could not tell.

I lay on my belly and panted. Kemp. Mother. Father.

'Lowell.' Moth took my face in her hands. Her eyes were red, her face hard from withholding tears. 'Lowell, we have to go. I'm so sorry. We have to go. It's gone. Maybe they escaped. The house is gone. There's nothing we can do here.'

A crash. Roof falling in. Our home. Moth dragged my fur and I stumbled, stood. Shouts washed over me. I could not tell if they came from Moth and Lycaea, or from my neighbours, or from our enemies. *Enemies.* I gasped for air. The ground slid beneath my feet. *Kemp. Mother. Father.*

Back to the trees, but they offered no sanctuary this time. I wanted to scream and keep screaming, but fear and pain left me mute. I was dumb in the darkness.

'We need a place to hide.' Moth's voice was threaded with grief. 'Lowell. You need to show us where to hide. Please. I know. I know, but we have no time.'

I Shifted, found the clothes Moth had dropped when she saw the burning house. I pulled them on, clumsy in the dark. My fingers fumbled with the laces. Lycaea hissed her frustration, but I could not focus on her. I fixed my attention on my fingers, and then my legs as I started to walk. For a misty moment, I had no idea where we were going.

'Caves,' I managed. My tongue was numb and heavy.

'Caves at the foot of the mountains.'

'Good enough,' Lycaea said. 'Lead. Derry, move.'

'Lass?'

We all turned. Dodge and Moth met, almost knocked one another to the ground. They fused closer than a soul-bond, neither of them able to speak. Moth buried her face in his shoulder, hands clenched about his shirt. Dodge shuddered and managed to whisper something in her ear. She nodded.

My heart stuttered. Wild hope. If Dodge was alive, my family might be. Kemp. I wanted to wrap him in my arms, rough with him, listen to his constant questions. 'Dodge?'

He looked at me. He closed his eyes and lowered his head.

'I was out at the well,' he said in a hoarse whisper. 'I'm sorry. I didna see anyone get out. The soldiers barred the door. I tried. I tried, lad.'

My body folded in on itself.

'We need to go.'

Lycaea. Unshaken. Driven. I managed to lift my head. Her eyes were fixed on me. I almost hated her.

'Wake up, Sencha,' she said. 'We. Need. To. Go. Show us the way.'

'Give the lad a chance to breathe, Lycaea,' Dodge said.

'Why? Leldh's men won't.'

'Give him a moment!' Moth held Dodge's hand tight.

'No.' I straightened. Breathed. Acrid smoke stung my eyes, and tears streaked my cheeks. 'No. She is right. We need to go.' Pain knotted my chest and made speech painful. I managed. 'The caves.'

Moth reached out for my arm, but I moved away from her. Comfort would have shattered me.

We stole through the Valley. When the Valley was first settled, before the houses and barns were built, our people had sheltered in the caves. Now, so many years later, they were obscured by trees and vines. They were a perfect place to hide. I had loved them as a boy, all the children did. Kemp loved them. Had loved them.

We heard screams as we went through the forest. From the incline leading to the caves I could see amber lights springing up through the Valley. Other houses destroyed. Other people murdered.

We were slow, painfully slow. Every few paces, we found ourselves ducking into shadows and behind trees. Sometimes waer passed us by, white-eyed with fright or agony. No one stopped. I stumbled over a body. *A body.* I did not stop to identify the corpse. I felt nothing.

Finally, we pushed through trees to the entrance of the caves. I cleared the vines and squeezed through the narrow mouth of a cave. I moved away from the others, as far as I could, and sat. Grief ran along my spine and forced my head into my hands. Sorrow was a tide, and I was just a stone in its path.

Lycaea

My stupidity had killed the family that sheltered me. I should have left as soon as I could walk. Fool. Complacent fool. A child, a little boy. And the Sencha parents, killed because of my cowardice.

I tried not to look at Lowell Sencha. His world was gone. He sat hunched at the edge of the cave, still and silent. His face was grey. He had stopped crying, but only for the moment. The grief would hit him in waves, seemingly endless, until he was smoothed by them and could be worn no more.

I sat. My head spun and nausea held me fast. The sickness was better than the fear, though. I had been this sick before, but I had never been this afraid. Leldh would follow. He would destroy everything between us, until I was back in Caerwyn.

I had to go back to Caerwyn. To Leldh. *And Kaebha.*

But not alone. Not this time. This time, I would go back armed. And with an army.

First, I had to go to Luthan.

We were safe for now, while the soldiers went on their rampage. They were always undisciplined on the first night of a hunt. They just went through destroying, and burning, and enjoying it, until the grey hours of day. Then, they would search properly. Round up survivors and bring them back to Leldh. Interrogate people. Someone would let loose about the caves, if they were well-known to the Valley people. I had to leave before then. I knew they needed time to grieve, but if they did not come with me now, I would go on my own.

I leaned my aching head back against the cool stone wall. *Luthan*. At least it was a direction.

While Moth and Dodge talked, I crouched by Lowell. I had caused the death of his family, indirectly. I had to face it, and him. I waited until he met my gaze. His eyes were hollow. I would not let myself look away.

'They did not deserve to die,' I said. 'You all deserved better. I'm sorry we were too late. I'm sorry the soldiers followed me here. I should have left sooner.'

'Why?' He was not asking me why I should have left, or why I was sorry, or why he deserved better. It was the 'why' of a child, struggling to comprehend, for the first time, the unfairness of things. I had no answer for him. It was the nature of life to devour the living. Time eats all bones.

Lowell dropped his head again, weighed down by grief.

'What now?' Moth and Dodge sat close. They had not released hands since finding one another again.

'Luthan,' I said. 'We'll need to leave soon. Before the soldiers can learn of these caves.'

Lowell's head jerked. Bewildered eyes. Swallowing

confusion. I forced myself not to see.

'That's a long way to go, lass.'

'Yes. We will need to get supplies from the soldiers.'

Moth dragged a hand through her hair. 'A flawed plan to say the least.' She spoke softly. 'Lowell needs...he needs rest. You are still not recovered from your injuries.'

'We can hunt in the mountains.' Lowell cut into our conversation, surprising me. 'Hares, mountain-goats. The elements would be our real enemy.'

'The chipre-folk will have moved on by now,' Moth added. 'Otherwise they would help us.'

'So we need clothes and rope.'

Moth hesitated, then nodded. 'And tinder and flint.'

'Good. What else?'

'Weapons.' Dodge grimaced when we stared at him. 'Aye, sure, most of us can scarce use them. But you can, Lycaea, and we can learn. If you can get weapons, do so.'

'When?' Moth asked.

'Before dawn. They'll be drunk and glutted of their killing, and they'll be lazy for a few hours.'

'Are you certain?'

'I've seen it before.' Flat, tired sentences from all of us. The terror was gone. Replaced, for the moment, by resignation. The worst had happened, but we had survived. We had to keep surviving.

'Just before dawn, then,' Moth agreed. She touched Dodge's shoulder. 'We should sleep in shifts. Lycaea, you should sleep first. And you two, Dodge, Lowell, you need to rest. I can take the first watch.'

As soon as she spoke the words, my limbs and eyes became

heavy. Lowell's shoulders slumped. He lay on his side and closed his eyes. I knew what Moth was doing; so did Dodge, but he did not fight it. He kissed her cheek and leaned against the wall to sleep. I glared at Moth, accusing, barely able to focus on her as my eyelids threatened to close.

'I know,' Moth whispered. 'But you *do* need to rest, dear. I'll wake you when the time comes.'

I fell into the arms of sleep. At least I did not dream.

Moth touched my shoulder to rouse me. She was gentle, but I jerked awake and almost struck her. She was prepared for it; her arms were around her face before I even moved.

'It's just me,' she whispered when no blow fell. 'It's time to go, Lycaea.'

I breathed out. My body was stiff and sore. I climbed to my feet, having to stoop for the roof of the cave.

'I'll be back,' I said. 'Probably. If not, take Sencha and Dodge to Luthan. Tell Hemanlok he owes me Leldh's death.' Always a risky move, to tell Hemanlok he owed you something. But if I died, at least I could stir him after my last breath was drawn. And if they captured me and I did not die, at least there was a chance someone would come for me this time.

This time.

Rage warmed my belly. It was the greatest weapon I had. It smothered fear.

I pushed aside a curtain of leaves. It was dark outside, but my sight was better than a human's. There were small benefits to being a waer. Heightened sense of smell. Better night-vision. Better instincts. I knew, also, that with the Shift came regeneration of the body, and healing of certain wounds. I could not bring myself to do it, though. I did not know what I dreaded more: Shifting, or being apprehended by Leldh's men. Both brought insurmountable pain, and a loss of control.

Lowell, in his wolf shape again, trotted towards me. He regarded me with steady, sad eyes.

'No,' I whispered. 'Go back, Sencha. You'll hinder me.'

He shook his head and slunk past. I could understand it, in a way. The need to do something, to not sit around and wait for pain. At least his colouring was dark; I almost lost him in the shadows. I considered arguing with him further, but there was no time. I left the mouth of the cave, followed him through the trees. I could smell blood now, and burnt flesh. Soldiers nearby. More fires. Metal. Lowell and I went with soft movements. His head was low, but there was control and focus in his walk.

'Stay with me,' I muttered to him. 'No running off on half-sung death-bids.'

His tail swayed in acknowledgement, but it was hard to know how much he registered. I rolled my shoulders back and closed my eyes as we came to a stop in the shadow of a tree. I could hear soldiers now, and when I glanced around the tree I could see three of them ahead in a clearing. Three lounged on the ground, sleeping. Two on guard. Manageable.

When I looked closely, I could see other figures there as well; bound and huddled on the ground. Waer prisoners. I lowered into a crouch and put a hand on Lowell's shoulder. I hated the touch of the rough fur, but I needed his attention on me.

'Do you see the prisoners?' I breathed. I felt his muscles tense under my hand. His hackles lifted. Anger. Good. 'I want you to get them loose. Any way you can. We kill the guards, we free the prisoners, and then we run for the caves.'

A quiet growl of assent. I stood. I did not give myself time to think it through. I walked forwards, stayed away from the light of the fire. I saw the prisoners move, scenting one of their own. One of the soldiers kicked at them.

Lowell surged forwards. He was silent, but impossibly fast. I jerked into movement. A soldier jumped to his feet and I slammed my elbow into his belly. He bent double and I grabbed his head, smashed it against my knee. His face was broken. He did not have time to hit the ground before I drew the sword from his belt. A thrust, and he bled. I turned in time to catch another soldier as he swung his blade at me. Metal clashed. I darted to the side and swung down, releasing his weapon. He stepped in and I reached around. The blade gleamed red in the light of the fire. The stench of blood. I sliced the back of his knees. He screamed as I cut him down.

Howls. Dark shapes darted through the clearing. One of the three remaining soldiers stuck a wolf with a sword and Lowell fell upon him before he could draw his blade from the corpse. Snarls and rips. The man screamed, gurgled.

Two more. One went for Lowell. Blood beat honour down. I stabbed the man in the back. The last soldier ran. Lowell started after him, but I held my blade in front of the wolf and would not let him pass. No time for a hunt. Survivors first.

'Done,' I snapped. 'Free the waer, then head for the caves.'

Lowell went to the remaining waer, used his strong teeth to loose their bonds. They gave him no thanks. They pelted into the shadows. I looted the bodies. Warm clothes, tinder and flint, swords and a knife. A water-skin. A lucky afterthought;

we would have struggled without one. I sheathed the sword I had taken. I would clean it later.

'Move,' I said to Lowell. He stank of blood and sweat. His first kill. His tail was between his legs, ears pressed flat against his head. His eyes were whited with panic. Nausea rose in my gut, but I choked it back. My head ached. My body wanted to fall into another shape. Growls bit the inside of my throat. I straightened, gritted my teeth. Lowell was immobile. '*Move,*' I urged. When he stared at me, bewildered and unhappy, I shoved him forwards. One paw set in front of the other, and finally he broke into a run. I struggled to keep up. My head swam. As we skidded to a stop in front of the cave, I bent and retched. Not because of the violence. I had not baulked at a fight since I was a child. It was the movement. My head.

Lowell skulked past me. I let him go in. He had much to absorb. It would probably take our whole journey to Luthan for him to understand what had happened that night. If we survived.

When I was composed, I joined him, Moth, and Dodge in the cave. Lowell was pulling on his shirt. When he was done, Moth wrapped her arms about him. He dropped his head onto her shoulder.

'Bundle up,' I said, handing some of the clothes to Dodge. 'Time to go.' All I wanted to do was lie down and sleep, but one soldier had escaped, and he would tell others. 'There was a witness. Couldn't be helped.'

A hiss from Lowell. I looked at him, realised he felt horror at the takings.

'You looted the bodies.' His voice was hollow.

'That was the point,' I reminded him. I tried to gentle my

voice. 'You and I both killed tonight, Wolf. But so did they. Let's not get sentimental.' I drew the sword and cleaned it.

'Did you get the tinder and flint?'

I tossed them to Moth. She tucked them into the pocket of her yellow frock. *Yellow,* of all colours. I tossed her the black cloak I had retrieved from the man Lowell killed.

'Put that on,' I told her. As she did, I turned to Lowell. There was bruised flesh around his eyes. He seemed old, and impossibly young.

I crossed the distance between us and held a hand out to him. 'Stand,' I said. 'Dawn will be on us soon, and we need to be well into the mountains before they start searching.'

He recoiled from my hand and stood on his own. He walked past, and the hot sting of humiliation crawled over my skin. I set my teeth. He could blame me if he wanted. I was not concerned with his approval.

Kaebha

The soldiers lined the yard, their spears held in salute. They were clad in crimson and black, their faces shadowed by helmets. The soldiers were straight-backed. Their chins were lifted and although their eyes stung from the dust picked up by the late autumn, they kept their gazes ahead.

Daeman moved past them. He stopped in front of Cooper. The man hailed from Pelladan, the grey island off the eastern coast. He was handsome, with fine blond hair and blue eyes. Like all Pellish men, he had been drafted into the navy at the age of fourteen and he had climbed his way through the ranks with brutal ambition. When he could climb no higher he came to the Mainland, and Leldh had found him.

Then Leldh had found Kaebha, the newest addition to his coterie.

The door to the chamber at the end of the yard swung open and the prisoners were brought out one by one. Soldiers bent to shackle each prisoner to the iron bar that ran across the stretch of land. The prisoners were cowed and silent, cringing away from each contact. Daeman halted a soldier before the prisoner could be chained. He took the prisoner by the arm and hauled him over to Kaebha, tossing him at her feet. Kaebha's eyes flicked downwards and then ahead once more. Daeman chuckled.

'You obey my every order, do you not, Kaebha?' he asked.

'I live to serve.' She was built like an acrobat, but she stood like a soldier, and Daeman knew she would obey like one.

'And this waer?'

'My will is yours.'

'And if I order you to beat the wretch to death?'

Kaebha paid the man's sobs no heed, her attention now focused on Daeman. She gave a tiny bow and Daeman's eyes, the same golden sheen as his hair, lit.

'Proceed,' he said and stood back. Kaebha stepped forwards and lowered her spear, her eyes on her victim. She paced around him. He braced his hands on the ground, trying to push himself up, and Kaebha swung her spear in a swift arc over his head, bringing it down upon his back. The man cried out and collapsed to the ground, huddling into a ball. Kaebha struck him again, her movements precise. The other soldiers gave way to muttering, and then to jeers. Kaebha grabbed the front of the man's shirt and jerked him to his feet.

'This is a better death than you deserve.'

The man gibbered in fear. Kaebha felt mild disgust, but little else. She proceeded to hit the man with precise, brutal strokes until he fell once more. His cries became whimpers, and his whimpers became silence.

Kaebha stepped back. It was her first kill. She turned her eyes to Leldh. His golden eyes flashed, and he inclined his head. She had pleased him.

Lowell

You and I both killed tonight, Wolf. Let's not get sentimental. Lycaea's words condemned me. In the night, I had lost my family and my honour. When she offered her hand, I could not bring myself to accept it. I could not look at her.

Moth found rosemary just outside the caves and returned with bundles of it. I burned a sprig, cupped the ashes in my calms. Moth poured the water into my hands and I drank. It was a poor excuse for the Dawn Worship, but it was all I had. The rest of the rosemary I gathered into the bag Lycaea had snatched. My movements were sluggish. I had run out of tears, and grief lodged in my belly, cool and hard. The rituals of the Dawn Worship brought no comfort. They made me think of my parents, and Kemp, and all the mornings I had dreaded going with them to the worship-house. Thankless fool.

Shame followed me through the mountain-pass and, as we ascended, along the precarious mountain ledges. To distract myself, I watched Lycaea step up rocks and crags. She used the small trees and bushes to hoist herself up, grabbing them low so they would take her weight. I could smell sweat and blood on her. Her eyes were set ahead. I tried to follow her course, but it was not long before I held a branch too long and it snapped. I stumbled, sending rocks skittering downwards. I choked down a shout as I fought to find another grip. When none came to hand I closed my eyes.

Long fingers wrapped about my arm and hauled me onto a safe ledge. I wavered a moment before finding my balance.

'Keep your eyes open,' Lycaea said. 'We are all tired, but if you do not focus you will fall.' I leaned against the cliff face, shaking my head.

'We should rest,' Moth put in. She and Dodge were slow, and lagged behind Lycaea and myself. Dodge was nimble enough – Tadhg, his home, was framed by craggy peaks and sharp crevasses. Moth, though, needed his help.

'No,' Lycaea said. 'We keep going until nightfall.' I sensed her impatience with Moth.

I braced my head on the rock for an instant, willing frustration not to best me. We had been travelling almost two days, up at first light and walking, often climbing, deep into the hours of darkness. We paused only so I could perform the small rituals of the Dawn and Grey Worship. I was sparing with the rosemary Moth had gathered, and glad I only needed it for the Dawn Worship. The Grey Worship was easier to adapt. I burned a stick, then blew out the flame to signal my surrender to the time of shadow. Pressed the cooling ash against the base of my neck to protect me from Hollow's harm. Felen was not like Freybug. Felen demanded the Grey Worship, would give no help or protection without it. Freybug helped us unconditionally, and so the Dawn Worship was an expression of pure thanks.

I performed the Dawn Worship on our way through the mountains, but my heart was not in it. Freybug had not been able to save my family. Had not protected our Valley. It was difficult to find things to thank her for.

Where I struggled to fumble through in the dark, Lycaea seemed to have no limit. She climbed tirelessly and ignored her injuries until Moth tended them in the evenings. She was driven. In some ways, I was glad of it; the constant travel left me with little time to think about what had happened to my family. Even so, I fell into grief numerous times during the day. Something would remind me of my mother, my father, and hot pain would rise in my chest. Heaviness throughout my body. Sometimes it took me a moment to remember why I was grieving. My heart knew the absence of my family before my mind did. It was a crushing, exhausting pain.

Moth sometimes tried to talk to me about them, but I preferred not to. Dreamless sleep, at least, was a blessing. By the time darkness fell at the end of each day, I was too tired to dream.

On the third day, we climbed until the last traces light began to fade. The sky seeped from a warm gold to crimson as clouds scattered their way across the horizon. The air was thick with the scent of rain and cool mountain air. I paused on a flat section of rock to pull my cloak tighter about my shoulders. *A dead man's cloak,* part of me whispered. I ignored it. My eyes were on the mountains before us. They pointed accusatory peaks into the bloody light. Behind, all that was visible of the Valley was a thick plume of smoke.

Lycaea was level with me. She stopped also, tilting her face towards the light. Her jaw locked.

'Red sky at night, sailor's delight,' she murmured. 'Red sky in the morning...'

'Shepherd's warning,' I put in, glad to have someone draw me from thoughts of home.

'Shepherds have nothing to do with it,' she said. 'Shepherds took on the saying after some storyteller drew it inland. It originated at sea. With sailors.' She opened her mouth, closed it again, then shook her head and changed the subject. 'There's a series of caves ahead. We can stop for the night. Be prepared to leave before the sun rises. We lost time today.'

It felt like an accusation. I lowered my head and pressed on towards the caves. Like Lycaea, I could smell their musty air before I saw them. The moss. Traces of animals. My muscles ached. Somehow, it was all the worse knowing respite was so close. My legs shook.

Lycaea drew her sword before she stepped through the mouth of the cave, ever cautious. She nodded over her shoulder and I joined her. When I sat, I could hear my legs click and groan.

'You should stretch them out,' Lycaea said. She did not sit. 'Keep moving slowly.'

I rotated my ankles. I dreaded the rest of the journey. My boots were too thin for mountain-climbing, and my feet were covered with blisters and cuts from the rock. My hands were raw and red, though I could not tell if it was due to the cold or the climbing. I performed the rituals of the Grey Worship in silence, too tired to speak.

Dodge eased to the ground beside me when he and Moth reached the cave. It was harder on them both; they did not have our youth, and Moth in particular seemed ill-suited to such activities.

'We need to hunt,' I said, at length.

'Yes.' Lycaea squatted and started to clear an area at the mouth of the cave for a fire. 'You and I, Sencha. Moth cannot, and Dodge lacks the stomach.'

I dared a glance at Dodge. He winked at me.

'Will you Shift?' I asked Lycaea.

'Don't be ridiculous.' She did not spare it a thought before she moved on. 'Fortunately, Moth is a decent cook, so I imagine whatever we catch will be somehow palatable. Derrys, you should look for herbs and greenery. I'm trusting you both not to poison us all.'

I expected Moth and Dodge to be offended by her tone, her words, but they were unmoved. Moth was massaging her calf-muscles, and Dodge leaned back against the rough wall of the cave. They swapped a glance. I knew they could not be bound as waer couples were, but there was something in them that made me think of it.

'We rest first, dear,' Moth said, when Lycaea's silence made it clear she was waiting for an answer. 'I think it's time we gave Lowell an explanation. Much has happened, and much has been left unspoken. He needs to know about Daeman Leldh. Who and what he is.'

I watched something pass over Lycaea's face; an expression I could not define.

'I'm going to hunt,' she announced. 'Join me when you're done here, Lowell.'

She snatched a dagger from where we had set out meagre supplies, took her sword, and left the cave.

'No surprises there,' Dodge sighed. 'I figured she wouldna much want to revisit this.' His dark eyes found me. 'If you dinna want to hear it just now, lad, say so. I know it's hard. If it gets too much, let me know. I dinna want to cause you further pain.'

'We think you should know why they hunt Lycaea. How she came to be involved with these people in the first place.' Moth leaned her head on Dodge's shoulder and they laced their fingers together. Her voice was soft. 'It will not help, at least not in a practical sense, but it may give you some sense of peace, at least to know why.'

'Thank you.'

'Lycaea used to work for a man named Hemanlok.' Although Dodge was the one speaking, he used none of his usual embellishments and flare. For once, he privileged content over delivery. I was grateful. I did not think I could stand a performance. 'The man we're going to see in Luthan. He's a powerful man, and a dangerous one, but he protects the city.'

'He is not nobility,' Moth interrupted.

'No. There isna rank nor title for what he is, lad. He's the soul of Luthan. Do you know who Luthan's king is?'

'Kirejo?' I felt my ignorance, doubting my answer, but Dodge nodded.

'Kirejo, aye. He makes the laws, but Hemanlok dictates what passes and what doesna in Luthan. He has a network of folk working for him; Rogues, criminals, the like. His closest allies call themselves the Own. Lycaea was one of them.'

'In Luthan? Then how did she come to be captured in Caerwyn?'

Dodge nodded. 'Hemanlok keeps informed on all the most powerful folk in Oster. Even Moth and I sometimes go to him with intelligence of happenings in various places. He keeps himself in the know so he can protect Luthan, you see. In any case, he got wind of a man setting up in Caerwyn. Getting mighty strong, mighty quick. So Hemanlok needed information.'

Dodge seemed hesitant. I had heard his stories all my life, and he had never seemed so uncomfortable telling one. Perhaps the subject was too close to home.

'Hemanlok decided to send Lycaea in to get that information. She was young, and quick, and the only member of the Own not yet known to Daeman Leldh. Lycaea leapt at the chance. She adored Hemanlok. I think she wanted to impress him.'

It was hard to imagine Lycaea desperate to impress anyone. It was hard to imagine her adoring anyone.

'How old was she?' I asked.

Moth's eyes hardened. She answered for Dodge. 'Fifteen. We should have told Hemanlok it was too young.'

'For a while, Hemanlok had correspondence with her. Then, after a few months, it stopped. We tried to contact her. Tried to get her out. Seemed to us they'd killed her, because we sent people in and they either came out with no word, or they never returned. Three years passed, and we didna know more until your mother wrote us to come and help Lycaea.'

Mother. Her worn hands, her dark eyes. Her wry smile and busy movements.

'Tell me about Leldh.' Vital to stay away from thoughts of home. I think Dodge sensed it. He rushed into an answer.

'He hates the waer. Hates them, and is fascinated by them.'

'Why?'

Moth took in a breath too sharply. Dodge pressed a kiss to the side of her head.

'Do you remember the stories I used to tell you, lad?' he asked. 'About the Kudhienn?'

'Of course,' I replied. The golden men and women who had once enslaved Oster. I always loved the story because they had been defeated, in the end, by the waer of the north and the south. The three Watchers, though I believed the Watchers to be no more than a myth, were added to the story for the sake of fantasy. The Kudhienn, according to Dodge, had long life-spans. They were able to see as many as six generations of a human or a waer. They were youthful and beautiful then, and cruel. But they had been wiped out hundreds of years ago, and had long become little more than stories to frighten or inspire children with. I hardly knew if I believed half the things Dodge said about them.

I frowned. 'What do the Kudhienn have to do with it?'

'Everything,' Dodge replied. 'Daeman Leldh is one of them.'

The storyteller was grim and silent. He let it sink in. I tried to read Moth's face, but she was not looking at me. Her eyes were on the mouth of the cave.

'He isna full-blood, I think,' Dodge said. 'But he is Kudhienn. It was one of the reasons Hemanlok sent Lycaea to Caerwyn; to confirm it. It seems she discovered much more.'

The thoughts would not fit inside my head. I breathed out.

Moth rose and excused herself, saying she wanted to gather some dry wood before any rain fell, and some herbs before Lycaea came back with her hunt. I was left staring at Dodge, trying to work out if he was mad.

'It makes sense, lad,' Dodge told me. 'You know it does. Especially his hatred for the waer.'

'How do you know all this?' I asked.

'I'm a storyteller, lad,' he said. 'I collect tales, which means it's my job to get people to tell me things. Hemanlok told me some things. Others, I pieced together from folks in Luthan. Moth told me a bit, too.'

'Tell me what the Kudhienn could do.' I bit my tongue. '*Can* do.'

'They have long lives. They're experts at manipulation. They can worm their way into your head, make you think their thoughts. Sometimes they can disguise themselves. Sometimes, they can keep people away from them; repel them, almost.'

I rubbed my face. I did not know what to think. I wanted to find Lycaea and ask her about it, but I doubted she would give me any answers.

'I…need time to think,' I told Dodge. 'I should help Lycaea to hunt.'

'Too late.' Lycaea's voice, cool and flat. 'Nice work with the fire,' she added, with a pointed glance at the empty area we had designated for a fire. She slung a goat off her shoulder and sat to clean the blood from her sword. She must have been fast as a hornet, to catch and kill a goat with the blade. 'Where's Derry?'

'Gathering herbs and firewood.'

'Fine.' She handed me the knife she had taken. It was an ugly, hooked blade. 'Skin the goat, Sencha.'

I had no qualms about skinning an animal. It was a skill I had put to good use at home. I took the knife and gathered rope to hang the goat from.

'Outside the cave,' Lycaea snapped. I opened my mouth to argue, then saw her face and realised she could not skin the animal. I wondered how hard it had been for her to hunt without Shifting. I moved outside and thanked Freybug for the gift of the goat before I began my task. It was difficult to string the goat up, more difficult than it would have been at home.

I was so hungry, it was all I could do not to pull off a chunk of meat and eat it raw. But Valley waer did not do such things. We never ate raw meat. We hunted, and then we brought our food back so it could be cleaned and prepared. Civilised and decent. I restrained myself, and forced my thoughts to other things.

The Kudhienn. The *Kudhienn*. A story so old, it was close to myth. I shuddered, those tales suddenly too close. Murder and torture. I had forgotten how much the stories frightened me as a child, even as I was entranced by them. Once or twice, after I had woken up crying from nightmares, Dodge had been sternly rebuked by my parents. The nightmares lingered in my mind now as I skinned the goat.

Moth rejoined us as I finished. Her arms were laden with wood and herbs, and I set aside my task to help her carry them inside. I was surprised she had managed to find so many things to eat. Vegetation was sparse in the area, though other parts of the mountains were lush and green as the Gwydhan

Valley itself. Still, Moth had always been clever with plants. I supposed it was the combination of being a healer and loving to cook.

Dodge built the fire just outside the cave, and I finished with the goat, deferring to Moth's cooking expertise when I was done.

'I could tell a story to pass the time,' Dodge suggested. 'Lowell, would you want to hear a story of the Watchers?'

Moth looked at him sharply, and placed a hand on his arm. 'Not tonight, love,' she said. 'No more dark stories tonight.'

Lycaea nodded. She prodded at the fire, keeping it alive through the evening. A subdued peace fell between us. I knew the Derrys were trying to let me absorb some of what they had told me, but I found I did not want to dwell on it. We needed something to stand in the stead of the story Dodge had told before. The darkness and worldliness of the Kudhienn. All I could think of were the Valley tales, which were so full of hearth and home.

'Did you ever hear the story of Felen and the goat?' I asked. Surprise awoke on Dodge's face, became delight.

'Nay, lad,' he said. 'Tell us.' I suspected he was lying, as he seemed to know all the tales of the Valley, but I did not contest him on it. I glanced at Lycaea but could not tell if she minded. She kept the fire alive while Moth cooked the meat.

'Felen saw the beginning of the world. The creation of the stars, and the first steps of man.' I was not so skilled as Dodge at the art of storytelling, but I had always loved the story of Felen and the goat. 'She thought herself very wise. Over the years, humans and animals worshipped her, and so her vanity grew. One day, however, she heard that there was an animal who boasted of being more wise than she. Felen was furious. She sought out the creature, and found it was a goat.'

Lycaea raised an eyebrow. I faltered. The story suddenly felt home-spun and childish.

'Go on, Lowell,' Moth said, turning the goat. 'Did she challenge the goat?'

'Yes,' I said. 'She told the goat he would have to prove himself. She said if he was truly wise, he would be able to find the precious stones she had hidden in the woods. The goat was delighted, and went through the woods to find the precious stones. In spite of all his boasts, he was not very wise.'

'Those who make claims of wisdom rarely prove it,' Dodge grinned.

I nodded. 'So: he stuck his head in rabbit holes and bushes, scraped his hoofs at tree-bark, and almost drowned himself in the river. Eventually, he saw the gleam of those stones secreted beneath the jutting roots of a tree. He jammed his head through the roots, and then found himself stuck. Now was Felen's chance. She coerced the roots of the tree into growing, and sharpening, and she drove them into the goat's head.'

Moth cast a reflective glance at the goat we were cooking, her lips tilting. 'Poor thing.'

'Felen left the goat for dead, but she had not counted on the soft heart of Freybug, the wren, who was watching from nearby.'

'The wren?' Moth asked. 'I always thought Freybug was a wolf.'

'A dog, sometimes,' I corrected. 'But Freybug could take all manner of shapes. In this story, she was a wren. She felt sorry for the goat and when Felen left, she went to him, healed him as best she could, and tried to pull the roots from his head. But she lacked the strength, so instead she called the woodpeckers to her, and they pecked at the roots until the goat could wriggle out from the tree. And there he was: left with two large roots sticking out of his head, but at least he was free and alive.'

'Goat-horns,' Lycaea muttered. 'Quaint.'

'It was not long before Felen realised what had happened. Outraged, she chased the goat out of the Valley, and into the mountains. His hooves were too large and ungainly for the narrow ledges, so he scraped them against rocks until they weathered into delicate cloves. Felen was relentless. She would not let him set a foot in the soft slopes of the Valley. Eventually, he learned to stay away, and so he remained in the cliffs and mountains.' I stopped, a little sheepish. 'That is all I know of the story.'

'It's a fine tale, lad,' Dodge reassured me. He was being kind, but his words still warmed me. 'And a grand homage to the poor beast we're about to dine on.'

'I'm sure that's a great comfort to the goat,' Lycaea said.

'Do you have a story to tell, Lycaea?' Moth asked with a small smile.

Lycaea's eyes flicked towards her. 'Do *you*?' Her frame was tight and hunched. Anger lurked in her features, though I could not tell why.

Moth watched her a while. She said nothing, but her expression spoke for her. Sadness. Disappointment. Caution.

Lycaea threw another log on the fire. 'Let's just eat,' she said, and we did.

Kaebha

She was learning. Techniques, timing, the right questions to ask, the right games to play. Cooper was helping her, in his own combative way. They despised one another but they served a common purpose. Cooper knew Leldh wanted her to help with his experiments, and as part of his workings against the Watchers. Likewise, Kaebha knew Cooper was a fine torturer and an exemplary soldier. Leldh needed them both. It was their job to support him. Even if it meant tolerating one another.

'Pick it up.'

It had been a long time since she'd fought with a sword. She picked it up with shaking arms. Cooper's eyes were lit. He fought with a rapier, the traditional weapon of Pellish swordsmen. His back was straight, legs flexed. Impeccable posture, precise movements and no imagination.

Kaebha picked up her blade.

'As I was saying, cleanliness is imperative, especially when dealing with half-breeds. They carry disease. I am not just talking about the

waer, of course.' Their blades clashed and Kaebha leapt back. 'I mean all half-breeds. Elementals, changelings, the lot. In essence, the population of Luthan, and most of the scum in our cells.' Cooper fought from the wrist, delicate and quick. His footwork was spectacular. He must have trained relentlessly. 'So be sure to have a slave clean away any blood, and wash yourself thoroughly. When was your last kill?'

'Three days ago.'

'Half-breed?'

'Intruder.' She hissed as his blade knocked her hand.

'Too slow, Kaebha. Improve your footwork.' He let her shake out her hand before resuming position. 'You should hunt more. You cannot climb the ranks if you lack initiative. You need to show Leldh you are actively loyal.'

'Leldh needs me by his side.'

'He needs to know you are committed.' As Kaebha swung her blade, he caught her arm. 'You have been here long enough, Kaebha. You need to put the rest of it behind you. He will learn to trust you when you show him how much he means to you.' His voice softened. 'I know you feel the same way I do. I know how you admire him.'

Rare words from Cooper. Kaebha slowly lowered her blade.

It was a mistake. The hilt of his rapier slammed into her gut, bending her double. Kaebha wheezed and gasped for air. The Pellish man withdrew and sheathed his sword.

'You feel the same way I do,' he said coldly, 'but my loyalty has never been questioned. See that yours is equally unwavering, Kaebha. Or one day he may find he has no use for you.'

Lycaea

It sat beneath my throat. Always angry. A glowing coal I could not cool. Moth's expression made it flare, and the awful sounds almost tore from my lips. Whimpers. Snarls. They forced themselves through my body like vomit, and it was all I could do to choke them down again. My body wanted to change. The wolf inside me was pacing. It would tear me apart if it had the chance.

I would not allow it.

Needing the distraction, I turned my pain outward and sought someone to gnaw at. Lowell sat by the fire, listening gravely as Dodge continued to explain the Kudhienn to him. He had shrunk since the attack on the Valley. Where there might have been rage, there was only a deep and quiet grief. There was no anger to him. No evidence of a wolf struggling for blood and *meat*. He had skinned the goat without hesitation, seemed unbothered by the smell. How was it possible?

The stench of the goat haunted me. Should it have given me hope, this control of Lowell's? It was infuriating. Was it so easy for him to pretend there was no beast within? I wanted to hurt him until he showed he felt something. I wanted to *bite*. I had been able to control it in the Valley, and while we were travelling, but now I was tired. It was hard to keep fighting.

'Lycaea.'

The tone in Moth's voice buzzed in my ears, made my skull ache and my face flush. Pity, reproach. I hated her for it.

'You need to Shift.'

My body almost betrayed me, almost lurched forwards into her words and embraced the sick contortion of bone and flesh. I held myself rigid and still. The pain deafened me. I could smell my own sweat. I could smell Moth's, and I wondered if she feared for herself. I could not kill her, but in my other shape I could bite off her hand. What right did she have? She was not a waer. She had not been turned against her will. She did not know the impulse to attack, the bloodlust, the way my own senses attacked me at every moment.

She must have seen it in my eyes. She shrank back.

Time passed. The urge passed. My muscles relaxed. Ached as they unclenched. I finally willed my legs to move, and they carried me to snatch the waterskin from the ground by Dodge. The storyteller moved aside. A wordless invitation for me to sit by him. I stood by the fire instead, and sipped the water. It helped to clear my head.

When I felt human again, I sat by Dodge. He smiled at me. I returned my gaze to the fire. Dodge, I knew, would not press me towards Shifting. He tended to leave the mothering to Moth, and I appreciated that. I could tolerate his company for a while.

'How much longer is the journey to Luthan?' Lowell asked.

'Once we're out of the mountains, give it a good two weeks,' Dodge said. 'We'll follow the river right through. If we need to stop, we'll pass through Coserbest on the way south. We can get supplies and the like there.'

'How much distance between Coserbest and Luthan?'

'A week or so, on foot.'

'Along the coast?'

'No, lad. The river forks before Coserbest. One leg cuts through to Luthan. We'll follow that leg. It's a more direct route.'

'Can we seek aid from Coserbest?'

'It's too small,' I put in. 'And all their force comes from ships, and most of those ships are whalers, fishers, or traders. Besides which, we have no sway over Coserbest. Our strength and hope lie in Luthan.'

'Will Leldh and his people move on Luthan as well?'

'Doubt it. He was planning to attack in the spring. The passes won't let him bring an army through at this time of the season.'

'Is there anyone in Coserbest who will help us?'

'Are you done asking questions?'

He frowned and said nothing. I regretted my words. Reminded myself he had lost his whole family. His home. He had stepped into a much larger world. My world.

My fault.

My earlier resentment towards Lowell Sencha faded. Perhaps what he showed was not so much control as resignation. I resolved to be more patient with him.

I cleared my throat. 'There are people in Luthan who will

help us,' I said. 'Leldh is becoming too powerful. He'll strike there, in the spring, when the mountain-passes are clear. Luthan has the biggest population of half-bloods in Oster.'

'And Hemanlok is in Luthan,' Moth added. 'Leldh hates Hemanlok.'

He hates you too, Moth, I wanted to say, but I bit my tongue. Moth Derry had her own secrets. It was not my place to expose them.

We had to travel east around the Valley to reach the southern pass of the mountains. It took longer, but it was safer than crossing the Valley itself. It took four days to put the Valley out of our sights. I was grateful when we could no longer see it. I could not say for certain if Lowell Sencha felt the same way. When it was in sight he was pale and grave but when we left it he looked continuously over his shoulder. Searching for what he had left behind. I did not know what to say to help him. In the end, I held my tongue. If he wanted comfort, he could get it from Moth.

We left the mountains that framed the Valley and the winter rains swept in. The wind made wolfish noises as it whipped past us. I worried we would not find caves to shelter in or animals to hunt. The way was slippery and difficult, and at the end of each day we were freezing, spent. I was coming to feel grateful for the deep sleep Moth could give us. Possibly exhaustion would have prevented ill dreams in any case, but I was glad not to chance it. We needed whatever rest we could claim. I worried we would grow weak and sicken with the cold and battering elements. Moth's presence, alleviating the edge of our discomfort, reassured me.

I had to remind myself how mercenary she could be. Moth, like Hemanlok, like their associate Melana, played a long game. The only difference was Moth had learned to hide it better. She and Dodge appeared for all the world like a wandering couple, devoted in their middle years. A little eccentric, but harmless. It was certainly how Lowell saw them. He helped Moth over crags and rocks, gathered herbs for her, and lent her his cloak when the cold grew sharp. I wondered what he would think if he had any idea what Moth Derry was capable of.

'Please don't tell him.'

Moth came to stand beside me. Her dress was plastered to her with the rain, and her spectacles were so spotted with water I doubted she could see anything. Moth Derry, the Healer of Oster, and she still had to squint to see without those glasses.

'Get out of my head, Derry,' I growled.

'I'm not in your head, dear,' she said. 'I have no wish to know exactly what you think of me. But you are not difficult to read, Lycaea; you never have been. You look at me, scowl, look at Lowell, look at Dodge, look back at me, and then back to Lowell again. It hardly takes a scholar.'

I had not realised I was so obvious.

'Lowell Sencha has known us all his life, Lycaea,' Moth said. 'Much as you have. He does not know the things you do, though.' She looked over her shoulder at Dodge and Lowell. The two were collecting firewood as they went, trying to find something dry enough to burn without smoking us out. 'His world has expanded far enough over the last week. Perhaps you do not care to keep my secrets, but I hope you will show him compassion by holding your silence.'

'Your secrets are your own,' I said. 'He'll find out soon enough, though.'

She pursed her lips. 'Lycaea, there are other things we need to discuss.'

'I suspect you'll be discussing, and I'll be resenting having to listen.' I picked my way over a rotting log and found the path again. It was narrow and winding, but there was a good rocky ledge on the other side that protected us from the worst of the wind and made it safer to walk.

'How long has it been since you Shifted?'

Again, my body coiled and readied itself. Panic made my blood hot. I walked faster. Moth struggled to keep up with me.

'Almost ten months,' I said, because I knew she would not let me be if I refused to answer. She hissed in a breath.

'Ten months of torturing yourself,' she said. 'Why?'

'That's a stupid damn thing to say, Derry, and if you were a waer you'd know it.'

'I have spent a lot of time with waer.'

'And you've spent a lot of time watching women give birth, haven't you, but you still don't know how it feels.' Harsh words, regretted as soon as I saw Moth's expression. She and Dodge had wanted children desperately. It was one of the cruel ironies of her life that she, bound for so many years to deliver and care for children, could never have one of her own. My mother, on the other hand, hated children and had brought me into the world unwelcomed. And there I stood, throwing it in Moth's face. Guilt made a nest in my stomach.

'You have always been blunt, Lycaea,' Moth said. 'You were never cruel.'

'People change, Derry. Perhaps it's the wolf in me.'

In the silence following my words, I could feel her question gathering. I had known it would come.

'Lycaea. Who is Kaebha?'

Kaebha was never far from my mind. After all she had done, it made sense Moth would ask about her.

'Leldh's torturer.' I kept the words steady. *Hold her still. The metal warms. Look at me, dog.* 'She and I came to know one another well, over three years.' The mountain air was bitter, but I sweated and suffered in the heat of fear and shame. 'Why? What have you heard?'

'Whispers.' The word sounded old. She had that look in her eyes. Other-worldly. Distant. I turned my gaze away.

'Storm's coming in.' Dodge's voice was loud, warning us they were almost close enough to hear our conversation. 'We'd best see if we can find shelter before it breaks.'

'Do you get weather like this further south?' Lowell asked. His arms were full of kindling. 'In the mountains around Tadhg?'

'No, lad. It doesna get so cold in Tadhg. The further south, the warmer it gets. Even Luthan will be different to what you're used to.' The two of them passed us. I was glad of Dodge's presence. He took Lowell's mind off the tragedy in the Gwydhan Valley in a way I would never have been able to. A good man, Dodge Derry. He had to be.

We found no caves that night, but a copse of stocky trees and a rocky outcrop gave us shelter from the storm. A fire was impossible, but we managed to keep our kindling dry. We slept on the ground, huddling together for warmth as the weather battled the air about us. I tried not to think about the crowded space too much. It seemed Lowell shared my discomfort. He slept facing away from the rest of us, in his wolf shape. When I woke the next morning, sodden with rain and numb with cold, he was padding about the area, stretching his legs. I stood and clapped my hands against my arms, trying to get the blood flowing. The Derrys were still asleep, hands clasped.

'Bad night,' I remarked to Lowell. He nodded and shook himself, sending water flying. I refrained from making a comment about wet dogs.

The sky was clear, and though the day was cold, the sun would soon dry us. The wind had settled enough for a fire, so I gathered the kindling and used the tinder and flint to bring us some comfort. While my back was to him, Lowell Shifted and pulled his clothes on.

'How did you sleep?' he asked.

'Long enough and deep enough.'

'So did I.' Something in his tone made me turn. His brown eyes were level on me. 'And have done, every night since the Valley was attacked.'

He was starting to emerge from his grief and put things together. Good for him. Not so good for Moth Derry.

'This sort of travel does that to you,' I said.

I wondered if he could smell the falseness on my breath. Why was I bothering to lie for Moth Derry?

He gave me one of his slow, quizzical smiles. It made me uneasy. The man didn't have a single damn thing to be smiling about. The fire leapt high, and I busied myself tending to it.

'You must be glad to be going home,' he said at length.

'Home?'

'Luthan.'

'Oh.' I shrugged, tried to mask the surge of emotion I felt at the thought of Luthan. Hemanlok's city. *My* city. Warm and vibrant, life in every corner. I had not let myself think about it until now, not properly. I suppressed my tone. 'Yes.'

'Such enthusiasm.'

'We have a long way to walk until we reach Luthan, Sencha. I won't be glad until I walk through the gates.' The thought of being apprehended before we reached Luthan was unbearable. I wanted cobbles beneath my feet again. I wanted the warmth of the sun on my face. I wanted the intoxicating scents of the market.

'And then we come back to Caerwyn.'

I started. '*We?*'

'Yes.' Something hardened in his face.

'*You* are not coming back to Caerwyn.'

'I am.'

'You're a farmer.'

'I *was* a farmer.' There was a growl in his voice. It was the most wolf-like tone I had heard him take.

'Has anyone ever taught you how to fight? How to stab a man?'

'I killed a man back in the Valley.'

'And you bawled about it afterwards!' Moth and Dodge were stirring now, roused by our conversation, but I did not lower my voice. 'It's a noble sentiment, Wolf, but we don't have time for noble sentiments. We don't have time for sentiment at all. When we get to Caerwyn, there will be more than five damn soldiers there. They'll tear you apart.'

'Then teach me to fight.'

'It would be a waste of time.'

'I learn swiftly.'

'You can learn as quick as you want, Sencha, but it won't give you a heart hard enough for warfare.'

'They *burned my brother alive*.'

There it was. The creature in his eyes. I saw it, and he recognised that I saw it. His chest rose and fell, struggling under the weight of his anger. His pale cheeks were flushed. His hands were clenched, but he eased the fingers out. He tried to calm himself.

'My little brother,' he said, voice quiet. 'He was just a child. My parents. All sent to Hollow too soon.'

'Daeman Leldh and his people kill many children.' I knew I fell short of gentle, but he needed to understand. 'Leldh, and his captain, Cooper. And his torturer Kaebha. They are merciless, Sencha. All Leldh's soldiers are. I will not be responsible for your death.'

'Then teach me how to fight, and give me a chance. Because I will follow to Caerwyn, Lycaea. There is nowhere else for me to go. I need to see this through. If you teach me, I will at least be able to defend myself.'

It was difficult to argue with his logic.

'Dodge could do with some instruction as well,' Moth said.

I rounded on her, blood shooting to my face. Would she never let me be? She went on, unyielding. 'We won't be fighting in Caerwyn, but if they find us before we reach Luthan, he needs a chance.'

'I can use a sword,' Dodge said, indignant.

'Holding one isn't the same as using one, dear.'

'Hemanlok taught me.'

'Hemanlok was being unkind. He was making fun of you.' She kissed his cheek. 'Learn, love.'

'The things I do for you,' he yawned. He stood, rumpled with sleep, and joined Lowell and me. 'Teach us,' he said.

'Not now.' Moth and Dodge would never let it rest. I could not refuse them; I could only stall. 'I don't want either of you doing something ridiculous like falling off the side of the mountain. When we get to the plains country.'

Stalling. As best I could. I did not know if I could teach them. I did not know if it was safe.

Lowell

I had always been fond of the Derrys, but during those days in the mountains they were the hounds that guarded the flock, kept me safe from the terrors of the darkness. It helped they had known my family so well. Sometimes, when I was overwhelmed and wept, Moth sat with me, crying her own tears. Dodge would leave us, then, letting us rest in the gentler melancholy that comes with shared grief. When we had dwelt on our pain too long, he would come back and comfort us with riddles and stories.

Lycaea, for her part, stayed away. I could not tell if she felt guilty or just lacked the patience. She had not truly known my family or the Gwydhan Valley, and to her it was just another example of the destruction Leldh could wreak. And he was searching for her.

She was difficult and distant until we left the steeper climbs and descended into the plains at the foot of the mountains, to the south-east of the Valley. It was the furthest south I had ever been. Already, the land had changed beneath my feet. The soil was harder, the grass less green. I had to force myself not to turn around, to search for what I had known.

The land ahead was vast. Grass and fields lounged before us, impossibly wide. In the distance, on the rise of a gradual slope, I could just make out the fringes of a forest. To the west, I knew the river lay nestled between grassy banks; I could hear it, but I could not see it. When we reached the road protruding from the mountains, I sat and stared at the world ahead. I had known it was much bigger than the Valley, but having it before me was a different matter.

I wanted to go home.

'We have to stay off the road.' I would have expected the comment from Lycaea, ever-vigilant, but instead it came from Moth. 'If they have finished searching the Valley, they will come through here.'

'Yes.' Lycaea released a long breath. 'We're exposed here, too. Too open. We'll have to push hard until we reach those trees.'

'What do we do in the event of an attack?' Dodge asked. He took a swig from the water-skin and handed it to Moth.

'We scatter,' Lycaea answered. 'Though I imagine you will have to stay with Moth.'

Sometimes I wondered about Moth; whether perhaps she was more frail than she seemed. I supposed she had to be well enough to travel with Dodge, but I worried there was something wrong with her, something no one had told me. I resolved to be kinder to her, and more watchful.

Lycaea was correct, we did have to push hard to travel

across the plain by nightfall, but was much easier going than the mountains. The grass reached my knees as I walked, and although it was different from the grass at home, if I ignored the scent I could pretend I was back in the Valley.

I put my head down and walked. Rain fell. Dusk stretched over our heads, cool and welcoming. I thought of the day Mother realised she was pregnant with Kemp. Father had taken me out to the forest and we had camped there, just the two of us. The forest had been dark and brisk, and the next day we ached to the bone with tiredness and the cold, but I was jubilant. It was the first time I had felt admitted into the adult world.

I would have given anything to have them back.

I went about the Grey Worship as soon as we were sheltered by the trees. The others waited for me; I knew Lycaea was impatient to make camp, but said nothing.

'I'll take the first watch tonight,' she said as we started off once more, seeking a good place to stop for the night. She pushed low-hanging branches aside and held them back so they did not snap in our faces. The gesture was small, but it surprised me, and reminded me again that perhaps she was not so callous as she sometimes pretended.

'If you are tired, I can take the first watch,' I offered.

'It's fine, Wolf,' she said. I wished she would call me by my name. 'You and Dodge will need your sleep for tomorrow.' I frowned. Lycaea glanced at me. 'No longer so keen?' she asked. 'I thought you wanted to learn to fight.'

I felt my features draw back in surprise. 'Really?'

'I said I would, didn't I?' She sounded irritated. 'Or perhaps you've changed your mind.'

'I want to learn.'

'Well, we'll see how long that lasts.'

'Not everything you touch ends in disaster, lass.' Dodge rocked Lycaea's shoulder with a friendly hand. She shrugged him off, but not before I noticed the twist of her lips. Almost a smile. She creased her face into a frown, hiding any traces.

'Here will do,' she said, changing the subject and shedding her sword and cloak as we came to a clearing. 'We can meet up with the river tomorrow afternoon. There are enough trees running along the banks to shelter us. Is everyone capable of going straight through to Luthan without stopping in Coserbest?'

'I think we should stop,' Dodge said. 'We need blankets, lass, and some proper supplies. It's a miracle we made it out of the mountains, frankly. We're all a good sight thinner than we were when we left the Valley.'

He was right there. Moth was more bird-like than ever. The sharpness of Lycaea's face was pronounced. Dodge's cheeks were becoming hollow.

'I agree,' I said. We all looked at Moth.

'I think we should stop to get supplies, but not overnight,' she said. 'We need to make the best time we can to Luthan. We go in, we visit the market, and we get back on the road. Coserbest has sailors and chipre-folk passing through all the time. Hopefully no one will look at us twice.'

'Very well.' I could tell Lycaea was displeased, but she was outnumbered. She scraped a clear space in the dirt with her foot, then used the tip of her stolen sword to sketch out a map. 'We follow the river east, all the way to where it splits. We take the upper river road to the coast. After that, it's about half a day to Coserbest, on the coastline. We pick up supplies, and then double back to take the lower river road, all the way to Luthan. It should take us about fifteen or sixteen days, including the detour to Coserbest.'

'Fourteen, at our pace,' Dodge disagreed.

'Our pace will be slower if I'm teaching the two of you how to fight. Moth, do we have any of the rabbits left?' I had hunted for us three nights before, revelling in the peace and the freedom of my wolf shape. I was glad when Moth shook her head.

'I can hunt for more,' I volunteered.

'Are you sure?' Moth asked.

'It is as invigorating as sleep,' I told her. I made sure Lycaea heard my words. Her refusal to Shift disturbed me. Perhaps she feared the pain. If so, the only cure was to practise Shifting until she overcame it and her body adjusted.

Lycaea, stoic and stone-faced, looked away as I Shifted. I wanted another waer around. I wanted to run with her, to hunt with her. The wolf in me recognised her as pack, yearned for the rough play and closeness of our own kind. She held back. Everything about her screamed she was holding back. I could not understand.

I left them, and went to hunt.

The next morning dawned with just a whimper of rain and we managed to find dry rosemary for the Dawn Worship. Though the skies remained heavy, it did not seem we would have wild weather for the rest of the day. I was relieved; I knew the lessons were going to be hard enough without the rain.

Moth sat at the fringes of the clearing, the waterskin freshly filled. Dodge played the fool for a short while, larking around to elicit Moth's laughter. Once Lycaea was ready, however, he stopped and focused, dark eyes on the angular young woman in front of us.

'Before you learn to land a blow, you need to learn to take one,' she said. 'We can start with hand-to-hand combat, and then work with the two swords we have. Stretch and warm yourself first.' She took us through different ways to ready our muscles for the exercise. When she deemed us ready, she showed us how to roll with a fall, to prevent breaking bones, and how to lessen the impact of a blow. In spite of her warnings, I was surprised how painless the experience was. She was careful and matter-of-fact in her instruction. She taught us how to throw someone off when they had you pinned to the ground, and how to twist your hand out of someone's grip, no matter how hard they held you. She also instructed how to knock someone out with your head, though she declined to have us demonstrate on one another, as Dodge suggested.

By midday, all three of us were sweat-drenched and exhausted, and Lycaea called an end to the lesson. We drank from the waterskin, packed our belongings, and walked again. Moth gathered various plants as we went; she seemed happier in the forest. Even Lycaea was in good spirits, letting Moth check her head wound without scowl or complaint. And Dodge was correct; although we delayed for the lessons each morning, we reached the fork in the river a day earlier than expected. Moth begged some bread from a local farmer, much to Lycaea's horror, and we ate well that night. Rabbits, chestnuts, and watercress gathered from the streams coming off the river. Worth the risk, I thought, for full stomachs.

*

By the time we reached the fork in the river, Lycaea decided it was time for us to try using swords. We only had the two she had stolen from the soldiers in the Valley, so we had to learn this one-on-one. I was glad when Dodge opted to learn first. Lycaea had been a good teacher thus far, but I could smell her nerves and it made me edgy. I went to sit by Moth. She seemed agitated herself, picking at stray threads on her yellow dress.

'Have you seen Lycaea use a sword?' I asked.

'Yes, dear. Many times. She prefers a bow-staff, but Hemanlok has all his people trained in a number of weapons.'

'I saw her fight the night we left the Valley.' I could not forget the blood.

Moth took my hand. Her fingers were long and worn, knotted with years of toil.

'Whenever you need to talk about it, I'm here,' she said.

Dodge and Lycaea finished stretching and picked up their swords. Slowly at first, they started to drill. I found myself watching their feet more than their swords. Lycaea was never still, but never moved without purpose. Each motion was clean and precise. After a short while, I could smell Dodge's sweat. He was not a young man, and Lycaea was relentless. Their breathing became audible. The swish and clank of metal, previously slow, was starting to quicken.

'Faster,' Lycaea snapped.

'Easy, lass.' Dodge tried to laugh, but he was breathless. I felt Moth's hand tighten about mine.

'Faster,' Lycaea repeated. 'Will your enemy slow for you?'

'Lass.' His voice grew sharp. 'I canna keep up.'

'Lycaea.' I pulled my hand from Moth's and stood. 'Slow down.'

She did not reply this time, but she swung the sword down at Dodge's foot. He jumped and the sword hit the dirt. She swung it up, sending soil spraying as she came back to position.

'Lycaea, stop!'

She stepped in and drove the hilt of her sword into Dodge's gut. When he doubled over, she grabbed his hair and dragged him down. He fell. I raced forwards. Lycaea kicked Dodge in the ribs and spun to face me. I snatched Dodge's sword from where it had fallen. Just in time, I met her blade. The clash of metal shook through my arm. Her eyes were flat, unseeing. Dodge lay gasping on the ground. I had never used a sword before. I gripped it with both hands, trying desperately to meet each swing. She clipped my arm. Pain shot through me. I almost dropped the sword. Lycaea stepped back, then lunged in. I fell to a knee and lifted the sword, pushed it up and aside. My arm bled. A blur in front of my eyes. My head screamed. My back found the dirt. The world was water, and Lycaea rippled as she stood above me.

Moth, behind Lycaea, put her hands on either side of the woman's head. A flash of green light. Dodge pried the sword from Lycaea's grip. Lycaea tensed, then swayed, then fell.

I stared at Moth. Her hands were still raised, and the air around them glowed. Her eyes were ancient.

Kaebha

Leldh pressed the hilt of the sword into her hand. His face was close to hers. He smiled, and his teeth gleamed in the light of the torches along the wall.

'Your strike, Kaebha,' he said.

She curled her fingers about the sword. It was cool in her hand. The woman on the floor, bleeding and broken, stared at her with dull eyes. She was young, perhaps a few years younger than Kaebha herself. Dark hair, dark eyes. Just another one of Leldh's prisoners. A waer, as so many had been.

Kaebha circled the woman on the floor. Her boots met blood, came away sticky and wet. Her lip curled. Unclean. She would have to do as Cooper had suggested and scour everything once she was done here. Waer blood was filthy. She could not afford to be infected.

'Kaebha.' Leldh's voice was stern. 'Focus.'

Kaebha tested the sword in the air, twisted it in a figure-of-eight. The waer-woman whined, twisting on the floor, and covered her head.

Her feet were bare and dirty. Half her fingers were broken. She was skinny, hair shaved and skin raw, her lips swollen and cracked. The band of silver about her ankle kept her from Shifting, and burned deep welts into her flesh. She shivered and whimpered, her leg kicking in a feeble, futile attempt to push the silver away.

Kaebha could not move.

'Kaebha!'

She lowered the sword. Flashes of her old life choked her. She remembered. Her body screamed. There had been days before Daeman Leldh. Days of summer and salted air. Her hands faltered.

She stepped away.

'No,' she said. She could feel Cooper's sneer, twisting into the back of her neck. She could feel Leldh's displeasure. He cleared the distance between them, grabbed her arm.

'Deny me again,' he whispered. 'Just once, Kaebha.'

'I cannot do this. She is an innocent. Scarcely more than a child.'

Leldh wrenched her arm. The sword clattered to the ground. Kaebha cried out. There was a loud snap. Broken bone. Kaebha cradled the limb, knowing worse was still to come. Leldh spat on her and stood back.

'Cooper,' he said. The Pellish man strode forward, snatched up the sword, and ran the waer woman through. Kaebha heard a scream and a gurgle, watched as the prisoner curled on the ground and died slowly. Leldh's attention was on Kaebha. He crouched before her and grabbed her chin.

'Loyalty,' he said. 'Loyalty, Kaebha. You have failed me.'

She did not argue. She knew it was true. She had no explanation for her inaction.

'I hate to punish you.' Leldh rose. 'You show so much potential. But you need to learn obedience, and loyalty. The canine qualities.' He

seemed thoughtful, golden eyes mild. Kaebha lowered her head. Sweat beaded on her brow and rolled down past her cheeks. Leldh let her wait.

'My lord.' Cooper was too eager. He wanted to see her punished. Kaebha could read the irritation in Leldh's reply.

'Yes. Very well.' She heard his boots clip the floor as he walked towards the door. 'Beat her, then bring her to me. Keep her conscious. I want her to feel every moment.'

Lycaea

'Get up. Get up and try again.' Hemanlok threw the stave at me. My limbs were heavy and sore. The air was stale with sweat.

'Pathetic.' A low, melodious chuckle from my mother, leaning on the railing to watch us train. She was waiting to deal with Hemanlok; one of the few occasions she was allowed onto his turf. 'Why did you take her under your roof?'

'She wouldn't leave me alone until I did.'

I tasted dust again as he knocked me flat onto my belly. Hemanlok's lip curled. He was embarrassed, I realised. Embarrassed by my failure, especially in front of my mother.

'Control,' he said. 'You need – to learn – control.'

The training-ring disappeared. A flash of gold eyes. The stench of burning flesh.

Kaebha.

I woke screaming her name. Damn her. Damn him. I would never escape them. Daeman Leldh and his pet torturer.

I was shamed by the sweat staining my clothing, slicking my hair. My hands shook. My head reeled. All I could hear was the boot-like drum of my heart, and the sound of my own ragged breaths.

'Lass.'

I saw Dodge, and a new shame rose to replace the old. I had swung the sword at him, unable to stop myself. I remembered knocking him to the ground. Kicking him, a man who had never done me harm. Guilt made me mute. He sat by me, cross-legged. Bedraggled. Hesitant. Afraid to see who would look out at him from my eyes. I swallowed to clear my dry throat. Moth had done the only thing she could. I was grateful to her. I could have done so much damage.

It was an effort to move my hand. More of an effort to take Dodge's, to try to convey my remorse. His palm, rough and weathered, was warm. He squeezed my hand and pulled me into his arms. I hunched over and let him hug me. My lungs eased. We sat in silence, and then I pulled away from him. It was all I could do to school my features and speak calmly.

'It won't happen again.'

'Past is past,' he said. 'I know you didna mean to, and there's no lasting harm done.' He touched my cheek, fatherly and forgiving. 'We have new problems to address, though. Moth had to make you sleep. Lowell saw.'

I winced. 'Where is he?'

'Hunting. He willna speak to her. He's frightened, lass, and alone. First you scared him witless, and then Moth did. We've known him since he was a child. It's too much for him to realise that *he* hasna known *us*. You'll have to be the one to explain.'

'I will.' I owed him. Dodge, whom I had known since I was a child myself. Dodge, with his stories and his unyielding love for Moth. Dodge, who had almost been cut open by my sword-strike. 'Are you sure he'll come back?'

'He doesna have anywhere else to go.' Dodge reached for my cloak. He eased it around my shoulders and fastened the clasp. 'Listen. We're only a day or so from Coserbest. I think it's best if Moth and I go on into the town to gather supplies. You and Lowell can walk on without us or stay here. We'll catch up with you either way. I believe he needs some space from us. This will be a lot for him to take in. I remember hearing it for the first time.'

I nodded. I had been raised with the knowledge of Moth and Hemanlok's dark business with their third associate. Lowell had not. I remembered Moth's words about his world expanding too far.

'You're best staying out of the town in any case,' Dodge said. 'What do you think?'

'I think you're a wise man.' The words were stiff on my lips, but they brought a warmth to Dodge's eyes. He leaned forwards and kissed my forehead. My eyes stung.

'Chin up, lass,' Dodge said. 'You're almost home.'

Home. The thought washed away Kaebha's darkness. Soon we would be in Luthan. It helped to look ahead.

I stood. My legs were heavy, my body still shaking off the sleep Moth had put upon it. I nodded to Dodge.

'I need to speak with Moth,' I told him. 'Then I'll find Lowell Sencha.'

'Good lass,' he said. I managed a smile, though it felt foreign to my features. Dodge winked at me, and I moved across the clearing to where Moth sat, on her own. She had been crying. I could smell the tears. Her narrow shoulders were high by her ears, and her light hair was unkempt. The wolf in me felt a surge of the old anger, the resentment. I pressed it down. Moth had sent me into danger, but now she was walking me away from it. I had almost killed her husband, the man she had fought so hard to stay with.

'Derry.'

She removed her spectacles to wipe at her eyes before she turned to face me.

'I had to.' Her tone was defensive, her chin high. 'You would have killed Lowell Sencha, and then you would have killed my husband. I cannot harm anyone, Lycaea, but neither will I stand passive and helpless while others do. Not if I can help it.'

'I'm not blaming you,' I said. 'You did what you had to. I understand. I don't want their blood on my hands.'

Silence hovered between us. The walls between us were my doing. She had tried to breach them, and I had rejected her.

'May I sit?' I asked. Moth moved aside to give me room. I sat beside her. I noticed, for the first time, how old she looked. Bird-like and fragile, though her eyes were steely grey. I remembered afternoons of fresh bread, tea, and laughter. We had been friends, once. We had spent late nights poring over maps and talking. She had taught me how to stitch a wound, and had intervened on my behalf to spare me Hemanlok's temper.

'I'm sorry,' I said. Not just for Dodge. For everything else. She had loved the Valley, too. Of the Three, Moth was the most human. She tied herself to people and their places. She suffered when they did.

Moth said nothing, but she rested her head on my shoulder. I breathed out the resentment I had been holding so close. She was the Healer, but she could not heal the irreparable. She could not undo what had been done to me, or her part in it.

'It's been a long time since I feared losing him,' she said at last. 'We're usually so careful. I forget he's growing older. One day, I might not be able to protect him.'

'Nothing bad is going to happen to Dodge.' I was surprised by how fierce my voice sounded. Moth lifted her head from my shoulder.

'I once swore nothing bad would happen to you,' she said. Her words were halting and careful.

'Past is past.' I echoed Dodge's words. 'I need all the Three on my side if we're going to defeat Leldh. So we need to put this behind us, Moth. You and I, and the other two. There's been wrong done on all sides. We can't erase it, but we can move forward from it.'

'I am glad to hear it,' she said. 'I want Leldh gone as much as you do. He's a threat to all we have worked so hard for. I cannot fight him the same way you can, but I will resist any way I know how. And I will help you as much as I can.'

'Thank you.'

'What of Lowell Sencha?'

I explained Dodge's suggestion and she nodded.

'It might be for the best,' she agreed. 'When should we leave?'

'Before he comes back from the hunt. This needs to be managed sooner rather than later. We need to get a field-dressing on the damage.' I paused. The phrase brought back the scuffle with brutal vividness. 'Did I hurt him?'

'You gave him a nasty cut on the arm and a bruised head,' she said. 'But Shifting heals the worst of that sort of wound. It's helpful for all but silver-burns, really. I'm more concerned about the state of his mind. Be careful with him, Lycaea. He is suffering.'

'I know.'

She stood and went over to Dodge. I felt lighter. It was hardly a joyous reconciliation, but it would hold us steady for long enough.

By the time Lowell returned from his hunt, Moth and Dodge were gone. He stood in his wolf form, hackles up, watching me with wary eyes. I held both my hands at my shoulders, showing him I meant no harm. After a while, he Shifted and pulled on his clothes. His eyes latched onto the ground. I could see the bruise on his brow, but Moth had been correct; it was less severe than it would have been without the Shift.

'I'm sorry I hurt you.' The word was becoming easier to say.

'You did not seem to see us at all.' His words were small and hard, loaded with accusation. 'You were someone else, Lycaea. I thought you were going to kill me.'

'I might have,' I confessed.

'Where are Moth and Dodge?' He forced the words out.

'They went on to Coserbest to get supplies. They'll meet with us tomorrow evening. They wanted to give you time to absorb and adjust.'

He gave a bitter breath of laughter. 'Did they? How kind.'

He sounded like me, then. I did not like it. Acidity did not fit his mouth, his temperate features.

I decided to be blunt.

'Moth and Dodge are concerned for you,' I told him. 'They want me to explain matters to you, and help you…understand.' I shook my head. 'Don't search for the logic in that. I'm clearly not exactly stable myself.'

'I have seen what Moth can do.' His voice was hollow. 'Her power. Did you know? Did my parents know?'

'I doubt your parents did. Moth likes nothing better than to pretend she is normal. She hides her strangeness under layers of domesticity.'

'What is she?'

'Sit down.'

'I will stand.' There was the wolf again, flaring behind his eyes. 'What *is* she, Lycaea? Is she a Kudhienn?'

'The opposite.' I rubbed the back of my neck. 'Do you know what a Watcher is?'

'Everyone knows the Watcher stories. Master Derry tells them all the time. Children's tales.' His last sentence thought to be dismissive. It came out desperate, as if he longed for me to confirm they were, indeed, just fables.

'That's how the story goes.' I met his gaze. 'Dealer, Assassin, Healer. Three people with impossible powers who guard the balance between good and evil.'

'Of course. That's…'

'Which means without them, the world would be immersed in one or the other, yes? And the good is as dangerous as the evil. It poisons and corrupts itself over time, without opposition to balance it.'

He was silent now.

'We don't need them all the time. Usually, we're able to

balance things ourselves. But sometimes – with great tyrants, with revolution, even natural disasters – things become uneven. And without the help of the Watchers, we plunge into darkness.'

I knew how grudging I sounded. We needed them, yes, and it made their failures all the more difficult to bear. I watched Lowell. He was stiff and pale, his eyes fixed on me.

I went on: 'Some say the world would unmake itself if the scales tipped too far one way or the other. Most have forgotten the old stories now, but without the Watchers and the balance they maintain, the world would be ash and dust. They have lived for hundreds of years, though one would never guess it by their appearance. Years ago, they rallied Oster to fight the Kudhienn and won. You know that story at any rate. Did you know it almost destroyed the Watchers? Cost them so much power they were helpless to prevent what happened next, when the people of Oster turned, and slaughtered the remaining Kudhienn. The children, the elderly.'

'Dodge said that. I did not believe…I thought…'

'It happened. But some of the children must have escaped, at least, because Daeman Leldh was one of them. The Kudhienn do not live so long as the Watchers, but they can still last out hundreds of years and seem unmarked by time. Leldh grew, knowing what had happened to his people and knowing who caused it. He put the blame on the waer people, who were instrumental in the destruction of the Kudhienn. Deeper than his hatred for the waer, though, is his hatred for the Watchers.'

'Lycaea, *stop*. This is not *real*.'

'It is.' He tried to turn away from me, but I caught his

wrist and held it fast. 'Lowell. This is the truth. Think about it. If you can believe Daeman Leldh is a Kudhienn, you can believe this. Moth Derry is a Watcher. There are two others. Hemanlok, and the Wytch named Melana. Individually, they are weak, compared to what they once were. Leldh has wards, ways to keep them out of Caerwyn if they are separate. But if we can convince all three to help, we can get into Caerwyn and destroy him. That's why we are going to Luthan. For Hemanlok and Melana.'

'Stop *lying!*'

I knew he believed me. I fell silent. Lowell's shoulders were hunched, his fists clenched. There was a flush high in his cheeks. He sat and raked thin hands through his hair. 'It is too much,' he said, voice low.

'It changes nothing, Wolf.'

'It changes *everything.*'

I knew what he was thinking. The similarities between the deities of his faith and the Watchers were strong. I did not share his faith, but I knew it was important to him. He had lost enough in the last few weeks. 'It changes nothing,' I repeated. 'Who is to say your gods did not make the Watchers in their image? The Watchers are not deities. They are people with long lives and terrible duties. They did not shape this world; they just try to keep it in balance. Hold your faith, Sencha. It does not have to falter because of what you have learned tonight.'

'Madam Derry...'

'Moth is still Moth. A healer with a storytelling husband. She's older than you thought, and has seen more. Perhaps she is more cunning, less honest. But at her essence, she is unchanged. She still cares deeply for you, as she cared for your family.'

'All it took was a touch, and you were unconscious.'

'And she has been easing our sleep since we left the Valley. She could not do us harm even if she wanted to, Sencha. As the Healer, she is forbidden to hurt anyone. It's why she couldn't intervene with the fight, and one of the reasons she couldn't prevent the events in the Valley from taking place. Her powers are limited in form, and weakened since the business with the Kudhienn.'

Exhaustion and confusion lowered his head. 'What else have they lied about?'

'Not much, I'd say. The story about Leldh is all true. Hemanlok, the Assassin, sent me to find out if Leldh was Kudhienn. Once Leldh has built his power, he will strike Luthan, because it is the heart of the Watchers. The Assassin and the Dealer both live there. I was supposed to bring back information of his plans, of his strategy for attack. I was intercepted on my way out, and now I remember little of what I saw. Three years at the hands of Kaebha...' My voice faltered. Lowell met my gaze. He was calming. I cleared my throat. 'Leldh wants me back so he can punish the Watchers, because he knows I mean something to them. He also wants me back so he can prevent me from bringing them information.'

'And for that reason, he killed my parents and my little brother.'

'Yes.'

'How are you connected to the Watchers, Lycaea?' he asked.

'I worked for Hemanlok. He took me in when I was a

child, taught me how to fight. Partly because Moth begged him to, and partly because he was glad to get some hold over my mother.'

'Why could you not stay with your mother?'

'She's insane. Unsafe.'

He absorbed that in silence. Changed the subject without betraying his thoughts. 'What of Master Derry?' he asked.

I raised an eyebrow. It was not the question I had expected from him. 'What about him?'

'What is he?'

'Human,' I replied. 'A human man with a human lifespan. Watchers aren't supposed to fall in love. Moth had to fight hard to win the right to be with him. Fight against Hemanlok, and the Dealer. Fight against the Balance. It'll end in tragedy, of course; she'll outlive him by many, many years.'

He pushed a hand over his face. His misery was tangible.

I took up a stick and poked at the fire. Sparks flew into the air, brightened the night. 'At least they're on our side.'

'Do you think they can defeat Daeman Leldh?'

'If they can't, we're dead.' No point lying to him. Not about this. 'But they defeated the collective Kudhienn force, once. If we can get all three of them working together again, we have a good chance. Even if they're weaker than they once were.'

'Will they cooperate? All three?'

'Hemanlok will, most likely. Moth will. The third...' I shrugged. 'Difficult to say. Of the three, she is the most powerful outside of Luthan. But she lost her mind years ago. Even Moth can't heal her. If the Dealer can't be convinced by Moth, I'll have to try.'

'Why would she listen to you?'

'I can tell her things about Leldh. And I've dealt with her before; I know the chinks in her armour.' It sounded weak, even to my own ears, but I was more than willing to distance myself from the Wytch. The Dealer.

I stood, restless. I had no wish to talk about Melana at great length. She had a knack for turning up when her name was spoken too often, and I wanted to be fully prepared before I confronted her. She was treacherous, slippery to deal with. 'You don't need to concern yourself with her, Wolf. If you're lucky, you won't have to meet her at all.'

'If I was lucky, I would still be in the Valley. And my family would be with me.'

We let the fire crackle between us.

'All I can offer you is revenge,' I said at last. 'And it's not a certainty, and it won't bring back what you lost.'

He stood. 'It will have to be enough,' he said, extending a hand to me. We shook. Lowell's face was grace, but his eyes gentled, and there was no animosity between us when he went to sleep.

For once, the wolf in me was quiet. Watchful, but still.

Lowell

I had not expected Lycaea to be a comfort, but her honesty gave me solid ground to walk upon. There was something reassuring about her bluntness, even if at times it seemed cruel. She was not malicious, as I had first suspected. Rather, I think she was reluctant to forgive the world around her for the cruelty she had been dealt. I could understand that.

We waited for Moth and Dodge to return, rather than leaving without them. I struggled with the new knowledge of Moth's identity. It was difficult to accept, though it made sense on many levels. Moth's apparent frailty. The way she and Dodge latched onto one another as though they had a soul-bond, as though they could whisper soul to soul. The deep sleeps we had all been blessed with, even after the carnage in the Valley. Moments from my childhood occurred to me: fevers vanishing mysteriously, broken bones healing quicker than anyone expected. Everyone put Moth's skill down to her being more worldly than the single healer of the Valley. How worldly, none of us had guessed.

'What supplies do you think they will bring from Coserbest?' I asked.

'Food, blankets, hopefully shoes. And, knowing Moth, tea.'

'How will they pay for everything?'

'They have friends in Coserbest. Besides, people happily pay for Dodge's stories.' She stomped out the fire and went about the clearing, scattering leaves and dirt to eradicate traces of our presence. I helped her. I buried the remains of my hunt from the night before. It had been a poor excuse for a meal; I had been too distracted to catch more than one rabbit. Lycaea, to her credit, had not complained, though by noon she must have been as hungry as I was. She paced as the sun crept over our heads. Agitated. I wondered what she was thinking.

'We bring tea.'

Lycaea coughed, covered a grin. I forced a smile, though I did not feel it. Dodge came through the trees first, two bags slung over his shoulder. He handed one to each of us. It was as much a peace offering as anything else, from his expression. I nodded and opened the bag, searching through it. Potatoes, onions, salted fish, a blanket, and a pair of walking-boots. The small comfort of those items made my resentment fade.

'Thank you,' I said. 'How did you manage to afford all this?'

Moth stepped into the clearing, holding another two bags. She did not meet my eyes as she answered. 'Dodge told some stories, and I did a few healing jobs for some old friends. We're lucky; everything is less expensive in Coserbest than it is in Luthan.'

I faltered, not knowing what to say to her. After all these years, I did not know her at all. I remembered the flash of green light, and Lycaea falling. Moth's eyes, old and otherworldly.

Lycaea pulled her new cloak about her shoulders, tucking the older one into her bag.

'Good,' she said. 'Let's go. We have a few hours along the river before sun sets. Dodge, tell me how things went in Coserbest.'

She started ahead of us. Dodge took Moth's bag from her and kissed her, then went to join Lycaea. I watched them walk ahead of us, through the shadow of the trees framing the river. It was clear Lycaea had left Moth behind with me to settle the tension between us. Moth cleared her throat, twisting the sleeve of her dress.

'How has Lycaea been?' she asked in a low voice. She still could not meet my eyes.

'Surprisingly well,' I told her. 'We had a long discussion. It cleared the air somewhat. Lycaea...explained matters. I understand now.'

'I am glad you know the truth, Lowell. Few people do.' Her eyes searched my face. She was full of caution.

I offered her my arm as we started to walk. It was instinctual, but she was so grateful, I was glad I had done it. I reflected on how kind she had always been to my mother, and how much Kemp had loved both the Derrys. Her arm felt thin and delicate linked with my own.

'Tell me about Coserbest,' I said.

It was a chance to move away from discussion of the Watchers, and Moth took it eagerly. She described the small fishing town so I could almost see it when I closed my eyes;

the squat limestone buildings, the rickety jetties and the fat, rugged ships in the harbour. I had never seen the ocean, but I had seen paintings the chipre-folk sold, and Dodge had described it enough times. I could smell the salt the Derrys had carried back in their hair and clothing, and traces of fish. There was a warmth to the scent. Something wholesome and vivid, far from the delicate sweetness of the Gwydhan Valley.

The weather started to change as we moved further south. The chill was taken off the air, and the rain fell less frequently, but with more weight. Grass became scrub, and the trees thinned. Moth said the air would only get warmer as we neared Luthan. She said they had never seen snow there; much different from the Valley, where we saw snow every other winter.

Home was too far away to think about. I forced my mind away, to the journey ahead. And Luthan.

As we drew closer to Luthan, we were forced to take the dirt road. It became cobbled, and filled with people as we neared the city. I felt the old grasps of panic at the sight and smell of so many people. Lycaea was straight-backed, her eyes gleaming as she took in her surroundings, obviously familiar with them. The limestone buildings ahead were dense and uniform, with few windows and grey roofs. The city was so populated, houses were built on top of one another – entire families lived above others. For a waerwolf who had come from the Valley, where everything had been spacious and clean, this was an alien concept. The skies were thick with smoke and the smell of salt and fish lay heavily upon the air, indicating the main trade within Luthan.

People passed us pushing carts of fish, and I saw someone carrying what Dodge told me was a shark. It looked monstrous, and I said as much to Lycaea. Unusually conversational, she told me sharks were nothing compared to durlows. Durlows were enormous, furred creatures who inhabited the north-east seas and often came as far south as Coserbest. Lycaea told me they were as large as a whale, which meant little to me; I had never seen a whale. Both whales and durlows were hunted by the Coserians, for oil and meat.

The city loomed above us, pale and weather-beaten. It stood on the top of a hill, which cut down sharply to the ocean. I had never seen so many buildings before. They were surrounded by a large sandstone wall, but from what I could tell passage through the city was largely unrestricted. There were guards, but they did not check the caravans and wagons in front of us, and they waved us through with less than a cursory glance.

We stepped into a narrow street, framed on each side by high walls of thick limestone. There were a few gaps in the wall on either side, offering glimpses into the sprawling districts on either side, and guarded doors. The houses in the north-west corner of the city were barely standing, held together with dubious materials, mostly scavenged. Sounds of brawling came from behind the wall. Men and women shuffled out, pushing carts and hauling bricks. Small children peered through the gaps in the wall or walked along the top, nimble as kittens. They were thin, with big eyes and grubby faces. They called to us as we passed. They knew Moth and Dodge; I heard some of them of them asking for stories. Dodge laughed and waved them away, promising to return.

The doorways of the second section were guarded by armed men in uniforms. Any person to enter the upper section had to present identification and proof of birth, to indicate they were worthy to enter. I watched elegant men and women walking though, attended by servants.

'That's the Primero,' Dodge told me. 'It's for the high and mighties, anyone with a title.'

'And the other section?'

'Ultimo,' he said. 'The slums. Powers that be decided it would be best to separate the city into classes. So one night, about a hundred and fifty years ago, they herded the poor and the helpless into this section, closed the gates, and put guards on them. You need a pass to leave the section, and you need *serans* to get a pass.' *Serans* were coins used by most of Oster. They were made out of fish-scales, packed together tightly. We sometimes used them in the Valley, but more often we bartered and exchanged goods. They were only really useful when the travellers and chipre-folk came through the area.

'And if you cannot obtain *serans?*'

'Then you're trapped.'

I stared at Lycaea. 'You live in a place like this?'

Her lips tilted. 'Wait,' she said. 'Just wait, Sencha.'

'To the south side of the city, beyond the Mercado, are the Grinaja and Ciadudan districts,' Dodge went on. 'The Grinaja is a prison quadrant, and the Ciadudan is for the regular civilians.'

The Mercado, the market, sprawled out before us. I stopped at the wall separating the corridors from the square. Sweat prickled my brow. I could smell animals, and hear them squawling behind the wall. People. Children. Strong aromas burned my nostrils. I stumbled. Too much. Too many. It was hot, and my hands shook. The acrid combination of urine and smoke hit my nose. My wolf growled, and it rumbled through my throat.

'Lycaea? Lowell?' Dodge touched my shoulder.

Lycaea's jaw was clenched. I knew she felt it too, though perhaps not the way I did. The assault on the senses. I forced myself to move. My hand broke the space between us and brushed hers. She did not move. She took two deep breaths, then spoke.

'Keep walking forwards. Mind your pockets. Don't get waylaid, and don't stop for anyone.'

She thrust her chin up and walked forwards. Ignoring the scream of every instinct, I followed her.

The square was large, framed by taverns and inns. Bright colours flooded the market – tents and flags, ribbons and gilded wagons. At the far end of the Mercado was a row of cookeries, roasting goat and beef and pig on spits. A man sat to our right, peddling roasted almonds and chestnuts. A child with orange hair streaked past me, barefoot and shouting obscenities. Perched on the roof of a tavern, a group of men and women sat with their brown legs dangling. They were drinking and calling out to passers-by. I turned in a slow circle, lost in the swarm of activity. A woman bustled by me, a goose under each arm. One honked, making me jump. Lycaea clamped a hand on my shoulder and steered me through the crowd.

Moth was waylaid already, bent to speak to a group of children. They bounced around her, calling and laughing and reaching to touch her hair. Dodge wheeled around and joined her, hoisting a young girl onto his shoulders. Moth took off her spectacles and placed them over a boy's nose. Her laugh rang out clear. I felt a pang of sadness for them both. They would have been so suited to children of their own.

'They'll catch up with us when they've finished playing,' Lycaea said over the noise of the crowd. She kept her hand on my shoulder. It grounded me. I walked, forcing my way through pressed shoulders and waving arms, past carts and stalls and musicians. Someone tall Shifted to my left, and I felt the burst of energy expelled from the action. I stared as a large wolf prowled through the crowd – a souther-waer. Simultaneously, I felt the call of the pack, and utter reprehension. My kind, and yet not my kind.

'Watch out for them,' Lycaea said. 'Sometimes they eat people.'

Not my kind at all.

A juggler wandered by, a path cleared in front of him as he tossed flaming batons. Lycaea dragged me after him and we walked a few paces behind in the clear spaces wrought by his work.

'Pattern and flow,' Lycaea said. 'You learn to follow the beat of the crowd. Keep up, Sencha.' In spite of her initial pause, she seemed to be enjoying herself now.

I could not see where we were going. I had lost all sense of direction. Moth and Dodge had long been swallowed by the milling masses. How could one place be so full, so alive? I made myself breathe steadily. Followed Lycaea. The people around us were deafening. I was lost, could not string together my thoughts.

'Here. Here, Wolf.' She pulled me forwards and we

broke out of the crowd. We stood in the shadow between a temporary weapons-stall and the permanent inn standing behind it. I braced my hands on my thighs and dragged in several lungs of air.

'Is it always like that?'

'Mostly. Can you breathe?'

'Yes.' I straightened. 'Sorry.'

'Never apologise.' Her voice was brusque, but I was learning not to mistake that for unkindness. 'Not for things beyond your control. Come. We still have a way to go.'

'Moth and Dodge?'

'They know where we're going. They'll catch up.'

'Where *are* we going, Lycaea?'

'The Grinaja.'

I stopped, trying to remember if the Grinaja was the quadrant designated to the prisoners, or the civilians.

'The Grinaja?'

'The prison district,' Lycaea confirmed. 'Keep close. Be careful.' She ducked into an alleyway between the inn and another building. I followed, glad to leave the rush of the Mercado behind. We walked through the narrow alley, shaded by the roof-ledges. The sun glared through the cracks, shining onto the cobbles. I squinted at it, unable to believe this was winter in Luthan. It was warm, even in the shade.

We came to a fence and Lycaea climbed over. It was high and metal, but not difficult to scale. On the other side lay a bare street and an imposing wall. Lycaea nodded towards the wall.

'The Grinaja is beyond,' she said. 'We'll have to go in an old way, through a broken fountain. Assuming it's still there.

Guards patrol most of the streets, so be alert. If they catch you out, you'll get a beating. Or locked up.'

'Have you been caught before?' I lowered my voice as we neared the wall.

'Three times. The first two times were unpleasant. The third time was different. I was one of Hemanlok's people by then, established. The lawkeepers let it slip, because it was better than crossing the boss.'

'Does everyone in Luthan know who he is?'

'Of course.'

We rounded a corner, into a dead end. The old fountain was there as Lycaea had said; several limestone horses standing on a platform. Lycaea climbed onto the platform and ducked between the legs of the horse. She was lost in the shadows, and I hastened to go after her. I had to crawl. It should have smelt musty and foul in the tight space, but instead I caught traces of clean air. I wriggled through the darkness and found the statue legs replaced on either side of me by brick. When I clambered out, I was on the other side of the wall.

The Grinaja was quiet. Still. The buildings were large and rectangular, regular, with barred windows. There were some lights, but it was mostly dark. I wondered that a whole district could serve the purpose of housing criminals. Were there so many?

Lycaea seemed to read my thoughts. 'The criminals and their families live here,' she said. 'If your parents are both imprisoned, for example, you get moved to one of the Crims' Orphanages here in the Grinaja. Awful places. Half the time, the children would be better off on the street. If your spouse is imprisoned, you're forcibly moved here and given a job washing or whoring or breaking up bricks or maintaining the streets. Either that, or you're forced to pay an extortionate tax to keep yourself out. Some people go so far into debt to avoid imprisonment in the Grinaja, they end up in the Ultimo. Couldn't rightly say which is worse.'

'Regardless of their innocence?'

'It's supposed to be more of a deterrent to criminals if their spouses suffer too. I don't know. You force people into the criminal district, pretty sure you'll just get more criminals.'

'Why are we here?'

'Because I'm a criminal. Hush now.'

We stole around buildings. My heart pounded with the same mingling of fear and delight associated with childish hide-and-find games. Felen only knew why I trusted Lycaea. She seemed determined to give me reasons not to.

Shouts and wails were faint in the Grinaja, but almost ever-present. I could hear two people shouting at one another. Every so often, a face appeared at the bars, or an arm stretched through. I wondered at the children who were kept in such a place. I tried not to imagine Kemp there, though it was the first thing to spring to my mind. My poor little brother.

Lycaea took my arm and pulled me into the shadow of a wall. She was alert; her hand gripped me tightly. I could not tell if she was frightened or exhilarated.

'Do you smell that?' she demanded.

I lifted my nose and breathed in the sharp tang of leather, blood-like traces of metal. Sweat and dirt. The sounds reached me now; footsteps rounded the corner. Lycaea was frozen. It was her sweat I could smell. We pressed closer to the wall, just out of sight. I held my breath.

The footsteps were heavy, booted. There was more than one person; I heard softer steps following, and a light sound of something brushing against the wall. Maybe three of them, from the scents. Murmurs reached my ears. I heard Lycaea's sharp intake of breath.

'Wik said she saw them coming though the Mercado. Healer and storyteller both, and our girl.' A woman's voice with a strong Luthanese twang. 'And some norther-waer blood. Wik didn't know him.'

'Is she sure?' A man, also Luthanese. His voice was thin and reedy. 'Is she sure it's *our* girl?'

I looked at Lycaea. Her face was white. She did not move.

'Boss?' The woman again. The heavy footsteps had stopped. 'What is it, Boss?'

A large hand grabbed the front of my shirt and yanked me away from the wall. I shouted and kicked, found my feet hovering off the ground. The man holding me was immense. He held me with little effort. I clutched at his hand, trying to free myself from his grip. He shook me. A wolf shaking prey. I tried to remember what Lycaea had taught us and hit out at his neck, tried to claw at his eyes, but he swung me around and slammed me against the wall. My teeth clacked together. Though my back took the initial impact, my head was forced back until it knocked against the bricks. His hand was at my neck then, cutting off the air. I kicked and struggled. My lungs ached. I could feel blood gathering in my face, swelling it.

The man brought his face close to mine. His skin was nut-brown, but his eyes were white. The white of blindness. He bared his teeth and spoke. His voice was impossibly deep. My vision hazed.

'I could hear you breathing, blood.'

'Put him down, Hemanlok.'

The man's grip on me tightened with Lycaea's voice. I closed my eyes. Slowly, I felt the hold on my neck slacken. He dropped me and stepped back. I slid down the wall, holding my throat. Lycaea pushed past Hemanlok to my side, grabbing my arm and hauling me to my feet.

'Are you hurt?' she asked.

'No.' My voice was thin, but I could breathe.

'Brat.' The man's voice jerked our attention back to him. Lycaea straightened. She kept her hand on my arm, and I did not pull away. I suspected she needed the support as much as I did.

'Not easy to catch you unawares,' she said. 'Either I'm getting quieter, or you're getting slow.'

'That's not her.' It was the other woman, her voice hard and clipped. 'Our girl wouldn't talk to you like that, Boss.'

'Pipe down, Flick.'

'*Boss.*'

'Flick.' Although he did not raise his voice or address me, his tone made me shrink back. The woman, Flick, set her teeth and lowered her head. I dared a glance at Lycaea, and wished I had not. I had never seen her so frightened. Her features were pinched and tight. One fist was clenched, and the other hand still gripped me.

'Where's Derry?' Hemanlok asked.

'In the Mercado. Playing with the street-urchins.'

'She could've just heard that from what we was just saying,' muttered the third person, a short man with lank hair and cracked teeth. 'She's carrying a *sword*. Our girl didn't carry a *sword,* not in habit. Bow-staff, every time.'

'I didn't exactly have a gleaming selection to choose from,' Lycaea snapped. Her fear was getting the better of her.

'Shut your mouth, Shard.' Hemanlok's attention never wavered from Lycaea. He stepped towards us. Lycaea dropped my arm and wrapped her fingers about the hilt of her sword. I heard it rasp as it dragged an inch from the sheath.

Hemanlok heard it too. He smirked. 'Think you're quick enough, girl?' he asked.

'Quicker than I used to be.'

'That ain't so hard.'

She said nothing. Hemanlok drew back. His lip curled.

'It's her,' he said. 'But she ain't ours anymore.' He turned away. 'Walk on.'

Lycaea stared. Shock melted into hurt on her pale features. She looked at the ground as the three started to walk away, and her shoulders hunched. My stomach clenched. My wolf had hackles, was growling, wanted to bite.

Without thinking, I scooped a loose stone from the ground and hurled it at Hemanlok's retreating back.

'*You owe her!*'

Kaebha

She lay on her stomach, tasting dirt and blood.

'How much do you know about the waer, Kaebha?' Leldh had stopped expecting her to answer by now. 'Do you know what they did to my people?' He stepped around her. She could not crane her neck to look at him. Her eyes fixed instead on his polished boots. Her mouth was too dry to spit on them.

'They joined with the Watchers,' he went on. 'Which was natural for them, as they were wrought by the Dealer. But being cowards, and lacking the discipline and talent to fight with weapons, they reverted to their animal nature. They attacked our people in packs. Used their mind-speech to confuse us. My people retaliated by using the soul-bond against them. We broke their pairs. When the war was over, it was the waer who attacked us most savagely. If they could not kill us, they turned us.'

Kaebha focused on her breath. Everything was a haze of pain.

'The waer blood works like a disease. When mixed with regular

blood, it corrupts. Like a pestilence, like a plague, it spreads through the body. Finally, once it has claimed every drop of your blood, it forces you to Change. To take the shape of the deformed mongrel. Many of the Kudhienn killed themselves rather than allow that. But it did not matter either way. The shape was too much for them to sustain. Those Kudhienn who were turned, died.'

He crouched before her and pulled her head up.

'I wonder what it will do to you.'

She did not have time to scream. He slashed open her ragged shirt and the flesh beneath it. Kaebha choked, and squirmed.

'Blood,' Leldh said. Cooper handed him a small vial. There was a pop as Leldh unstoppered it. Liquid splashed across her flesh.

For a while, there was no pain. Her skin went numb. Then it started to tingle, and it was cool before it became icy cold.

Kaebha started to whimper. Before long, she was shrieking.

'There is nothing you can do to stop this,' Leldh said. He made sure she could hear him, spoke in the lull between each scream. He straightened. 'Truthfully, I just want to see you writhe,' he admitted. 'It gives me the greatest satisfaction. This is the cost of insubordination.'

Kaebha's bones ripped free of ligaments. They clicked under her skin. A terrible sound tore from her. Her backbone elongated.

Then all was sound, and smell, and agony.

Lycaea

Lowell Sencha was a mad fool. I could not stay his arm before he let the rock fly. It was the last thing I had expected from him. I grasped his wrist, yanking his arm back and pulling him behind me. Even as I did, I knew he was a dead man. No one attacked Hemanlok and lived.

Hemanlok strode towards us. All muscle and power. I should have waited for Moth and Dodge. I should not have brought Lowell into the Grinaja. I should never have returned to Luthan. I should have known Hemanlok would see through me, make me a pariah.

I faced him. Lowell, behind me, was silent. Not afraid, but angry.

'Say it again, boy,' Hemanlok drawled. His voice was lazy, but he was ready to strike. I heard Lowell take a breath and I cursed his audacity, knowing he was going to press on. Mad and *brave.*

'You owe me.' I spoke before he could, the burden shared between us. 'You *owe* me, Hemanlok.'

Flick and Shard, standing a few paces behind their boss, cringed. Hemanlok was too close. He did not touch me. He towered. I thrust my chin up and tried to stare down the blind man. My legs felt heavy. My palms stung where my nails bit into the flesh. I had to clench my fists and press my lips to keep both from quivering. Hemanlok said nothing. The silence weighed on us, and I struggled against it. When I spoke again, it was through gritted teeth. Childish repetition of the words. I hated myself for sounding petulant and small.

'You owe me.'

'You always get others to fight your battles for you, girl?'

'Do *you*? I don't remember you walking into Caerwyn with me.'

His hand jerked back and I threw my arms over my head. If he struck me, the damage would be devastating.

'I have spent weeks healing that girl's head, Lok. If you cave it in, I'll be terribly upset.'

Moth's quiet voice spoke into the heart of Hemanlok's anger. I lowered my arms. She stepped between us and put a hand on Hemanlok's chest. There was no force in the touch, but I knew he would not be able to move past her. I heard the smile in her voice.

'Calm, brother,' she said. She always called him 'brother', as if their shared years of enslavement linked them by blood. 'We have travelled a long way.'

'Get your people under control, Derry.'

My shoulders eased. I heard Lowell's breath resume behind me.

'Will you take us below?' Moth asked.

'If you dinna, we'll come along anyhow,' Dodge added cheerily. I flashed him a grateful look. He and Moth were two of the few people who could diffuse Hemanlok's sweltering rage.

I stepped around Hemanlok, forcing myself out of fear's paralysis. I was no longer the child who had blindly followed the sightless Hemanlok into danger. I dragged danger behind me now. I dragged Lowell Sencha, too. He glared at Hemanlok. I was acquainted with anger, but Lowell carried himself with *righteous* anger. Hemanlok, if he felt it, ignored Lowell. He stormed down the street. Moth kept pace with him, speaking in a low voice. Dodge trailed a few steps behind. Lowell and I were left with Flicker and Shard, who had once been my family. They eyed me now with undisguised hostility. Lowell threw it back at them. Flicker sneered and turned, swaggering after Hemanlok. Shard watched me with ratty black eyes.

'Is it you?' he demanded.

'Who else would bother?' I retorted. His broken teeth sprang out in an ugly grin and he sprang after the others.

I punched Lowell in the arm. 'That was the stupidest thing you have ever done, Wolf,' I told him. 'You have never been so close to death before.'

He rubbed his arm and shook his head. 'He had no right to speak to you like that.'

'No one tells Hemanlok how to speak. Not even Moth.'

'Then his behaviour is unsurprising.'

'Let's walk.' I was surprised at how grateful I felt. A mad fool, yes, but one who had put his head on the block for my sake.

Lowell fell into step beside me. I kept my attention on those walking ahead. Flicker was a few years my senior, and as lethal as she was condescending. Our affection for one another had always been complicated by her competetiveness. She had resented me for having the chance to go to Caerwyn. Now, I would gladly have changed places with her.

Shard, the short man with the bad teeth, would be close to forty years of age. He had been with Hemanlok since he was a ratty adolescent, and he would probably be with Hemanlok until he was a ratty old man. He had taught me how to pick a pocket, helped me tend weapons and sort information. He was not a good man, but he had always been good to me.

Hemanlok.

I wondered how much the Watcher knew. How much he could guess. He walked ahead, broad-shouldered and tall, clad in black. He was a man who knew exactly the impression he made on other people. He had spent years creating and maintaining the face he showed the world. He and Moth made a strange pair, walking down the street together. Her tattered yellow dress and his black coat. Her bird-like frame, his bulk.

'Where is he taking us?' Lowell asked in undertones.

'Below.'

He shot me an exasperated frown and I shook my head. Navigating Luthan was a complex game of alliance and trust, and knowing when to keep your mouth closed. Lowell would have to wait for his curiosity to be sated.

The roads were narrow and twisting. The sounds of prisoners shouting grew louder as dusk fell, and we stepped around the heart of the Grinaja. I had to suppress a shiver. Familiar scents washed over me, uncanny in their strength. The moss, the stench of the prisoners, Flick's perfume. I shrank back as a law-runner walked past us, then recognised her as Pallo Hoss. One of the many men and women who wore the lawman's uniform but answered to Hemanlok. They had a tidy business, being paid both by the city and by the Rogues. Pallo recognised me, and her eyes widened, but she did not question us. Her job, as far as we were concerned, was to be as blind as Hemanlok.

We rounded a sharp corner and faced a narrow building. The windows were boarded, the door was locked; on one side was a brothel, on the other was an old warehouse. It was used for storing food taken from the docks to be distributed amongst the children in the Crims' Orphanages. Hemanlok pulled out a key and unlocked the door. Flick sidled past Lowell and myself, standing guard at the end of the street while the rest of us went in. The narrow building looked as though it should smother us with dust, but the way was clear when we walked in. Hemanlok liked to keep his walkways in order. Lowell drew closer to me, uneasy. I had walked this path so many times, I did not have to think. My feet carried me down the rickety stairs, into the basement at the end of the hallway. Hemanlok pulled up a rug, unbolted the trapdoor, and lifted it. He swung himself down, making his way below with swift certainty.

'Hollow's eyes,' Lowell murmured. It was the first time I had heard him curse.

'Shut your mouth, blood,' Flicker said, elbowing him aside as she joined us and went ahead. She flashed me a dark look before she climbed down.

'Mind yourself,' Moth cautioned Lowell. 'The way grows

slippery here. Watch your hands on the ladder.' She lifted a smile to Dodge as well. 'You too, clumsy.'

He winked at her and took the ladder. Moth gave Lowell an encouraging nod and left us with Shard.

'I'm going last,' the small man said. To secure the trapdoor. I realised I had expected to do it myself, and I fought back a bite of unhappiness. It had always been my job. I set my teeth and went in before Lowell. Moth was right; halfway down, the rungs of the ladder became mossy and cold, slick with the damp. I was slow and careful. When I stepped away from the ladder, my feet splashed ankle-deep in water. Stale sea-water, by the smell, rather than sewage. The Grinaja was on the eastern side of the city, close to the docks. During high-tide these underground passages flooded. The first time I'd walked out of them, I waded through waist-deep water and as soon as I emerged in the Grinaja, Hemanlok sent me down again. My sodden clothes would have given me away.

I could hear Lowell slipping on the ladder, trying to grip it. He was slower than I had been, and Flicker snorted with impatience before he was even halfway to the tunnel level. There were faint splashes ahead; Hemanlok was already on his way home.

'Faster, Wolf,' I growled. I did not want him to seem a fool in front of them.

Finally, his feet splashed into the water. I took his arm and guided him to the narrow ledge at the side of the tunnel.

'Here,' I said. 'Put your left hand on the wall and follow the curve of the wall to your left. Even if you lose sight of the others, keep your path. Come on.'

I watched Moth and Dodge as they walked a few paces

ahead of us. Dodge walked in front, the ledge too narrow to accommodate both of them side-by-side. Moth stayed close to him. They were holding hands.

I released Lowell's arm and he steadied himself on the wall.

'How many people know of this tunnel?' he whispered.

'This one in particular? Just Hemanlok's Own. And Moth, Dodge and myself.' I forced myself to exclude my name from the Own. 'Just under a dozen people. There are hundreds of tunnels, though. Beneath the whole of Luthan. This is the safest. Some of the others are dead ends, to throw off the lawmen. Others have traps and guards.'

'Is your tongue always so slack?' Shard spoke behind me. My shoulders jerked. 'Hope you didn't run your mouth off in Caerwyn, girl. We don't really need the whole of Oster crawling through our tunnels.'

Anger ignited me. Hackles, teeth, the howl. I reined them back, but I could not rein back my human response. I swung around and slapped my palms against his chest, pushing him back. He lost his footing and slid into the water, rattling curses at me.

'None of you can have cared too much,' I snarled. 'Otherwise someone would have come to help me.'

'Lycaea.' Lowell took my arm.

I left Shard and kept walking. My face was hot. *Hope you didn't run your mouth off in Caerwyn, girl.* Three years of Leldh, and Cooper, and Kaebha. Of course I had. It had come to a point where I told them anything they wanted, anything at all, to make it stop.

I wondered if that had been what Hemanlok could sense about me. Whether he could smell the betrayal on my breath.

We reached a fork in the tunnel and took the left path. I did not remember the walk being so long. Three years had warped my memory of the route. I kept my head down and my mouth shut. I did not want another altercation with one of Hemanlok's people. There would be plenty of time for it once we reached the Den.

We descended further. Winding stairs. More tunnels. New scents started to drift past us. My body registered them before my mind did. My breath quickened. My heart sped. I walked taller.

'What is that?' Lowell asked.

Home.

I could not say the word aloud. It came to my mind unbidden. Unwanted.

We stepped into the dim glow of Luthan's secret district. The Debajo. The pull to Shift was stronger than ever. I choked it down, focused on my surroundings. The tunnel had widened into a cavern. It was one of a series, a whole network under the city, but this was the biggest. There were lanterns along the wall and buildings, many of them. Some carved into the stone, some wrought out of wood and brick. Men and women worked and lounged on the corners, drinking or smoking, or striking deals. Half-bloods, half-breeds, runaways and criminals. Anyone who needed to escape the glare of the sun and the lawmen.

I glanced at Lowell to glean his reaction. His eyes were wide and his mouth was agape. He took half a pace forward, then retracted his foot. A smile split his features; sudden understanding, sudden appreciation. His wonder was infectious. A grin itched my lips. I remembered seeing the Debajo for the first time. Peeling back the layers of Luthan and finding complete freedom, far removed from of the smothering threat of the Grinaja or the Ultimo. Running through the tunnels. Hassling local vendors and traders.

Dodge was already striding forward, clasping hands with a Tadghan man he knew. Moth smiled as people acknowledged her. Hemanlok ignored most of them, and they kept their respectful distance. I lowered my head. These people knew me. Had known me. I was unsure if I wanted to be recognised.

'Keep moving, Wolf,' I said. We followed the others through the great cavern, then took another narrow tunnel and came out into a second, smaller cavern. The buildings here were less dense, too; this was Hemanlok's domain, and people knew to give him space. It was sparse and functional, like the man himself. One large building, half worked into the rock, served to house his Own. It jutted out from the wall, ugly and square, with only a few windows on the upper level. Metal stairs ran to the top level. At the side of the Den was a smaller building, for some of Hemanlok's runners and clerks. He ran quite an operation. It accumulated enough paperwork to keep any scholar happy.

'The walls could do with some painting, Lok,' Moth commented, voice mild. 'The place is starting to look tatty.'

'The boss is blind, Derry,' Flicker drawled as Hemanlok unlocked the door. 'Do you think he cares?'

The Healer snorted. 'I know he's blind. That's why I'm informing him.' She smiled and stepped through the door after Hemanlok. The others filtered in, and I forced myself to join them. Ran my hand along the door, and the internal wall. Smells I had never noticed before, and could not shake from my mind now. I put names to the scents. *Donovan. Mitri. Salvi. Hywe.* It was all I could do not to run through the Den and call their names. These people who had been mine.

'Boss?' A ginger-haired man stuck his head around a doorway, mouth full of food. 'I spoke to Tollins – hello, Derrys, welcome back – and she said the Wharfer-gang still wants a bigger cut than they're entitled to. They're pushing this season. You want that I should…' He trailed off. It was hard to meet his gaze. Mitri. Warm, wonderful Mitri, who had once sat up with me when I had a fever. Mitri, with his tricks and jests. He was almost ten years my senior, but I had been closer to him than I had been with anyone else in the Own.

He came into the hallway now, scratching the back of his neck as he stared at me. He swung to face Hemanlok.

'Is it her?' he demanded. 'It is our girl?'

'Yes,' Moth said, before Hemanlok could reply.

Mitri crossed the distance between us and caught my shoulders. He searched my face.

'I would hardly know you,' he said. He pulled me into his arms. I wished he had been the one to meet us in the Grinaja. He smelled of spices and metal, of salt and sand. Mitri dealt with sailors and the wharf-gangs. He was the voice of the Own when Hemanlok was too heavy-handed for a situation. He rounded before I could stop him, and shouted through the Den.

'Hywe! Salvi! Donovan, she's back! *She's back!*'

Hemanlok had mounted the stairs to his own quarters. He wanted nothing to do with this. Moth and Dodge were on his heel; it was clear Moth still had much to tell him. Flicker leaned against the wall, her arms folded and one eyebrow raised. Shard had his hands in his pockets. He had kept his distance since I pushed him in the tunnels, and rightly so. Neither of them spoke. Mitri swore impatiently and squeezed my shoulders.

'Stay here,' he said. 'I'll get the others. Stay here.' He trotted through the Den.

'Mitri's more beauty than brains,' Flick commented. 'And that's not saying much. Don't expect us to all welcome you back with open arms, girl. I for one would like to know exactly how you spent your time in Caerwyn. How much you told them. What happened to the people we sent in after you.'

'And what happened to *you,*' Shard added.

'Perhaps we should question how *you* would be after three years of imprisonment and torture.' Lowell put his hand on my shoulder. I was surprised by how much of a comfort he was. 'We have travelled for weeks to get here. We have neither rested, nor washed. Is hospitality a thing only practised in the Gwydhan Valley, or have you heard of it here as well?'

Flicker pushed off the wall. Her dark eyes blazed.

'You talk far too much for a stranger,' she said. 'Don't make me take your tongue.'

'Try it,' I said to her.

'This ain't your turf any more, girl.'

'Lycaea?'

Donovan's voice interrupted our conversation. Mitri's cousin was tall, but he was muscular and solid where Mitri was skinny. My anger at Flicker melted away when I saw the Pellish man. He had grown a beard since I last saw him, and had suffered at least one broken nose. He almost broke me with a hug. I had to wriggle free from his arms before they crushed me. He released me, then took my shoulders again and held me at arm's length.

'We have heard murmurs for weeks,' Don agreed. 'But the whole story can wait until tomorrow. Come through. You look weary and bone-thin. Wash, eat, rest. In such an order.' He caught my hesitation and his smile softened. 'We kept your room as it was,' he said. 'Flicker made us. Just in case.' He caught Flicker's hand and kissed it. Unsuited as they were, the two had been in love since I had known them. It was good to see one thing at least had not changed.

'I did *not*,' Flick snapped as she left the room. The muscles across my back eased. Perhaps I had not been so far from their minds as I had believed.

Lowell

The night we arrived in Luthan, I remember neither lying down nor closing my eyes. Sleep devoured me. I slept on a pallet on the floor, in Lycaea's room. It was only when morning came I had the opportunity to lie in the quiet and take in the surroundings; to get some idea of who she had been before Caerwyn. Glass, smoothed by the sea, hung from the ceiling on coarse string. The room was cluttered with books and oddities; a carved ship furred with dust sat atop a chest of drawers, and what looked like a red flag was bundled over the bedpost, with a corner draping to hang by Lycaea's face. Jars of shells and polished stones lined the crooked shelves, propped into place by pegs or chucks of wood. The room smelled of the sea, and of the bright mess of the Mercado. Not what I would have expected from Lycaea.

I lay somewhere between sleep and wakefulness. We were underground, so there was no way of telling what the time was beyond how far the candle on the dresser had burnt down. Early hours of the morning, I estimated. I could hear people moving around in the other rooms, but there seemed no urgency to rise. After weeks on the road, the pallet was a luxury I wanted to enjoy. I tried not to stir too much, for fear of waking Lycaea. She had been reluctant to share the room, I could tell. It was not, I think, that she did not trust me; it seemed she just wanted time to be in the place she had once called home.

Shortly after I awoke, I heard Lycaea swing her feet onto the floor and walk past me to splash water from a bowl over her face. She brushed her fingers along the shelves, flicked her nail against one of the jars. She left the room, letting the door click softly behind her. I gave her time to wander the building – the Den, I reminded myself – on her own. Then, when the candle met another mark, I pulled myself to my feet and washed my own face in the water-bowl. The last night I had spent indoors was back in the Valley. Now we had stopped moving, the grief had shifted from hot pain to a stubborn melancholy, always lodged somewhere behind my ribs. I tried to imagine bringing Kemp to Luthan, or showing my mother around the Mercado. Bringing my father through the tunnels.

Even as I tried to conjure the images, I knew they did not fit, could never fit. They were like me. They belonged in green hills.

'Wolf, wake up,' Lycaea called through the door. 'Moth's cooking.' I pulled open the door and she shouldered past me. 'Thought you'd like to know,' she said. 'Go on, let me change my clothes.' Her hair, much of it grown back now, was still hay-spiked from sleep. She kicked aside a trunk. 'Look at this place. Don't know how I lived in such a mess.'

'I like it,' I told her.

'Go eat. Straight down the hall, and on the right. You'll be able to smell your way there, I guess.' She closed the door. I followed her directions, and the smell of frying bacon and mushrooms. Moth had a talent for occupying kitchens, and this seemed to be no exception. When I walked into the room, she had herbs spread out along the bench and a pan over the hot coals. I frowned at the hearth and chimney.

'Underground?' I asked.

'Hop out of the way, dear.' Moth moved past me and set the pan on a wooden slab. 'There are wind-tunnels above us, and vents cut into the stone from here to there. Smoke gets swept right out. They're not safe to walk in, of course.' *Kemp, smothered by black clouds.* 'How did you sleep, dear?'

'A roof, and a soft bed. It is what I have been dreaming of.' I leaned against the table and watched Moth. I had learned years ago not to interfere with her cooking unless she asked for help. She made the space her own, and I would not intrude upon that. I could tell she was enjoying the well-equipped kitchen and abundant food after our difficult journey. Sometimes she paused to breathe in the scent of a herb, or to taste something. I could smell bread in the oven. I wondered how long she had been awake.

'Did you speak to Hemanlok last night?'

'At great length. I explained to him the situation. I think he is waiting to have things out with Lycaea, though.'

'He was cruel to her.'

Moth sighed. 'Hemanlok has forgotten what it is like to be human,' she said. She ladled bacon from the pan onto a plate, then brought the pan back to the hot coals and tossed mushrooms onto it. 'He has no concept of what it is for a human to be imprisoned, or frightened, or tortured. He has no understanding, in particular, of what those things will do to someone who is little more than a child, as Lycaea was when she was locked away. He senses great change in her, and he is disappointed. Lycaea, on the other hand, cannot forgive him for not coming to rescue her. Not tearing Caerwyn apart with his bare hands to get her out.' She shook her head. 'They need time. Time to lick their wounds, fight it out with one another and forgive. Things will be much better now she is home.'

'Not for long,' I pointed out as Dodge joined us in the kitchen. 'There is still Caerwyn. Leldh. Kaebha.'

'Hm.' Worry creased her brow. She went to the oven and removed the loaf. It was just risen, so she must have been awake and working for quite some time. I shook my head.

Moth cut the bread and handed me a steaming slice. 'Eat, dear.'

Others filed into the kitchen, and I came to know the different members of the Own. Shard, casual and lazy. Mitri, the charming con-man. His cousin Donovan, from the island of Pelladan. Flicker, who had married Donovan the year before, making the greatest mismatch I had ever seen in a couple. They could not even share a soul-bond to smooth the ragged edges of their thoughts. I could not think how they managed.

Finally there were two men I had not met the night before: Hywe and Salvi. The former, to my shock, was a man of the Valley. I scented it even before I saw him. He sent me a dark look and kept his distance. Few people left the Valley to live elsewhere. I imagined he must have had a good reason. The second man, Salvi, was languid, uninterested.

All of Hemanlok's Own treated Moth and Dodge with a casual familiarity. There were even two rooms in the building set aside for them; one to sleep in, and the other as a work room. The latter was filled with manuscripts and vellum for Dodge and healing materials for Moth. The Rogues of the Own seemed genuinely fond of them. Mitri waltzed a laughing Moth around the kitchen as Hywe peppered Dodge with questions about Tadhg. The Valley was not mentioned. Either they had found all they needed to know from Hemanlok or the Derrys, or they were being tactful and waiting until one of us raised the issue. I hoped they already knew. I did not want to explain my loss to strangers.

Lycaea joined us a short while later, clad in a grey shirt and black breeches. They would have looked well on her, had they sat better; they were too big, and made her face look even smaller and more angular. It was improved, though, by the sudden grin sparking across her features when she stole bread from Donovan's plate. The big man pulled a face and gave a tolerant smile.

'You need to put some fat on those bones,' he teased. 'Look at you.'

'She has *muscle* now, though,' Mitri chimed in, poking Lycaea's arm. She swatted him away, but she did not seem to mind. I caught a glimmer of a smile on her sharp features.

'Enough mountain-climbing will do that, I suppose,' she muttered.

'You kept up your training?'

Lycaea glanced at Dodge, guilty, and grimaced. Dodge snorted. 'Sort of,' he answered for her. At her troubled frown, he grinned and nudged her with his elbow. All was forgiven, on his part.

'Boss'll knock you into shape,' Flicker said. She looked pleased by the prospect. Lycaea ignored her, spooning mushrooms onto the bread.

'What did you do to the mushrooms, Derry?' she asked through a mouthful.

'Fried in bacon fat, dear.' Moth glanced over her shoulder at Lycaea and smiled. 'What do you think?'

'Feels unhealthy.' Lycaea swallowed and thought about it. 'Tastes good.'

'So,' Donovan said, as I finished eating. 'What do we need, Lycaea?'

'Boss's permission,' Flick said sharply, before Lycaea could answer. 'We ain't doing a thing until he says we are. This ain't our fight. Some dogs up north get themselves killed, what's it to us?'

'Flicker, mind yourself, *please.*' Donovan lowered his head, embarrassed. None of them met my gaze, but for Lycaea. She narrowed her eyes and returned her attention to Flicker.

'What's it to you?' she asked. 'Perhaps I should explain. Daeman Leldh entered the Valley searching for me – and wiped out the Gwydhan Valley in a night. *One night,* Flicker. I'd be surprised if he lost more than ten soldiers. He'll find Luthan more difficult, and many of your people will die if he attacks, which he *will.* There is nothing Daeman Leldh hates more than Watchers, and waer, and half-breeds. Rogues and misfits. Our people.' She lowered her voice. 'He knows about the Debajo. He knows how to get in. He knows about the vents, he knows which tunnels he could flood, he knows everything. If he strikes Luthan, he strikes the heart of Luthan. He strikes us all.'

Silence stretched across us. I could only imagine how difficult it was for Lycaea to admit such things. I admired her steadiness. Her voice, though quiet, did not waver or falter once.

Flicker, disgusted, stood and left the table. Salvi, Shard, and Hywe left with her. Donovan and Mitri remained as they were. Donovan looked torn.

'What we need,' Lycaea went on, as if nothing had happened, 'is the support of Kirejo, firstly. We need manpower, legitimate power as well as the hands of the Rogues. We need the Wytch and her people. And we need as many sailors, thugs, and fighters as we can get. We need them to have weapons, and we need them to be fed and sustained over the journey to Caerwyn.'

'How much time do we have?'

'As soon as we can mobilise Luthan's forces, we need to move. There's not a lot of time.'

'I can talk to the Wharfer gang, and some of the sailors,' Mitri offered.

'You ain't doing any such thing. Not yet.'

I had to fight a cringe at Hemanlok's sudden comment. For a big man, he moved softly. I had not heard him enter the room. He strode past Lycaea, throwing something to her. She instinctively caught it.

'Training room,' Hemanlok said. 'I want to know who I'm dealing with.'

He left the room and Lycaea held the bow-staff in her lap.

'He's going to beat me bloody, isn't he.' It was not a question.

Moth winced. 'Probably,' she admitted.

'Brilliant.' Lycaea dragged herself out of her chair and followed Hemanlok. I rose and cleaned my plate, then started after her. Moth caught my shoulder.

'Best leave her this time,' she said. 'It will be humiliating for her.'

'Is he going to hurt her?'

'Not badly.'

I sighed and helped Moth and Dodge to clear away the breakfast food. I was unsure how much a training session with Hemanlok would help Lycaea. I worried it would damage any confidence she had gained. I did not want to see her slide backwards.

When the kitchen was clean, I walked through the corridors of the Den and stood outside the training room. Through the open door, I could see Lycaea and Hemanlok. Their staves met, clacked together rapidly. Even with my limited experience, I could tell it was not going well. Lycaea was constantly on the defensive. In just a few moments, she was flat on her back, and he hit her across the stomach.

I turned away. Moth was right. Lycaea would not thank me for interfering, or for witnessing another moment of weakness.

At midday Lycaea emerged bruised, and bleeding from a split lip. She dodged Flicker's sneers, avoided my concern and busied herself instead making plans with Moth and Dodge. It was hard not to comment, but I knew I had to hold my tongue. This was her home, and her pride had already been beaten down.

We sat around a large table – not in the kitchen, but in a circular common-room with a high ceiling. The chairs were comfortable and cushioned, but from the table, the papers and shelves, and the behaviour of the gang, it was not a room designated for leisure. Maps were tacked on the wall, showing both Luthan on the surface, and the intricate tunnels and caverns of the Debajo. When I studied the latter, I saw script labelling different sections.

'What is this?' I asked Lycaea. She came over and pointed.

'We're here,' she said. 'See? *Own*. Over here, near the coast, is Wharfer Turf. The Wharfer gang operates there, and it's their responsibility. Up here is Isteri Turf – a group of women from Manon run it. There are about six more gangs.'

'And they're each responsible for the caverns in their area?'

'Also for the upkeep of the tunnels running to their caverns. And we have some responsibilities on the surface as well. Keeping the entrances secret, bribing the right lawmen, keeping tabs on powerful people who work in our area.'

'Who organises this? Do all the Rogues answer to Hemanlok?'

'To some degree. Each different group has its own leader, but they all follow the same code. If they break it, then they do answer to Hemanlok and the Own. Hemanlok put all this into place years ago.' She did not say 'centuries ago', but I knew she meant it. 'It's a ragged sort of justice, but it works for us. Sometimes Rogues step out of line, but it's never for long.'

I did not want to imagine what happened to Rogues who crossed Hemanlok. I changed the subject. 'So how does the surface match up?' I dragged my finger across the wall to one of the other maps. 'We walked such a long way through the tunnels. Are we still below the Grinaja?'

'No. We're to the west of the Grinaja, beneath the citizens' district.'

'The Ciadudan?'

'Yes.' The questions put her at ease; I could tell she was glad to be distracted from her bout with Hemanlok. 'Actually, we're directly beneath an inn called O'Shea's. Popular with the seafarers. I used to sail with the owner, Malley, when we were children. He's a friend to the Rogues. There's a tunnel at the back of Own Turf leading straight there. It's how we're going to get to the surface when we go to speak with King Kirejo.' Her lips twisted into a wry grin. 'His most royal and benevolent majesty.'

The jest was lost on me. I was unsettled. 'Wait. *We?*'

'Yes. You, Dodge, and myself.'

'Why me?' Panic was rising in my throat.

'King Kirejo loves Dodge Derry's stories. And Dodge is far more eloquent than you or me, so he's coming along whether he wants to or not. *You,* on the other hand, are coming because you are a man from the Gwydhan Valley. You are an eyewitness and a representative of your people. Don't look so panicked, Wolf. Just be grave and thoughtful and tell Kirejo the truth.'

'He is a *king*.'

'Oh, hardly.' She waved a hand. 'His brother was supposed to take the throne, but he died in a shipwreck before he came of age. Kirejo never had the spine to be a king. He does whatever Hemanlok wants him to do. He's only started to show resistance in the last few years, since he married. His wife actually has half a brain, so she's more of a challenge.'

'Will they help us?'

'I don't intend to give them much choice. We might not speak for Hemanlok just now, but there's no reason they need to know that. I intend to frighten them into supporting us.'

I ignored the questionable morality of this particular tactic, and spoke with care. 'We do not speak for Hemanlok or his Own, but do they support us? *Will* they support us, when it matters?'

'He is yet to decide,' she replied, voice stiff. 'Best hope so, Wolf. We have no chance of victory without him.'

I took a chance and put a hand on her shoulder. 'He will see sense,' I told her. 'Keep trying. There is only so long he can ignore the threat Leldh poses to Luthan. No matter the rift between you, I doubt he would see this city reduced to ashes, or the Debajo unearthed.'

'Perhaps.' She relented into a smile. It caught me off-guard, as it did every time, seeing the ghost of a happier person. I released her shoulder, not wanting to make her uncomfortable.

'How do we prepare to meet a king?' I asked.

'Well, you can borrow some clothes from Hywe,' she said. 'You're roughly the same size, and you'll need to dress with care. Well enough so Kirejo takes you seriously, but not like a city-man. If Hywe has nothing, Moth can alter some of Mitri's clothes for you.'

'Is Hywe from the Gwydhan Valley?'

'Thereabouts,' she agreed. 'He is a waer himself.' Her face closed over, but over the weeks her disgust for our people seemed to have lessened. I did not believe her internal struggle with her true nature was ending, but at least she was coming to see us in a kinder light. 'He lost control when he was young, and they cast him out. I think he hurt someone. I never had the whole story for him.' Her voice turned sharp suddenly. '*Don't* ask him.'

'I was not planning to,' I promised. 'It is not my concern.'

'Good. Because they won't hesitate to beat you senseless if you push them. Donovan and Mitri are gentler souls, but the others have all done their share of damage across the years. Hemanlok never took anyone in out of charity, and most of the people he takes in are criminals.'

'Were you?'

'Back then?' Her face softened. 'Not really. I was lucky. Hemanlok had some conflict with my mother, and took me in to get some leverage over her. It worked in my favour. She was not a good parent.' It was not the first time I had heard mention of Lycaea's mother. I was beginning to draw some conclusions. 'I was quick, though. Quick and willing. I would have followed Hemanlok anywhere. He values loyalty.'

'Then he owes you some.'

She was startled, then amused. 'Yet another thing you should keep to yourself. Come on, Wolf. We need to get you presentable for a king.'

Hywe was unwilling to do us any favours. Two days later, I was wearing Mitri's altered clothing, tugging at the shirt, uncomfortable and anxious. Moth straightened my collar and kissed me on the cheek. 'Try not to be nervous, dear,' she said. 'He is a man with a metal hat, and no more. He has not half your wit or common sense. Let the others do the talking; he likes Dodge, and he fears Hemanlok's people, Lycaea included. Both are advantages to us.'

'The man is a fool,' Lycaea put in. 'If he refuses to help, we can always knock the metal hat off his head.' She tugged a coat on. 'Are you ready? We don't have all day to waste.' She was already striding towards the door. Moth gave me a gentle push, and I followed Lycaea. Dodge met us outside, his eyes alight with excitement.

'Ever met a king before, lad?' he asked me.

'I feel ill,' I replied. 'How will we get in?'

'Can you imagine refusing entry to one of the Own?' Lycaea demanded. 'Kirejo is so scared of Hemanlok he nearly soils himself every time he sees one of us. He'll let us in. I'd respect him more if he didn't. Luthan has had a succession of weak kings, but Kirejo is the most pathetic by far. Makes our job easier, but the man turns my stomach.'

Dodge and I followed Lycaea through the Debajo, winding through narrow streets until we reached one of the many tunnels leading through to the upper city. I walked slowly so as not to slip; the ledge was covered with moss and slime. Dodge, behind me, was slow. He kept both his hands flat against the damp wall, though there was nothing there for him to grip and prevent a fall.

Lycaea, with none of our caution, moved swiftly, light on her feet. She would make a wonderful waer, if only she would Shift. I had an unexpected image of the two of us hunting together, wolf and wolf. It made my neck hot and I forced my eyes away from her.

After climbing a short, rocky stair, Lycaea and I pushed open a heavy metal door and stepped out into a cellar.

'Malley O'Shea is an old friend of the Rogues,' she said, 'but that goes two ways. We have to show him respect, too. Out of courtesy, we only use this exit for important business. Otherwise, he'd have thieves and criminals traipsing through his establishment too often, and it would attract attention. Be polite. Walk quietly and don't attract attention.'

Lycaea straightened her clothes, closed the door behind us, and shifted a few blankets and sacks over it. When we were ready, she climbed the stairs and pushed open the door to the inn. She walked through as if she owned the place. Dodge grinned and stepped after her. I was more hesitant. The inn was loud, filled with raucous patrons. They were mostly sailors, from the smell. Tar, salt, rum, sweat, fish. I was lost in the shove of men and women. There had been nothing like this in the Valley. The crowd closed my throat over as the wolf in me scrabbled to find a footing. It was hard to breathe.

A hand clamped over my wrist and tugged me through. I found myself face-to-face with Lycaea.

'I know,' she said, not needing to hear my excuses. 'I feel it too. The smell. The people. Just shove past, Wolf. Push through it. Keep moving.'

She had not let go, and I was not about to ask her to. I let her lead me through the crowd of people. She waved to a stocky Tadhgan man at the bar and then pushed me into the open.

'A'right, lad?' Dodge asked. He seemed oblivious to the stench, the pure force of so many people.

Lycaea stopped, realised I was still wild-eyed and shaken. She released my arm, then patted my shoulder. Her words were stiff and halting. 'You get used to it,' she said. 'Gather yourself, Sencha. I need you to have your wits.'

I nodded. She was right, though it took me a few streets to recover myself. I gave myself distance from Lycaea and Dodge, walked close by the walls of the Ciadudan to have time to breathe. By the time I had calmed, I had a new reason to panic; we had reached the northermost wall of the Ciadudan, and were about to enter the Primero. The nobles' quarter. I knew without asking that the nobles here would not be like our Lord Alwyn. I wondered, painfully, what had happened to him. What he had suffered for keeping Lycaea a secret.

There were guards on the gate between the Ciadudan and the Primero. More guards than I would have thought necessary. They eyed Lycaea suspiciously, but Dodge did all the talking and presented a sheaf of papers. He had certainly had no papers when we were travelling. Either they had been waiting for him at the Den or they had been somehow procured since our arrival. I avoided Lycaea's gaze and decided I did not want to know. We were admitted to the Primero, and nothing else mattered for now.

The nobles' district was too extravagant to be called beautiful. Vibrant, expensive-looking murals made the streets seem gaudy, and the gilded statues lining the streets were tasteless. Gardens cut through the centre of the roads but with pungent orchids and lilies growing in such numbers, they were overpowering and sickly. I tried to imagine the people from home walking these streets, and almost had to laugh.

'Feast your eyes, lad,' Dodge said with a sly grin. 'Bonny, aye?'

'It is certainly...vivid,' I replied. By Felen, the people were even more ridiculous, ranging between the impractical and the inconceivable. Ethereal dresses that hardly covered the women boasted long trails held up by attendants. Men sported wide-brimmed, purple hats with bright plumage. Even the horses were decorated, their manes and tails braided and their saddles painted. I saw some servants walking behind their masters with enormous birds in their arms. They were purely decorative. It was like a dream in which nothing made sense and yet everything purported to. I found it difficult to restrain my distaste. Lycaea made no such effort.

'Waste of air,' she muttered. Dodge chuckled.

We made our way along the gaudy streets. I remembered seeing on the map how they were arranged: streets fanned out from the centre like the petals of a flower. At the heart of the sector was the Bastion. I was breathless before it. Turrets spiralled towards the sky, wrought in smooth white stone. In contrast with the gaudy streets, the Bastion was sparse and elegant. The gates surrounding the palace rose on either side, imposing and strong. Guards in blue stood at the entrance. They were different from the guards I had seen at the gates to Luthan, and in the Mercado. They were alert and neat, and they watched us as we drew near. Lycaea and I stood back to allow Dodge ahead of us. He spoke to the guards, and one sent a runner while we waited. Lycaea propped herself up against a low wall and folded her arms.

'You may as well sit down,' she told us. 'Those gates won't open to us for another hour or so.'

She was right. The sun was high in the sky before the guards stepped aside and allowed us in. I squared my shoulders and walked into the palace of King Kirejo.

Lycaea

The Primero made me angry, as it always did, and I carried the anger into Kirejo's palace. Whcnever I walked through the garish streets, I was reminded of people starving in the Ultimo. Children locked away in the Grinaja Crims' Orphanages. Parents in the Ciadudan trying desperately to keep their families from being locked in the struggle between the Ultimo and the Grinaja. I could not shake the thoughts as I walked through the marble hallways. Kirejo was a man who perpetuated the struggle of his people. He allowed the Debajo, yes, but only out of cowardice. If he did better by his city, the Rogues would not need to be underground at all. There would be no need for such vast divides amongst the people of Luthan.

But we needed his help now. No way around it.

I focused on the tapestries lining the walls as we walked. Elaborate and bright, like the Primero itself; but these were beautiful, as well. Luthan at its best. The Mercado, rendered in all its chaos and colour. The sedate streets of the Ciadudan. Families helping one another in the Ultimo. The dark quiet of the Grinaja.

The guards opened a pair of blue doors and Dodge walked ahead of us into the greeting-hall. He was already performing, his arms spread wide and his expressions exaggerated as he announced himself.

'Dodge Derry of Tadhg, your majesty,' he said with a flourishing bow. 'Ever at your service.'

I looked past Dodge, at the king and queen. The former was native Luthanese, with tanned skin, dark hair and eyes. He was slumped in the chair, but as we came into the hall he sat up with a wide grin. I sighed. If Kirejo had not been a king, his flaws might have been forgivable. He might even have been likable.

'Master Storyteller!' he exclaimed. 'You are always welcome.'

Kirejo's wife, formerly Ela Darce, was unmoved. Queen Ela was almost twenty years younger than her husband. She was the daughter of a Pellish noble. Her father had once owned slaves, but during the slave revolt on Pelladan he had changed his ways. The Lady Governess of Pelladan, once in power, had bestowed riches upon the family and paid for Ela's education herself. Ela was the first woman to be educated at a Pellish university. It had always struck me as a shame it had not prevented her from being sold into marriage. She would have made a better ruler in her own right.

She sat, motionless, her pale eyes fixed on us. She all but ignored Dodge.

'You are most welcome.' She spoke in the refined monotone common to the Pels. Donovan, over the years in Luthan, had learned the tones and inflections of the Mainland, but Ela had only been married to Kirejo a few years. 'I was not aware of your scheduled visit.' Her voice was flat, but her words were pointed.

'We werena scheduled,' Dodge admitted, cheerily. 'But we appreciate your welcome.'

'What stories do you bring us this time, Master Storyteller?' Kirejo asked eagerly.

'Just the one, your majesty, and I fear it is both true and terrible.'

Kirejo beamed and sat back, under the impression this was part of Dodge's act. He tapped his palms together.

'Go on,' he said. 'Tell away.'

Dodge began our tale. Kirejo listened with rapt attention, his smile fading as he realised the severity of the situation. Soon, all pleasure evaporated and was replaced by panic. His shoulders rose and tightened. His eyes flicked towards the exits when Dodge detailed the attack on the Valley, and our desperate flight through the mountains. For the first time, he noticed me, and real fear entered his face. The last time he saw me, I had been standing at Hemanlok's shoulder.

Ela's eyes sharpened, but she showed none of her husband's fear. If she felt it, she did not betray herself.

'Your tale is tragic,' she said as Dodge came to a conclusion. 'We have heard much of the Lord Leldh, and his doings in the north. But the Gwydhan Valley is beyond our jurisdiction. The town of Herithes, I believe, has responsibility for the people dwelling there.'

'Herithes lacks the numbers to assist,' I said. 'And they have no love for the waer people. They cannot help. They *will* not help.'

'Neither can we.' Words tumbled from Kirejo's lips, betraying his uncertainty.

Dodge reached back and put a hand on Lowell's shoulder. 'Hear us out, your majesty. Standing with us is a man from the Gwydhan Valley.'

Lowell swallowed and stepped forwards. 'Your majesties,' he said. 'My name is Lowell Sencha. My family was slain in the attack on the Valley. My parents, and my younger brother. Please understand. My brother was five.' His voice wavered, and I worried he would lose control. Instead, he lifted his chin and went on. 'The Gwydhan Valley has always been a place of peace. We have never been at war. We have never wronged anyone. Leldh attacked a defenceless population and murdered my people.'

'So you have come to beg.' Kirejo gathered himself, thrust his chest out. 'We have had information, and a plea.' He levelled an imperious finger in my direction. 'Why are *you* here, Rogue?'

'To make threats.' I folded my arms and made no pretence of servitude. I was no longer one of Hemanlok's people, but I remembered how to act like one. 'You ain't exactly known for your bleeding heart, Kirejo, and your lovely lady wife here is about as warm as a Pellish winter. We didn't expect you to leap at a chance to save innocent lives, so I'm here to outline the alternatives.'

'Which are?'

'Firstly, the invasion of Luthan by Daeman Leldh and

his followers this coming spring. They hate half-breeds, and your city has the highest half-breed population in all of Oster. There are also particular enemies of Leldh living in the city, and he will stop at nothing to find and kill them. He will tear your city down, stone by stone.' I let my words sink in for a while before I went on. 'But I don't think even that information will convince you. After all, you can always hide behind your walls, or flee. Leaving your city to ruin and despair. So I have something much more immediate to convince you.' I walked forwards, up the stairs towards the thrones. Kirejo jumped to his feet, his hand shooting towards a ceremonial sword at his side. My lip curled. 'Don't bother,' I told him, my own hand on my sword-hilt. 'I could cut your hand off before you called for the guards. But I'm not the one you need to worry about. You know his name. I don't have to say it.'

Kirejo froze. 'The Assassin.'

'He's willing to protect the city, even if you're not. And if that means usurping you, or replacing you, or doing terrible things to you and your wife, he will take those steps.' Kaebha flashed through my head, vivid and terrible. I forced myself not to falter.

'We do not respond to threats.' Even Ela's voice sounded thin and weak.

'Then respond to the plea.' I stepped back. 'Keep your pride. Keep your kingdom. Send troops to Caerwyn.'

'Luthan has not been to war in over fifty years. Since before my reign.'

'Which would explain the flab about your stomach.'

Lowell's intake of breath reminded me I might have gone too far. I could not back down. I had to behave like a Rogue.

I held Kirejo's gaze. His hand still hovered by his blade.

'Be seated, my king.' Ela's voice was calm. She looked past me, at Lowell. 'Approach, man of the Valley.'

Lowell approached and took a knee. I thanked the stars for his natural courtesy in such a tense moment.

'We do not respond to threats,' Ela repeated, 'but we have heard stirrings, and we have had unpleasant missives from Leldh and his people. Long he has been a menace on the edge of our sight. And we feel both compassion and outrage for his actions in the Gwydhan Valley. Luthan has always been a place of refuge for the half-blooded. If we strike against Caerwyn, it will be for this reason only.' Her eyes flicked in my direction, the message clear. The city must be assured that their majesties had been moved by the plight of their subjects, and not by the impudent words of a shabby criminal.

'Everyone will know of your benevolence.' Lowell was even and quiet. 'The words of Master Derry carry power and appeal in this city and throughout Oster, I believe. You will be remembered as defenders of the weak, and protectors of the innocent.' Eloquent. 'If any of my people survive, they will be eternally in your debt of gratitude.'

'Within three weeks, you will see our city on the march.' Kirejo rallied, not wanting his wife to voice all their decisions. 'On three conditions. Firstly, you and the Own must be marching also. If you call the city to war, you must also go to war.'

'With all my heart.' Lowell kept his head bent.

'Secondly, we need confirmation of these events from others. We will send out emissaries to gather local intelligence, to ascertain the truth of your tale. Thirdly.' Once more, Kirejo pointed at me. 'If victory is not ours, the reparation will be her head. I will not stand insubordination of this kind.'

I laughed. Could not help myself.

'Your majesty,' I said. 'If victory is not ours, I will not walk off the battlefield alive. You have no need to burden yourself with my head.'

'Did you mean what you said back there?' Lowell was subdued as we walked through the tunnels leading back to the Debajo. 'About not surviving defeat?'

'Obviously.' I frowned at him. 'If we lose, there is no future for Luthan, Wolf. Certainly no future for me.' I could not allow myself to imagine a continuing future with Leldh in power. A future where Kaebha might have me in her grasp once more.

'And if we succeed?'

'What about it?'

'What will you do then?'

The question devoured me. I focused on the sound of echoing steps through the tunnels. There was no 'after'. There was me, and Leldh, and Cooper, and Kaebha, and Caerwyn, and one foot in front of the other until they all fell. *After?* Bitterness shuddered through me.

'I don't know.' I forced the words out. 'Move on, I suppose.'

'After'. Bitterness rotted me. I knew Kaebha would never let me walk away from Caerwyn alive. She had released me once. It would not happen again. There could be no 'after'.

'What about you, Lowell?' Dodge asked, cutting the silence. 'Do you have plans?'

'I am uncertain.' Lowell sounded unhappy to have the

question turned back his way, and I could imagine why. When the battle-dust settled, Lowell and I stood at the same gallows. Neither of us had a place to go.

'Back to the Valley?' Dodge asked.

'It depends on how many survivors we find.' Lowell did not add *if any,* but it hung between us. Dodge clapped him on the shoulder. I said nothing. There would be survivors, I expected, but I doubted they would ever recover. There was no 'after' for them, either.

The Den was dark and quiet by the time we returned. The Own kept surface hours, though there were always a few gang members awake and operating. They rotated shifts, depending on the season and Hemanlok's will. The Rogues lived a life of crime, but it was highly disciplined. We entered quietly and went to the kitchen to eat. I was surprised not to find Moth there. We had told her what time we would return. I realised I had expected to find her waiting for us, tea freshly brewed.

'She isna here, lass,' Dodge said, not needing to wonder at my pause.

'Where is she?'

'Dealing.'

'Already?'

'Time eats all bones, lass.'

'Dealing?' Lowell asked.

Dodge busied himself in the kitchen. I narrowed my eyes at his back. It was more his to tell than mine.

'She is speaking with the third Watcher,' I said. 'The Dealer.'

'Your mother.'

I choked and whirled to face him. My heart clattered about

my ribcage. Lowell watched me, his dark eyes intent. Dodge had turned from the bench, his own face lit with interest.

'How did you know that?' My voice was shameful, little more than a rasp.

'Moth once told me she used to be dear friends with your mother. Hemanlok took you in because of your mother. Daeman Leldh hates the Watchers, and he hates you.' He hesitated. 'It was a guess. But your expression confirms it.'

Dodge burst into laughter. 'Too quick for the rest of us, Lowell Sencha!'

He *was* too quick. I would have to guard myself more carefully. There were thing I did not want him to know.

'Very clever,' I drawled, trying to cover my attempts to regain my footing. 'Yes. Fine. My mother.'

'Why has Moth gone?' Lowell asked. 'Why not you?'

'Because the third Watcher is insane,' Dodge said.

'Insane?'

'Raving,' I confirmed. 'Moth is one of the only people who has been able to sway her heart in the past. You should see when Hemanlok tries. The years have driven a wedge between the Assassin and the Dealer.'

'Did she raise you?'

Dodge and I snorted simultaneously. The question did not merit an answer. My mother would have more success raising a mountain than a child.

'Do you have any of her power? Are the duties of a Watcher inherited through blood?'

'No and no. Thankfully.'

'Watchers are sought out and chosen by their predecessors,' Dodge said. 'Sometimes they hunt for years and years until the Balance shows to them the new Watchers.'

'Do you think Moth can convince the Dealer?' Lowell asked.

'No.' He sagged a little, and I shrugged. 'No one said this would be easy, Wolf.'

'But you said we need all three Watchers to attack Caerwyn. And Kirejo, and the Rogues.'

'We do.'

'Then what can we *do?*' His voice snapped in frustration.

'I'm working on it. There is no sense admitting defeat yet, Wolf. Our swords are hardly drawn.'

Lowell

Moth returned hours after we arrived at the Den. She was pale, and her eyes were red-rimmed from crying. She folded into Dodge's arms as soon as she walked through the door, and I could see her shoulders shaking. Dodge kissed the top of her head and held her close. I could not think what the Dealer might have said to upset Moth so. Feeling like an intruder, I retreated to Lycaea's room. The door was ajar, but I still knocked before entering.

'Door's open, Wolf.'

I stepped into the room. Lycaea sat cross-legged on her bed, poring over lists and maps. She did not glance at me as I entered. The daughter of a Watcher. I had suspected, but I had hardly been able to believe it. In hindsight, it seemed obvious. By the curse of her blood, she was caught in these events for Kudhienn and near-deities. I wondered if she had ever known what it was to lead a normal life.

'You should get some rest,' she said. 'We meet early with the Rogues and sailors. And souther-waer. I hope you don't mind if I keep the lamp glowing, though. I have work to do still.'

'Souther-waer?' I could not care less about the lamp. 'You said they eat people!' I was nettled, and it was impossible to prevent an accusatory note from entering my voice. Had she been laughing at my expense?

'They do,' she said. 'A rather useful habit, if they're on our side.'

'Are there many in Luthan?' I adjusted my tone, though I felt uneasy. Even in the Valley, we had heard tales of the souther-waer and their barbarity. They did not have our control or our moral code. They were said to be savages.

'Not in Luthan, but just outside. The Rustfur tribe lives on the river half a day south of Luthan, and at the moment their allies, the Greypaws, are there as well. They should put in with us if we explain the situation to them. They've had troubles with blood-purists before, and they'll understand the threat Leldh poses to Oster.'

'And the Rogues? And sailors?'

'They might take more convincing.'

I pulled over the sleeping clothes I had been lent by Mitri and cleared my throat. 'Do not look,' I warned Lycaea. 'I am changing my shirt.'

I saw the corners of her mouth curl upwards.

'I won't,' she said. I changed my shirt. When my head came clear of the collar, I noticed Lycaea looking. Blatantly. She grinned at me, and I tossed the old shirt at her.

'You take your clothes off every time you Shift,' she said,

with a rare laugh. 'What's the difference?'

'It is different. Wolves wear no clothes. We have no need for them. When I am human, I abide by human customs.'

'Makes *no* sense.'

'It makes all the sense in the world.'

'When you are a wolf, do you act entirely like a wolf?'

'Well, no,' I admitted. 'The human mind guides the instinct. It is a union.'

'Then when you are human, why be so fastidious about human customs?' I frowned at her and she lifted her hands. 'I'm just asking. It doesn't make sense to me.'

'Perhaps if you Shift, it will.'

She grimaced, and I felt the light atmosphere dimming. I swiftly changed the subject, not wanting to leave it tense and uncomfortable.

'You said your mother did not raise you. Who did, then? Madam Derry? Hemanlok?'

'Can you imagine Hemanlok raising a child? And you would have known if Moth had raised me. I would have gone with her and Dodge to visit you in the Valley, wouldn't I? No; I was raised at sea. My father was a Pel. A slave. When my mother abandoned me, he took me and fled to the ocean, took up with smugglers. He died when I was six. I was brought up for the most part by an old quartermaster. She was the closest to family I had for eight years or so after that. Until I left the ocean.'

'Why did you leave the ocean?'

'When the quartermaster died, there was little to tie me to the ships, and I was itching for the novelty of city life. I obviously could not go to my mother; she was too dangerous.

So I came to Luthan, found employment under Hemanlok. Sometimes I went with the other Rogues to different cities; Manon, and Tadhg. For the most part, though, I made Luthan my home.' She folded the maps and started to put them away. 'And yourself? What was your life before the attack?'

My tale was nothing so glamorous as sea travel and visits to Manon. I related the short, uninteresting story of my life. The one point that stayed in my mind was how different our families had been. Her mother, insane and unloving. Her father, dead when she was a child. I was lucky that I had been given the blessing of many a long and happy year with my family.

She listened as she worked, looking neither bored nor surprised. 'Do you miss it?'

I could not answer her for a while. I missed my family. I could remember the smell of grass and sheep, and incoming rains. My *parents*. My brother.

'Yes.' I could think of nothing else to say, and I felt the lack seep between us. That single word could not convey the loss of my home.

'Ah.' The syllable could have meant a range of different things. Lycaea cleared her throat. She sounded nonchalant, but she would not look at me. 'You know, you are welcome here.' She finished clearing the papers. 'If we survive battle with Leldh. I'm sure we could find you a place to stay. There's not much left for you in the Valley. And the other waer would be welcome in the Debajo as well, or we could find a place for them in the Ciadudan.'

In the mix and swell of the city. Far from the rolling hills and quiet forest. I could not suppress a shudder.

'That is a *no*. Am I right?'

She was looking at me. I averted my eyes. It had cost her a good deal of pride to make the offer. Still, the answer was the only one I could give.

'I can make no choices until I know what became of my people,' I said.

'They may not be alive.'

'I feel in my heart they are.'

'Of course,' she said, and though she said no more I could sense her cynicism. She looked away and resumed her work. Her jaw was tight.

'When it is over, I will visit,' I promised.

'No,' she disagreed. 'You will lose yourself to farming and domesticity. You will forget what it was like to be here. To live in the moment. Luthan may be a corrupt pit of depravity and immorality.' She lay down and pillowed her head with her hands. 'But it is *beautiful*.'

I was struck by her sincerity. I wished I could make her understand. 'If you could go back to the ocean with your old ship-mates and the quartermaster, and know everything would be the same, would you leave Luthan?'

She propped herself on her elbow and watched me again. I went on. 'Things will not be the same when I return home. But they can be repaired. I could never survive here. Luthan is far too big a world for me to live in. I would drown.'

'I know.' She reached over and dimmed the lamp, in spite of her earlier words. 'The offer is still there,' she told me. 'If the Valley becomes… if it is no longer home for you. There will be a place for you here.'

I felt unexpected warmth in my stomach. I was suddenly very aware of her. She stared at me, unabashed and direct.

Fruitless to try to fathom what she was thinking. Neither of us spoke as I felt the tension build. I broke it.

'Tell me about Manon, and Pelladan. I have never been beyond the Valley before. I know little of such places.' Dodge had told us much about the dry, hot city of Tadhg, but he had never told us much about Pelladan or Manon.

'Pelladan's not worth much,' she said. 'It's an island to the west of Luthan. A few weeks' sail. It rains there, almost constantly. Not a friendly place, either. The people are clever, I'll grant you, but years of civil war and slavery have made them bitter and withdrawn. Moth says they're way ahead of us in weapons and medicine.' She shrugged. 'Not worth much if the people aren't treated well, though. And they're not, even since the revolution. Women have a bad time of it, in particular. Even a Lady Governess in power can't stamp out centuries of mistreatment.'

'And Manon? Do you recall Manon?'

Her face relaxed into a slow smile. I could see the space where one of her teeth was missing. 'To the south-west of Oster,' she said. 'Not as far as Tadhg, which is two weeks souther still, but down from Luthan and Herithes by a long way. It's hot there, and humid. Impossibly green and vibrant. And the *food,* Wolf. Never tasted anything like it.'

'What of the people?'

'Different. It's a matriarchy, so a woman sits on the throne and women own most of the businesses there. Much of their culture is based around combat and honour. They have strange ways, to my eyes.' She paused. 'But then, I suppose we have strange ways to your eyes. Don't we?'

'Not so strange as I first thought,' I told her, and she

grinned. In a few moments, however, the grin faded, and her brow creased. Hard to tell what had stirred her thoughts, brought the shadows back to her face.

'Best get some sleep,' she said at length. 'We'll need our wits about us tomorrow.'

'Sleep well, Lycaea.' I knew there was no point in arguing, or trying to press her further.

'Sleep well, Wolf.' She flopped back onto her bed and rolled over, faced the wall.

I tried to sleep, but my dreams were haunted by men with golden eyes, and soldiers who set fire to thatches. Kemp wailed in my ears every time I closed my eyes. When the members of the Own rose for their morning meal, I was still awake.

The souther-waer were not like the waer of the Valley; they favoured open plains and the blue sky to caves and houses. They were nomads who travelled through the desert, known as the Parch, that stood between Luthan and Tadhg. Out of courtesy to them, we did not meet in the darkened tunnels and caverns of the Debajo, but instead beyond the southern wall of Luthan, not far from the main road. Lycaea and I sat in the long, spiny grass there and waited. Lycaea had a basket of dried and fresh meat under her arm. She had stopped at the Mercado on the way out, and bought it as a gesture of good-will.

The souther-waer smelled of smoke, blood and sand. They approached us in their human shapes, but they walked like wolves; all intent and coiled muscles. They towered above us. Four of them. Feeling vulnerable on the ground, I scrambled to my feet. Lycaea, chewing on a blade of grass, remained seated.

'Good of you to come,' she said. 'I'm Lycaea. This is Lowell Sencha.' She nudged the basket of meats over with her foot. 'We brought you food.'

The gesture and the words troubled me. It was the language of a submissive wolf, not one in charge. I felt we had to be stronger with these people.

'I'm Rog.' The brawny man at the front sat, and the other three followed him. 'This is Ariaf Greypaw, Keturah Greypaw, and Tarkin Rustfur.'

'Nice to know you.' Lycaea flipped the lid of the basket open. Rog sniffed at it, then nodded.

'Speak your piece.'

To my horror, Lycaea looked at me. I cleared my throat and looked between the four souther-waer. They were not armed; they did not need to be. It was obvious they could tear a man apart with little effort. The man who had spoken, Rog, had reddish hair and wore a pelt about his shoulders. A wolf-pelt, I realised, feeling ill. I wondered whether it was an honour custom, or whether it came from an enemy. The other three also sported wolf-pelts; grey for the Greypaws, and tawny for the other Rustfur.

I did not know how to speak to someone who was capable of skinning a waer, no matter their reason. I thought of skinning the goat, back in the mountains, and my stomach turned.

'Wolf.'

All five of us looked at Lycaea, but I knew she was speaking to me. With difficulty, I gathered my thoughts.

'I come from the Gwydhan Valley, in the northern mountains of Oster. We recently suffered an attack. A blood-purist named Daeman Leldh swept through my home with his army.

He slaughtered my people. He plans on doing the same to Luthan, when he has amassed enough strength. It will not be long.'

'We plan to strike at him first,' Lycaea said. 'We go with the men and women warriors of Luthan, but we need as much strength as we can gather. We've heard much of your skill in combat and the hunt. We would ally ourselves with you, and risk much to save all.'

The souther-waer took the meat and sampled it. They tore it with their fingers and ate the fresh meat still bloodied. They chewed with their mouths open. My mother would have shuddered to see it.

'We've dealt with purists before,' said the sinewy Greypaw woman, Keturah. 'Got no real wish to deal with them again. We can just go south. I'd like to see any mountain-fellow cross the Parch with his dainty army.'

'Would you hide in Tadhg?' Lycaea asked. 'You are not permitted within the gates of the city there. Luthan is the only city to allow you free walk of the markets. If you lose Luthan, you scrape out a living in the desert *forever.* There will be no sanctuary for you. And what if Leldh dams the river? What if he takes over the trade ports? He will wipe out the chipre-traders, you can wager on that. You rely on those traders for their wares during the hard months.'

'We rely on no one.'

'*We* rely on *you*.'

They were going to refuse. I knew it, and Lycaea could sense it. It was in the way Rog's shoulders eased back, and the way the others shifted their weight away from us. It was in the way Keturah's muscles bunched, in case we took issue with it.

I straightened and eyed Rog. He was a wolf, and I knew how to be a wolf better than Lycaea did. The souther-waer met my gaze, but only briefly. Size did not matter. Experience and nerve were everything. I reached for the basket and took some fresh meat. Pulled it apart with my hands and ate.

It was bloody and tough, chewy between my teeth. And it tasted…

No, I could not think about that. And I could not think about what the Valley waer would have said, either. *A kill had to be cooked.* The meat caught in my throat and I struggled not to gag. But it had the intended effect.

Rog growled. It was their food, given to them. I was not one of them, and in his eyes I had not earned the right to eat their spoils. I did not lower my gaze as I ate. The male Greypaw edged closer to me, and I let a growl rip through my throat. The sound gave him pause.

Lycaea opened her mouth to speak, but I shook my head at her. She watched us, intent. I let the silence hold. Then, when I was sure of their attention, I spoke again.

'Waer should help waer.' I sat back, threw the issue into their teeth. 'My people were slain mercilessly. Will you fight for yours like wolves, or will you let them die like dogs?'

'What do you know of fighting, little norther-waer?' Rog asked. 'Have you ever killed?'

'He has.' Lycaea cut through, her voice smooth and clear. 'He is a head and a half shorter than you are, and untried, but he is willing to march into battle nevertheless. He has as much courage as any souther-waer. Are you his equals? Or will you flee to the desert to suck lichen off rocks for the rest of your lives?'

The souther-waer said nothing. Lycaea and I waited, tense and motionless.

'We need to take it to our packs,' Keturah said at last. 'If we put their lives at risk, we need to give them their options. You'll be hearing from us.' She took the basket and stood. 'When do you leave?'

'Three weeks. If you're with us, meet us at the norther-wall of the city. We'll have an army with us.'

We rose and the souther-waer departed. I released a long breath.

'Fair, Wolf,' Lycaea told me. 'Fair.' She clapped my shoulder.

'They were wearing pelts. Did you know about that? They donned *waer* pelts, Lycaea.'

She waved a hand. 'It's not a violent thing for them. Those are the pelts of their fallen ancestors. It's a mark of respect and love. They keep their past with them. It's not supposed to threaten anyone. When they growled at you, though? *That* was a threat. One you managed remarkably well, I might add.'

I was both embarrassed and pleased by her approval.

When she spoke again, her words were short and sharp, jagged with nerves. 'How much control do you have over it?'

I did not have to ask what 'it' was. The inner wolf.

'The more you Shift, the more control you gain,' I told her. 'In the first few years, it is difficult. We have to watch our young ones with care, to ensure they do not cause too much damage in the village and Valley. Now, I feel it tugging at me sometimes. When I am distressed or angry, or wildly glad. I can suppress it with ease, though I prefer to listen to it. Usually, if I feel a compulsion to Shift, it is because I need to do so. I always feel better afterwards. For couples who are soul-bonded, it is an even greater joy. They run with one another as pack, and the Shift of one gives them both energy.'

'Does the Shift hurt?'

'No.'

She folded her arms and gazed out over the souther plains, the landscape stretching out towards the Parch and beyond. 'It *does* hurt,' she said. She sounded as if she was spoiling for an argument, her usual defense against vulnerability, but I kept my voice level and gentle.

'It is different when you have not been born a waer, and it is more painful the first few times.' She seemed unconvinced, and I went on. 'Especially if you have no care and comfort the first time, and no one to teach you. Newly turned waer have come to the Valley before, seeking our help. It is a terrible thing to undergo alone.'

Her lip curled. 'Kaebha was there,' she said.

I froze. 'Kaebha is a *waer*?' She nodded. Horror shot through me. 'A waer, who tortures other waer? Who helps her master to hunt us down and butcher us?'

'I don't want to talk about Kaebha.'

'How could anyone do such a thing?'

'I don't want to talk about Kaebha, Wolf.'

'But *why*?'

'Are you *listening* to me?' She rounded on me, eyes blazing. 'I don't want to talk about Kaebha. I don't want to talk about the things she did, or why. Bad enough we're walking right back into Leldh's arms, and two out of the three Watchers still haven't agreed to help us. *Bad enough* to think about what

Leldh did to me, that I can't escape what he did to me! He turned me into a *dog!*'

She was the one who had brought Kaebha's name into the conversation. In spite of what she said, I felt she *did* have a need to discuss it. But she was not ready, and I was unwilling to break the fragile trust growing between us.

I reined myself back, forced myself to remember how painful it was for me to discuss the death of my family. I lowered my head in a show of deference. Lycaea's breath was ragged, and her cheeks were flushed. She lashed out in fear, not in anger.

The rage faded from her slowly. She stepped back and took long, shuddering breaths.

'Sorry,' she muttered. 'I'm sorry. I'm trying, Wolf. You know I'm trying.'

'I do.'

'Kaebha is stronger than I am.'

'I doubt she has half your heart or courage.'

I think she was as uneasy with the comfort as I had been with the praise. She was paralysed in the wake of her own anger, possibly battling with the urge to Shift.

'We have Rogues to see,' I suggested, 'and sailors. We should return to the Debajo and ready ourselves. I imagine they will not be easy to convince, and their numbers might be great.'

I touched her shoulder. She flinched, then relented, let me put my arm about her. We walked together through the southern gates, back into the city.

*

The Rogues were not all Luthanese. One group was from Manon – entirely female in composition, they called themselves the Isteri. They greeted Lycaea in rapid Manoni. To my surprise, she responded fluently.

There were also Rogues from beyond the northern mountain ranges; and from Norest, islands off the north-east coast where fierce durlows swam and planes of ice were all that could be seen from miles around. There were few Pels. Lycaea explained that they preferred to concern themselves with the Primero and the nobler politics. But the Pels aside, Rogues seemed to come from every city in Oster, and beyond.

We sat and ate with them as we discussed our strategy; proper food this time, rather than the hunks of meat we had given to the souther-waer. I was fast falling in love with Luthanese food. It seemed decadent in comparison to the sturdy, thick foods of home. It was especially easy to get a taste for the honey-breads and the dried figs.

'We march on Caerwyn, then,' said a stout Rogue called Dice. 'We'll surely follow Hemanlok, long as he gives his support. But it'd be nice to know we got some aid, Lycaea. Are the Manoni on-side?'

'No.' Lycaea pulled apart a hunk of honey-bread. She did not seem to enjoy the sweet crust, but instead picked at the soft white insides. Her taste tended towards the savoury, like the salty olives and dried fish. Bright green nuts with crisp purple skins. 'We have more chance with the souther-waer, though. I'm hoping they'll fall in. But we need a real show of strength, which means we need all Rogues in, and the sailors too.'

Dice lathered his sweet bread with preserved sour cherries. 'It comes down to *seran* and gold, sweetheart. I can talk any

Rogue into any battle under the sun, but a golden tongue is nobody's use unless it can be bought and sold. You see my dilemma.'

'What do you need?'

Dice spoke through his mouthful. 'More turf.'

Lycaea tensed. I knew she could not promise him that. Turf control was entirely under Hemanlok's jurisdiction, and he had not put his hand in with ours yet.

'Can't do it,' she said. 'Everyone will be asking the same thing, Dice. You know that isn't fair.'

'*Serans*.'

'Leldh has those in abundance. If you come with us to Caerwyn, you can have free rein to loot the place. Not to mention there will be prisoners, and mercenaries, and all manner of people looking for jobs. Cheap labour. You're a Wharfer, Dice. You can never have enough labour.'

'And what can we offer you?'

'Blast-powder.'

I started. This was the first she had spoken of it.

'That could be difficult to get, Lycaea.'

Lycaea laughed. It was a warm sound, entirely infectuous.

'Don't give me a spin, Dice. You're Wharfers. Pels send blast-powder through your people every second week. Everyone knows you're the main suppliers in Luthan. We need it. Whilst the soldiers in Caerwyn are trying to hack at our Rogues and mercenaries, we need to line the courtyard with blast-powder or firesticks and blow the place to the stars.'

I forgot about the food and watched the two of them. Lycaea had been keeping her plans close. If she had discussed this with Hemanlok, I did not know of it.

'You always were ambitious, Lycaea.' Dice sighed and made one last effort to protect his interests. 'We'll still be short on men.'

'There will still be waer prisoners we can free.'

'Weak, hungered, injured.'

Lycaea's eyes were suddenly on me, though she still spoke to Dice. 'We have the Shadows.'

'Has the Wytch agreed to that?'

'Not yet.'

Dice smiled. 'Right,' he said. 'You get the Dealer on-side and you have yourself a bargain, girl. And don't doubt me for a moment, I'll talk every gang leader there is into joining us. Hemanlok can order them and they'll obey, but I can put their hearts into it.' He rose and wiped his mouth on his sleeve. 'Good eats, Lycaea. Send word when you have the Dealer.'

'You'll hear from me before the week is out,' she promised. Dice sauntered out, and Lycaea stared at her food for a while. I watched her, waiting for explanation. She raised her eyes. They were startlingly green, and focused.

'You better finish that quick,' she said. 'We still have a lot of work to do.'

Kaebha

Shame and agony sealed Kaebha's loyalty. She was unfaltering, unfailing. Four months she was held in Leldh's cells. By the time she emerged and returned to the ranks, she had no doubts or hesitations. She spent each moment at his side, to Cooper's chagrin. The competition between them resumed; though on Kaebha's part at least it was detached and controlled now.

Daeman watched their constant clashes with amusement. He saw new opportunities, now Kaebha shared the blood of his enemies. He tested her pain threshold on a regular basis; tried her with silver, and pushed her through the Shift with brutal delight. Kaebha endured. She had brought the repercussions upon her own head. She knew the price of defiance now.

After another month, Leldh brought her closer into his circle, admitted her once again into the fold of his coterie. This time, she was no mere soldier. Who better than Kaebha to deal with the waer? Who better to know how to hurt them, how to break them? She learned the artistry of a hot iron, the effects of silver on the flesh. Once, she skinned a dead waer and presented the pelt to Leldh. He was pleased; he wore the pelt about his shoulders.

Now she was put to more difficult tasks. Most of the waer she tortured had no experience with battle or hardship. They were easy to break because they had not been taught resistance. Because cruelty was alien to them. Such was not the case with the men and women of Luthan. Cooper and Leldh's other soldiers brought them in, fighting and cursing. They were the sharks taken in with a haul of fish. Sometimes they had been trying to infiltrate Caerwyn. Other times, the soldiers had attacked chipre-folk, and the Luthanese had been travelling with them. Half-breeds, vagrants, Rogues.

Kaebha was learning how to work on their kind too. Fire and iron and boiling water. Still, they were hard to break.

'Just think, Kaebha. This was once you.'

She looked over her shoulder at Cooper. Where her hands and tunic were stained with blood he was, as always, pristine. He leaned on the door frame. His lips pulled back into a slow, broad smile. Kaebha could have counted his teeth.

'Back in favour,' he went on. 'How does it feel to be licking Lord Leldh's boots again? Literally, this time.'

'I am working,' she said. 'Leave me. You are a distraction.' She turned back to the Rogue in front of her. A young woman: conscious, but only just. It was part of the skill, keeping them aware of the pain, preventing them from surrendering too swiftly to darkness.

She felt Cooper's breath on the back of her neck. She could smell him, his scent mild compared to the blood.

'How long this time, Kaebha?' he whispered. 'How long until you break and fall? And what, I wonder, will he do with you then?'

She stepped back from the prisoner. For once she was not torturing this girl for the sake of Leldh's curiosity. This time, she needed information. Cooper's words nettled her and pulled her attention away from the job at hand. She reminded herself that he wanted her to fail.

Never again.

She slapped the girl across the cheek, then reached for a bucket of cold water and splashed it over her face.

'Wake up,' she hissed.

The girl's eyes opened, rolled, focused on Kaebha. 'Please.'

Kaebha brought her face close. She softened her voice, touched the girl's cheek. Left bloodied fingerprints there.

'Are you ready to speak?' she asked. 'I am ready to listen. Just a few words.' She brushed the girl's hair back, sisterly. 'Tell me what I need to know.'

The girl started to talk, and Kaebha smiled. She hoped Cooper heard every word.

Lowell

Lycaea delayed visiting her mother. Instead, she spent her time sparring with Hemanlok and training me. Both were taxing. Lycaea's sessions with Hemanlok were in the morning, so by the time she came to me in the afternoon she was sore and ill-tempered. To my knowledge, they had made little progress; Hemanlok still withheld his support, and his forgiveness. Over the week after meeting with Kirejo, the waer and the Rogues, I could see it weighing on Lycaea. The Derrys had once told me how she craved the man's approval, and I doubted it at the time. But I could see it now. His rejection gnawed away at her. It would have helped if most of the Own did not follow his lead. Donovan and Mitri were kind, but Flicker, Shard, Salvi and Hywe treated Lycaea with varying combinations of cold indifference and blistering hostility. In their eyes, she had betrayed them.

'They have no right.' My anger spilled over one afternoon

following a heated exchange between Salvi and Lycaea. He had accused her of selling her body along with their secrets. She had thrown a plate at him.

Lycaea dropped into a chair. Her eyes fixed on the grain of the table. 'I don't care.'

I wanted to take her hand. Comfort her. 'I do.' All I could give was my support. Unquestioning. Unshaking.

Her gaze flicked to me. 'I expected it. I sold them out.' She rolled her shoulders back. I heard them click. 'Told Leldh everything I should have kept secret. Told him about Moth and Dodge. About the Debajo, and how to get here. Hemanlok's powers and restrictions. The Dealer's madness. Ways to get into Kirejo's palace. Any weaknesses Luthan has. He knows them all.'

'You were a child, Lycaea.'

'Doesn't matter how old you are. I'd do it again now.' She stood restlessly and went to rummage through the cupboards. 'When they start prying up your fingernails. Using brands. Scalding you with boiling water. Age makes no difference. It doesn't matter how many lies you tell. Chances are, you'll eventually give them what they want to know. Keep telling them anything until they stop.' She was lost in the memories. She shuddered, then turned around and held up a jar of spiced almonds. 'These?'

'Those,' I agreed, when I found my voice. I was not hungry, but she needed something to keep herself occupied. She sat opposite me and opened the jar, sliding it into the middle of the table.

'Thing is,' she went on, taking one of the nuts, 'they'll follow Hemanlok's lead. If he relents, so will they. For them, it's not really about what I did. It's about what the boss thinks.'

'He sent you there in the first place,' I said. 'A leader is only as good as his people.' I thought of Alwyn, respectful and kind, working alongside us in the Valley. 'If you are to blame for what happened in Caerwyn, Hemanlok is just as accountable.'

Her lips curved. She was laughing at me. 'He is a *Watcher*, Wolf,' she reminded me.

'All the more reason. He has a duty to the people who trust him, and he has the resources to keep them safe.'

'Gods don't have a duty to their people.'

'If they did not, there would be no point in them.' I took an almond. It was sweet and peppery, warm to the tongue. 'Besides, the Watchers are not gods. They are human, even if they seem to have forgotten. That is what Dodge said in his stories.'

For once, no argument. The tension eased from her shoulders, and she sat back in her chair. I wished she could always be so at ease with me.

'Will you approach your mother soon?' I asked her.

She threw an almond at me. I caught it, and she grinned. 'In good time,' she said. 'First, training-room.'

While Lycaea delayed, Moth continued to approach the third Watcher. She, too, was suffering continued rebuffal, and it took a toll on the little Healer. Most nights, she sat silent with Dodge, grey eyes distant. Arriving in Luthan had been a relief, but time and the upcoming battle were unkind to our spirits.

When I woke, I was exhausted. My muscles were knotted and sore. I ate in silence, knowing half the Own had risen already, and the other half would not be awake for another hour or so. Lycaea was awake, and I could hear the faint sounds of sparring from the training-room. I winced. It was going to be a long day.

Flicker walked through the kitchen, snatching an apple from the table as she went. She liked to watch the training sessions. I ground my teeth. Of all the Own, she was cruellest to Lycaea. I found it hard to believe she was married to Donovan, who was so mild and affable. She was certainly beautiful, but mischief and vanity made her ugly.

She pushed open the door to the training room and leaned against it.

'She's on the floor again,' she remarked to me. 'How is she supposed to fight in Caerwyn if she can't even keep her feet?'

'You should not mock her.' I finished my porridge and cleaned my bowl. I went to join Flicker at the door. 'I have never seen you sparring with Hemanlok. I would wager he could knock you flat.'

'I'm smart enough not to try. And I'm loyal enough not to have to.'

'How can you call her disloyal?' I watched as Lycaea sprang up, only to be sent flying back at least a foot. 'She came back here as soon as she could. And she has been desperately trying to make things right with Hemanlok since.'

Flicker nodded towards Lycaea and Hemanlok.

'She won't make things right with him. The person who came back from Caerwyn ain't the same person who left Luthan. She's a stranger to us. She ain't Rogue any more. He can't put his support behind her, because he can't trust her.'

'And he thinks he can ascertain whether she is trustworthy

through *this*?' Hemanlok's stave cracked against the back of Lycaea's legs, dropping her to her knees. She swore. 'Every day, he beats her. Every day, he weathers away the strength she has been building.'

'Then she ain't strong enough.'

'You underestimate her.'

Lycaea struck out at Hemanlok but he knocked her stave back each time. The third time this happened he caught her knuckle and she drew her hand back with a hiss. Hemanlok took this opportunity to strike, landing her a blow to the stomach with the butt of his staff. She doubled over and he hit her over the head, hard enough to make her stumble. As she lurched forwards, he slammed the length of the staff into her back, flooring her. I flinched.

'Get up.' Hemanlok's voice was firm. Lycaea did not rise. I could see her hands clench into fists. Hemanlok hit her with the staff again. 'Get *up*, brat,' he said. Lycaea took an audible breath and pulled herself up. She was barely on her feet when Hemanlok knocked her down again.

'He's taken all your talent,' he said, stepping back from her with disgust. 'All your pluck. I thought better of you, kid. I really did.' He nudged her with his boot. 'You used to have a bit of spark. Some courage. I thought it could last. More fool me.' His lip curled. 'You should have been left for dead. You're of no use now, in any case.'

She looked at him without speaking, blood trickling from her swollen lip. She lowered her head, pressing it to the ground. Hemanlok cast down his stave.

'You ain't one of my Own,' he said, and turned on his heel. He walked towards us with even, heavy steps. I took a step towards Lycaea. Flicker grabbed my shoulder and pulled me back.

'Don't even think about it,' she said.

'She needs help.'

'We don't pick up what the boss knocks down.'

'*Hemanlok!*'

Lycaea's voice cut through our argument. Hemanlok, now a step in front of us, halted. Lycaea stood. Her limbs were shaking.

'Don't walk away from me,' she spat. 'We're not done yet. *We're not done yet, Hemanlok.*'

She leapt forward and hit him. He spun without a pause, warding off the blows she dealt him with his hands alone. We watched, frozen, as she rained strike after strike at Hemanlok. The blind Watcher made no comment or retaliation, evading each blow. What he lacked in sight, he compensated for in other senses. Hemanlok snatched up his staff and they matched one another move for move, the staves locking. The crack of wood upon wood was fast and sharp, and the two moved so quickly the poles sometimes blurred. Occasionally Hemanlok would bark out a command, reminding Lycaea to spread her weight, lower her center of gravity, relax her hands and so forth. Soon, her motions became as fluid as Hemanlok's. The stave was an extension of her arm.

'Don!' Flicker shouted through the building. 'Come see this!'

Soon, all of Hemanlok's Own were crowded into the doorway. Moth ducked between them and stood by me.

In spite of the beating she had taken, Lycaea was full of energy, hitting out at Hemanlok with passion and precision.

I could have watched it forever. They were so graceful; they worked about one another as if they had been fighting the same battle since the beginning of time. When she stumbled, he would come in with a blow, but she would *know* he was coming, and block it. When she was behind him, he would move almost in time with her. It was eerie, and beautiful. It was more than a dance. It was a rebirth. She looked like a Rogue. She looked like a *waer*.

'Finally,' Moth breathed. 'I thought she would never start fighting back.'

A thump drew our attention and we turned to find Lycaea pinned to the ground. Hemanlok held the butt of his stave on her stomach, pressing it. He seemed as unruffled as ever. Lycaea was panting.

'I give,' she gasped. 'I give, Boss.' She coughed. 'Let up.'

He moved his staff to the side and pulled her up with a large gloved hand. 'Better, brat,' he said, clapping her on the shoulder. She leaned on her stave; I think she would have fallen without it. In spite of that, she allowed herself the smallest of smiles. It faded in a moment.

'We need words,' she said.

Hemanlok nodded. I left her, closing the door to shut myself and the Own out. The members of his gang swapped glances and made their retreat. Dodge would have stayed as he was, but Moth laughed and tugged on his elbow, pulling him away. I remained, and listened. It was unlike me to eavesdrop, but I needed to know.

'Thank you, Boss,' Lycaea said in a low voice. I heard them moving around in the room, presumably putting their staves away.

'I was expecting you to stay on the floor,' he drawled.

'So was I,' Lycaea admitted. 'But we need your help, Boss.'

'Do you?' He gave nothing away.

'Yes. Aye.' She corrected herself uncertainly, torn between the Own's patterns of speech and her own. 'We need firesticks, blast-powder, people to distract him, and fighters. If you help us, other Rogues will follow and we'll at least have a chance.'

'To do what?'

'To kill Daeman Leldh.'

'You want to do that, do you? Are you sure?' There was danger beneath his words now. 'You think you can take a knife and stick it in his belly, or set him alight, or saw his head off? You think you can do that?'

'You're the one who sent me after him, Boss. I'm going to finish what I started.' I wished I had never started to listen, or that I had stayed with her as support. 'Because if I don't, he will take over Luthan. He will find the Debajo, show it to every lawman up topside. He'll chase the Rogues out and burn every last one, because he knows it will hurt you, and Moth, and Melana. He'll make slaves of everyone in Oster, if he is allowed to go on. I can't let that happen.'

She paused. 'Neither can you, Boss. He hasn't touched Luthan yet, but he will.'

Hemanlok was silent. Eventually, his voice rejoined their conversation. 'I can't do much out of Luthan. Broke the Watcher laws one time too many; now I need the life of the city to draw on. There's things I can do, but I'm limited.'

'That's why we're getting Melana in.'

'*I* ain't dealing with her. Wytch gets crazier every day.'

'I will.' I could hear a pulse of relief in Lycaea's voice. 'I'll deal with her, or goad her into it. Does that mean you'll help us?'

'Not sure I have much of a choice. And what of your friend Kaebha?'

I pressed my ear closer to the door, but neither of them spoke for a long while. It was Lycaea who broke the lull.

'How did you find out?' Her voice was ragged.

'Melana's scry-pool.'

'Does everyone know?'

'Just Melana and me. Why did you think I tested you?'

'Thought you were punishing me.' A shuddering intake of breath. 'I'm trying to make it right, Boss.'

'You can't undo it.'

'I know.'

I drew back from the door. Their words were cryptic to me, but I imagined they were talking about the things Lycaea had revealed to Leldh under torture. I did not want to know the details of her torment, if she disclosed them to Hemanlok. I had listened enough.

The door rasped open behind me as I walked down the corridor and turned a corner.

'I'm on-side, Lycaea,' Hemanlok said. His voice was deep and firm, finally speaking the words I knew she had been longing for. 'Get the Wytch in, and I'm with you.'

Lycaea

The journey from the Den to Shade territory was easy and quick. Melana's gang, the Shadows, resided to the south-east. As the two turfs were side by side, I was unhindered for most of the passage. The change as I crossed over to Shade Turf was easy to see. The smaller tunnels networking within most turfs had lamp-posts situated at the beginning and end of each way. Shade Turf did not have these; in replacement, eerie grey-green lights bobbed about the alleyways, disappearing and reappearing at random. The place smelt mustier, and the distinct odour of Melana was in every corner. I could barely tolerate it. It was a strong perfume, cloying and overpowering.

The smell of my mother.

Melana had abandoned me when I was very young, and my father had taken me beyond her reach in case she ever changed her mind. I had few memories of my life with her before that. Being locked in a cupboard. Begging her for food.

Being slapped. My father's greatest gift to me had been taking me from her care so early.

There was a chance for negotiation with Melana nevertheless, and I had every intention of exploiting her power. If anyone could get us into Caerwyn, it was my mother – she was able to translocate people across short distances, and she was an expert in subterfuge. Her powers relied on bargains and binding contracts, which was where most of my reservations lay. The rest of my reservations concerned her insanity. It was not always obvious, but it simmered beneath the surface, in her malice and her erratic moods.

I turned down a street. The cobbled paving of the other turfs in the Debajo was replaced with soft, moist dirt. The walls of the buildings were a deep green with vines stretching from the ground. I knew Melana's passion for earth and greenery. It reminded her of her distant home on the island of Pelladan. She recreated the place as best she could in the middle of the city using glamours and enchantments. It did not work. There was something forced and unnatural about it. But then she had never been good at telling fact from fiction. Sometimes, I thought, Melana still believed she was on Pelladan.

Something moved behind me and I turned to face the Shadows.

No one in Luthan knew how many Shadows there were, or *what* exactly they were; they kept their faces obscured by masks and it was impossible to tell one from another. They reeked with the thick scent of Melana's magic and, as with their habitat, there was something deeply unnatural about them.

One of them gestured. I followed as they turned and started off into the darkness. The eerie green lights followed us, barely illuminating our way as we turned down winding alleyways and passed sharp corners. Something scurried across my path. It was neither cat nor dog, nor anything I had scented before. I was not perturbed. Such an occurrence was common in Shade turf. I thought back to the legend of the Watchers. I had heard it so many times from Dodge, I knew it by heart. The Morning, the Night and the Grey Hours Between. Moth, Hemanlok and Melana respectively. Melana's world was blurred; a mingling of reality and delusion. Nothing was certain. The creatures in her realm were neither one thing, nor another. They were caught in a permanent state of uncertainty.

We came to a small, dim building. The Shadows ushered me in, closed the door and were gone. Fading into the darkness that clawed about me.

I knew the small building well. I had made deals with Melana before. They came at a high cost, but she never broke a bargain. Melana was more honourable than Hemanlok or Moth in that sense. Hemanlok would break a deal under the right circumstances, and Moth would break one to save a loved one, without question. Melana held her word to the letter.

The Wytch made no sound as she entered the room but she was easy to see. The darkness did not need to touch her. There was enough of it within her deep blue eyes, the curve of her smirk. She was clad in a loose white slip, a good deal of flesh revealed where the simple garment fell short. Her black hair coiled about her shoulders and rippled gracefully as she moved to sit cross-legged on the floor. I followed suit. I had to watch myself for this was Melana's turf; Hemanlok had no jurisdiction. The situation was too precarious for me to make a mistake.

'My dear child.' Her voice was low and rich, amused. I felt a pang. There was no genuine affection in her voice. Once, I had craved her love. Now, I was sickened when she feigned it.

'Mother.' I met her gaze. 'It has been a long time.'

'Hasn't it just?'

'I want to discuss some business with you.'

'It always is business,' she chuckled. 'Otherwise you would never enter this place, would you? You find it repulsive.'

Her manner was cool, though madness sparkled in the sapphire of her stare. I spread my hands wide. 'Desperate times call for desperate measures. Daeman Leldh gains more power by the day, and he is a living defiance of everything you fought for, all those years ago.' I watched Melana. 'Everything you suffered for.'

'I have nothing to do with the Kudhienn,' she said. 'We lost enough last time. I wash my hands of this.'

'You battled the collective forces of the Kudhienn once,' I reminded her. 'Now, there is just one: Leldh. I am not asking you to confront him. That is my task and mine alone. Nevertheless, you are needed, all of you. Hemanlok and Moth have both pledged to help us.'

Melana relaxed, sitting back. Her lips curved into a slow, sly smile.

'Daeman Leldh,' she murmured. 'You were his.'

She could not have said anything more hurtful.

'I was.' Steadiness was the key with Melana. 'I know better now. It is time to claim vengeance upon him. The last of the Kudhienn, Melana. It is time to make a deal.'

'Oh, yes.' She sat forwards. A flush rose in her pale cheeks and she shifted her hips, drawing in a shuddering breath as she set her hands upon the ground between us. Her blue eyes glistened, bright and aware. 'So tell me, little fleshling. How much are you willing to sacrifice for the death of Daeman Leldh?'

Anything. Everything. Anyone, everyone. I watched Melana. She reached out a hand, grazing it along the skin of my cheek. I had to brace myself not to flinch.

'Tell me about Lowell Sencha.'

An unexpected turn of the conversation. Instantly wary, I pulled away from my mother's touch. Melana smiled and combed her fingers through her hair.

'Oh, would you look at that face! You used to look at me just so when you were a child and I refused to tell you a story.'

'Or when you refused to feed me.'

'Bygones,' she responded. 'I asked you a question, *Lycaea*. Hemanlok mentioned the fellow, and I know Derry is acquainted with the family. So who is this mysterious young man?'

'A farmer,' I replied. 'Of no interest to you.'

'Oh, but he *is*,' my mother said. 'Come now, my child, you know me.'

I clenched my jaw and answered her question. 'Sencha is a waer from the Gwydhan Valley. He and his brother found me washed up on the river, and the family took me in.' I shrugged. 'What more do you want to know?'

'How much does *he* know?'

My stomach sank. 'He knows all he is required to know.'

'Does he know about Kaebha?'

No. And he never can. I said nothing. I thought of Lowell Sencha, with his dark eyes and gentle smile. His quiet reserve and endless patience.

Melana took my chin in long-nailed hands and tipped my face to kiss me on the forehead. 'We have more in common than you are willing to admit.'

I leaned away from her. I could not lose Lowell. He was my ballast, my anchor.

'Tell him. Tell him everything, tell him who you are.'

'Is that a deal, Melana?' It was difficult to keep my voice level. Melana tucked her heels beneath her, her pose becoming childlike. She smiled. I looked away. I could not fathom why she would make this deal. Perhaps she had used her scry-pool and her shadows to see what would most torment me.

'It's hard to say whether you can be trusted, fleshling.' She stretched, fully in control now. 'Waerwolves are good judges of character, for the most part. They have good instincts. And he has no bias towards the person you used to be. If this Sencha stays with you after the tale is related, I will come with you. I will aid you in your battle against this Daeman Leldh. If he leaves, I will know you are not worth fighting for.'

My mind whirled. 'Lowell Sencha has no need to know.'

'And I have no need to come with you.' Melana rose, placing one hand on her hip and drumming her fingers along her upper thigh. 'This choice is yours to make, *Lycaea*.'

The choice was made. I could deny her. But I could not bring myself to make the deal, to lose what I had found in Lowell.

'So, you do not trust yourself either.' Interest sparked in her features and she took a step closer. 'Still, I find myself wondering why you are so afraid to tell him. Surely he is no great asset? A farmer is no advantage to you. You have very little to lose, dear daughter. Why the wild eyes?'

I did not know. He was unskilled in combat. He was a farmer. He was a *waer*. But…

'Wolf stays,' I said.

She laughed. The mockery edged under my skin, peeling it back and exposing old hurts. I fixed my eyes on the ground, reining my temper back as Melana laughed.

'You will never be fully healed,' she told me. My stomach twisted. 'Leldh has triumphed in one aspect at least. You will never be the person you were. In fact…' Her voice became a purr. 'There is, I believe, a part of you that is still…'

'Stop.' My chest hurt, though whether it was my heart or my lungs I could not tell. Melana waited. I shuddered. 'There is more I wish to deal for,' I said. 'I need information on the survivors from the Gwydhan.' If I was going to tell Lowell Sencha the truth, I wanted at least a chance to bear good news to him as well. If I could find the name of even one survivor, one person he cared about… 'Look in your scry-pool, Melana, and tell me who survived.'

'No.' She sat back, all business now. 'I do nothing for free. Allow me to counter-propose. I want Caerwyn.'

I rubbed my forehead. Hemanlok was right. She was getting worse. 'We're *going* to Caerwyn, Melana.'

'No, no.' She flicked a hand, irritated. '*No*. I *want* Caerwyn. Once Leldh is dead. Once his armies are routed. Once you are satisfied in your half-sung quest. I want Caerwyn to myself. I do not want Hemanlok to send in his little Rogues and people to establish a new colony. I do not want Kirejo claiming it for his own. Too long, I have slunk through the tunnels and caverns of the Debajo, underneath Hemanlok's thumb. I want a place of my own, as I once had on Pelladan.' She had been banished from Pelladan, and rightly so. Melana was not safe out in the world. But in Caerwyn, far from other cities and protected by the mountains...I considered it. Not to mention that she would be far from Luthan. Hemanlok would approve. Melana liked nothing better than to trouble him.

She went on.

'I want Caerwyn, and I want you to tell Lowell Sencha the truth about your time in Caerwyn. Those are the conditions for my support. And I will throw in a peek into the scry-pool for old time's sake.'

I hesitated. There had to be something I had not thought of. Melana's deals were often part of a longer game, and sometimes the simplest bargain could return to bury you.

But we needed her.

I extended my hand.

Melana clasped it before I could reconsider. A jolt sped up my arm. Blue sparks buzzed about our locked fingers. I caught my breath as Melana squeezed tighter. I became dizzy and dropped my head. Melana released me. All lies of tenderness were gone, replaced with intoxicated triumph. The deals gave her strength, but each one addled her mind further. One day, I knew, she would be beyond reach. She was already so far from Hemanlok and Moth.

She pulled to her feet and danced to the side of the chamber to take a clay bowl from the table. Placing it in front of me, she rubbed her hands together and breathed on them. I turned my eyes away as shadows poured from her mouth, entwined about her fingers. She shook her hands and the shadows dripped into the bowl.

'The Gwydhan Valley,' she said. 'Mm. Norther-waer.' She flexed her fingers over the bowl, drew shadows into formless shapes. They melded with the water in the bowl and Melana spun them once. When she moved her hands away, the shadows moved of their own accord. The Sencha house stood in darkness. Soldiers moved about it. I could pick out Dodge's lanky silhouette. It was the night of the attack. I leaned in as the shadows fanned out, depicting all of the Valley in inky detail.

Movement increased. I could not focus on all the shadowy figures, but I knew Melana could. I raised my eyes to watch her face. The mirth had died there, replaced by otherworldly peace. When she spoke, her voice dragged and slurred. Shadows weighed on her tongue.

'Many perished. Many fled.'

I forced myself to be patient.

'The soldiers came with fire and silver.' Her head drooped forwards, and shadows wreathed her head. She droned on. 'They took lives, and they took prisoners.' The black shapes writhed, gathered together, scattered again. 'Eight-seven. Eighty-seven prisoners. Men, and women, and children.'

'I need names, Mother.'

'Mmm.' Her head whipped back, eyes flaring black. I scooted away from her. Her voice was deep and resonant. 'Sencha.'

Frustration turned my stomach. 'I know this already, Mother. Sencha walks with me. I *know* he survived. Who else?'

She shuddered. The pillar of shadows moved. Darkness fell

away, and a figure emerged. I stared, then caught my breath, understanding. Sencha. She was not speaking about Lowell.

One of the other Senchas had survived.

'Go, daughter.' Melana's eyes, hooded and dilated, found me again. The shadows dissipated. She appeared old, now. Tired. I felt a stir of pity for her. She, like the other Watchers, was a slave to her own power. 'You have truths to tell, and vengeance to seek. I will join you on the road to Caerwyn.'

I was breathless by the time I reached the Den. Sweating and shaking. I knew what I had to tell him: the best and the worst things I knew. I pushed open the door and stepped inside. Stopped beyond the threshold. I could not will myself to go on. My stomach turned.

I leaned against the wall and breathed. The scents of the Own came to me, gentle and comforting. They grounded me and dragged my mind from Caerwyn. I was in Luthan. I made my own choices.

Forcing my legs to move, I went to my room. The door was open, and through the crack I could see Lowell Sencha. He was cross-legged on his pallet, and Mitri sat opposite him. They spoke of weapons and strategy. I knocked, then pushed the door open. Mitri grinned at me.

'How was the Wytch?' he asked.

'In fine form,' I told him. 'She's on-side. She marches with us to Caerwyn.'

Mitri whooped, and Lowell's face broke into a smile. I could not match their expressions. My head was spinning. I gripped the door-frame. It was hard to keep my balance.

'I need to speak to Wolf.'

Mitri and Lowell exchanged a quick look, then Mitri stood and passed me to leave the room. I released the door-frame and took his place opposite Lowell, my legs grateful for the rest. Lowell waited, ever patient, and I fought a fresh surge of horror. I had not realised how I had come to lean upon his calm and his quiet acceptance. I was going to lose it now.

'My mother had many things to tell me, and now I have two things to tell you. One is terrible for me to speak of. The other, I think will bring you much comfort. I want to speak of the most difficult first, Lowell. I...' My hands were shaking, and my voice caught.

Lowell reached over and took my hands in his.

'There is no need for haste,' he said.

His hands were warm and gentle. A comfort. I closed my eyes and began. 'Hemanlok sent me to Caerwyn to find out if Leldh was one of the Kudhienn. To discover his plans, and to know his strengths. I was young, Lowell. I was just fifteen.'

He nodded. 'Too young,' he said. 'Hemanlok never should have sent you.'

'I managed, for a month. I played my part. I had a false name. I pretended to be one of Leldh's soldiers. I spoke to prisoners, gathered information and stole things. It seemed to be a success, but someone was watching me. A soldier named Cooper. He took an instant dislike to me, and it grew as the month went on. Distrust led to outright suspicion. On the night of my departure, he caught me.' Hard to breathe. 'He caught me.'

Lowell squeezed my hand. I wanted to pull away. I wanted to run.

'At first, they locked me away, and I thought they would

kill me or leave me there. But…I was supposed to meet Hemanlok a week later, just out of the mountains. If they decided to keep me prisoner, I thought he would come for me, get me out in time. I waited.' *Four tight walls. The smell of blood. Hunger possessed me.* 'It was two months before they brought me in front of Leldh.'

'Hemanlok never came for you.'

'He couldn't. Not without the other two Watchers. Outside of Luthan he lacks the power, unless they are there to help him. Melana refused.'

'Why would she refuse? You are her *daughter*.'

'Her motives are her own. Impossible to say whether it was out of cruelty, or whether she felt her interference at that time would upset the Balance. Either way, I was left there. When no one came for me, I figured Leldh would kill me, but he had other things in mind. The torture began then.' *Fire, iron, deprivation.* 'I lost my mind, Wolf. I could not withstand it. I told them everything.'

He was pale. 'I am sorry, Lycaea.' The pity in his eyes seared me. 'You do not have to speak of it.'

'I have to. You have to know.' My throat closed over. 'I thought they wanted information from me, but they wanted more than that. They wanted servitude.' I drew a slow breath. 'When Daeman decides he wants you,' I said, keeping my voice low, 'there is nothing you can do about it. And the torture removes any essence of you. Your old life and beliefs fade. And once they are gone, there is a space inside of you.' I stopped, my mouth working soundlessly for an instant before I pressed on. 'Daeman filled that space with something loathesome. I resisted for as long as I could. But eventually, it was easier to not feel anymore. I shed my name, and my allegiance to Hemanlok. Leldh came to know me by the name I had assumed for my cover. It was his own little mockery of my failure.'

Understanding crept across Lowell's features. His hands were a dead weight on mine, limp and lifeless. I forced the words out. I could let there be no doubt in his mind.

'I was Daeman's torturer. I was Kaebha, Lowell. I was Kaebha.'

Lowell

Her hands were cool and clammy beneath mine. She sat with her legs crossed. Her hair, unkempt and unevenly grown back, strayed across her brow. Her green eyes were fixed on me, red-rimmed and hard in her angular face. Colour blotched her skin. I watched as sweat beaded on her forehead and tracked along her temple. The woman I had come to care for, and yet did not know at all. Lycaea. Kaebha. Daeman Leldh's torturer. A woman who had murdered people. Broken them with pain and fear.

I withdrew my hands. She sucked in a breath. My chest was tight with grief.

'You tortured people. You tortured *waer*.'

'Yes.' She spoke between her teeth.

'You killed innocent people.'

'Yes.'

'You served the man who slaughtered my family.'

Her head jerked up. 'Wolf. Your family...'

'No. *No.*' I stood. 'Lycaea. *Kaebha.* You served the man who *slaughtered my family.* Who destroyed my home.'

She shook her head. 'I just wanted it to stop. Wolf, there's something else. I need to talk to you about your family.'

'*Do not change the subject.*' My voice was harsher than it had ever been. Lycaea pressed her lips so tight, they whitened. I could not keep my words steady. 'I trusted you. I thought you were one of us.'

'I told you I wasn't.' She rose. She kept her hands at her sides, bunched into fists. 'I told you, Wolf. I am a waer, but I will never be one of your people.' Her voice dropped. 'It was as if I watched myself doing these things, and could not prevent it. As if Kaebha truly was another person, wearing my skin.' Her eyes were haunted. Distant. 'I'm not trying to justify it. I know there's no forgiveness for this.'

'What changed you?'

'I was supposed to head the attack on Luthan, along with Cooper. When he told me, I broke. I became myself again. I ran. His men pursued me to the river, and I jumped.'

'Who knows?'

'Hemanlok. My mother. I think Moth and Dodge guessed. You are the first person I have told. Hemanlok only found out because my mother told him.' She rallied, stood taller. 'I know what I did. There's no denying it or escaping from it. But I'm trying to make it right. I'll do anything to make it right.'

'You cannot.' Impossible to meet her gaze. I imagined I could smell the blood on her hands. *Murderer. Torturer.*

'Perhaps not. But I can ensure it never happens again. That's why I'm going to Caerwyn, Lowell. I will put an end to this.'

She reached out a hand, held it steady. 'I swear. But Wolf, you have to listen to me. Melana told me something else.'

I shook my head, and the words died on her lips. I could hear nothing more from her.

'Will you at least hear me out?'

'I will not. I am sorry, Lycaea. More sorry than I can say.' I walked out, and closed the door behind me. I heard something hit the door on the other side and shatter. Mitri rounded the corner and stared.

'What was *that*?' he asked. I shook my head and pushed past him. The tunnels and caves of the Debajo were suddenly oppressive. I wanted fresh air, and forests, and mountains. I wanted to go home.

In the days following I moved out of Lycaea's room, and shared instead with Mitri. He talked in his sleep, and kept strange hours. When morning rolled along, I was always exhausted. I had been training with various members of the Own instead of Lycaea. It was days until the army left Luthan, and I still did not feel ready.

I avoided Lycaea, and would not let her speak to me. She said she had pressing information for me, but I could neither trust her nor stand to be around her. It hurt. Somewhere in the darkness of the Debajo, I had to acknowledge how I felt about her. And I could not reconcile those feelings with the knowledge of what she had done. Perhaps she was no longer Kaebha, but Kaebha would always be staring at me out of Lycaea's gaze now. Lurking beneath the surface. I knew now, what I had seen during our flight from the Valley. When we killed the soldiers. When she attacked Dodge. Kaebha had never truly left, and I doubted she would.

To my relief, the Own busied itself with preparations for battle, and I was swept away with those plans. We met with soldiers and Rogues, trained relentlessly, and watched as the men and women of the city were mobilised. It was a rare occasion, I was told, that Rogues and lawmen worked together openly, but a truce of sorts had been called. It was clear Kirejo had received the confirmation he had been seeking. Daeman Leldh was now a declared danger, and we would face him together. To what end, I could not predict. It seemed impossible we could succeed against such a man; unthinkable that we should lose.

The night before Luthan's army left the city, I climbed the stairs and sat on top of the Den. I would march with them, among Kirejo's soldiers and Hemanlok's Rogues. I tried to prepare my mind for the conflict ahead. I knew I might have to kill. I would certainly have to fight. I might not even be able to recover any of my people. What were the chances they were still alive? What if Leldh had found them as malleable as Lycaea? I could not stand the thought of them being turned against one another. Turned against innocent people.

'Lad?'

Wincing, I moved aside from the ladder to let Dodge up. I did not want the company, but I would never turn the storyteller away. He sat beside me. Our legs dangled over the side. If I reached up, I could brush the roof of the cavern with my fingertips. My hands rested on my knees, useless. They felt like the rest of me. Heavy. Tired.

Dodge puffed out his cheeks and sighed. 'Heard it all through the Den, you know,' he said. 'Not what Lycaea said, but what you said. I havena heard you speak like that before, lad.'

'Did Moth tell you about Kaebha?'

'Aye. She'd heard rumours from chipre-folk about a woman named Kaebha. Pieced it together and told me before we arrived in the Valley. We werena sure, but the journey somewhat confirmed it.'

'You never said.'

'One of the great secrets of storytelling, lad, is knowing when a tale isna yours to tell.'

I wanted to remind him this was no tale; this was my life, and Lycaea's, and nothing seemed whole or complete any more. In the Valley, Dodge's stories had opened my world and made everything seem so much bigger. Now, they were reductive. They were small and trite by comparison.

We sat together without talking for a while. Though I had resented his presence, I found myself easing in his company. I knew he expected nothing from me. He was there to comfort, not to confront.

'Do you think she has changed?' I asked, when the time felt right.

'I dinna think she much cares what *I* think, lad. She cares what you think. But for what it's worth, aye. I dinna think she'll ever go back to what she was in there. She's trying hard, Lowell.'

'I do not mean to cause her pain,' I said. 'But Dodge.' I shook my head. 'What can I say to her? What can I do? She has so much blood on her hands.'

He sighed. 'When I first found out about Moth…' He lifted a shoulder. 'She's lived so many lifetimes. She's done bad things. She canna hurt anyone, of course, as the Healer, but indirectly she's done terrible damage. And she's wise, and has seen empires rise and fall. For a long time, it seemed knowledge of her past changed who she was in the present. As if I didna know her any more. I was angry. Her entire existence made me feel...small. Insignificant. Her world was too big, and if I shared her life I would have to step into that world.'

'What changed?'

He smiled. 'I realised I didna mind a bigger world.'

I tried to imagine how it felt, to be in love with someone bound to outlive you. Possibly by hundreds of years. To have no chance for children, even though they both wanted them. I felt an ache of sadness for the Derrys.

He rested a hand on my shoulder. 'She begged me to come up here and speak with you tonight.' I knew he was not talking about Moth. 'Not on her behalf, though. She had sommat else she wanted me to say.' I frowned at him. He took a slow breath. 'You need to brace yourself, lad.'

'What do you mean? What does she want?'

'When Lycaea went to Melana, she didna just ask for the Dealer to come with us to Caerwyn. She made another deal, as well.'

I shivered. I did not like the sound of it. 'What sort of a deal?'

'An information trade, of sorts. Lycaea would tell you about Kaebha, and in return Melana would tell her about survivors in the Valley.'

I faced him. I was mute. Dodge took my shoulders. He held them tight.

'Lad,' he said. He opened his mouth and spoke, but I could

not hear him above the roaring in my ears. I could see his mouth moving, but I could not connect with the words. I was conscious of my hands shaking and my eyes stinging, but I could not fathom why.

Somehow, we managed to descend the ladder and the stair, and to get into the Den. Dodge steered me inside and sat me in the kitchen. Moth was there in a moment, crouched in front of me with her hands on my knees. She repeated Dodge's words. Over and over again, until they sank in and I could work my mind around them.

Kemp is alive. Your brother is alive.

Words finally made it from my heart to my mouth. 'Alive? *Alive?* How? Where? Alive?'

Moth brushed tears from her own cheeks, then from mine. 'We do not know,' she said. 'We think he was captured with the other waer. Leldh may just have him at Caerwyn. But he is assuredly alive, Lowell. We can rescue him. We can get him back.'

Alive.

'Is he hurt?'

'I do not know.' She gripped my hands. 'If he is wounded, I will heal him if I can. Our focus now must be on Caerwyn, and the days ahead.' She kissed my forehead.

I caught Lycaea's scent, and turned my head. She stood at the door. Her eyes were a mystery to me. When she saw me looking her way, she retreated.

Lycaea

The nightmares worsened as the day of our march grew closer. I struggled to sleep. I was afraid all the time. In the end, I had to ask for Moth's help. She provided dreamless sleep. I tried to get through the days without thinking of Kaebha, or what lay ahead. I trained with Hemanlok and the Own. They were kinder now. Whether Hemanlok had spoken to them or not I did not know, but they followed his lead. They were beginning to accept me into their rank once more.

I left Lowell Sencha alone. He was justified in his retreat and I did not have the time to smooth things over with him. On the day before we marched out, I told Dodge and Moth what Melana had shown me, and they relayed it to Lowell. I meant to stay away even then, but I could not help standing in the kitchen doorway while he absorbed the news. He wept, and the Derrys comforted him. I backed away, and did not disturb them.

The Den was silent the next morning. Usual routine had been put on hold, and Hemanlok had ordered everyone to sleep. For once, I had not allowed Moth to dull my mind into slumber. I rested for a few hours, then went to the training room. It was dim and cool there. I lit the lanterns surrounding the sawdust ring and took up my staff. I would bring both staff and sword to Caerwyn, but over the past few years I had excelled in the latter and neglected the former. Leldh called the staff a 'Rogues' weapon', and would not have his soldiers using one. I stretched, warmed my muscles, and started to drill. The staff was worn and comfortable in my hands. I started slow, then forced my movements to gain pace. It would not do for killing Leldh, of course, but it might be enough to keep me alive until then. More importantly, it might keep me myself until then.

The thought of being under Kaebha's control again made my movements falter. I was capable of so much damage. Evil.

I set my teeth and spun my staff. I worked until my body was covered in a sheen of sweat, and my muscles had eased out from the day before. The boards by the door creaked and I turned, heart pounding. Hemanlok stood in the threshold. He walked in, took his own stave, and drilled with me. We did not speak I needed to stop for water.

'You ready, brat?' he asked as I sipped.

'Hope so.' I stretched my legs, then set aside the water-skin. 'I guess I'll soon find out.'

'We're with you this time.'

Something about his tone made me look at him. His jaw was locked. He stood like a soldier, back straight and facing front.

'Boss?' I asked.

'We should've been with you the first time,' he said. His voice was gruff. 'Shouldn't have sent you in alone.'

My throat closed. I had waited so long for the words. Agonised over them. Now they were being said, I could think of no reply.

'We'll make him pay, brat,' Hemanlok said, and shouldered past me, out of the training-room.

To my surprise, he joined us for breakfast. The last time he had done so, to my memory, was after a fire had swept through the Grinaja and killed some of the Rogues lurking in the streets there. Now, he sat at the table beside Moth, talking to her in a low voice. Usually Moth insisted on cooking, but this morning Donovan and Mitri had commandeered her place in the kitchen. They flipped batter-cakes and bacon, spilled hot fat on the ground and in general made a nuisance of themselves. Flicker, picking at dried fruits from the pantry, threw raisins at Donovan until eventually he abandoned the cooking and focused his efforts on stealing kisses from her. Hywe took his food and ate in the common-room; he was always a solitary type, not much given to company or mirth. Salvi and Shard sat cross-legged on the floor and ate there, laughing at the antics of the others.

The merriment felt forced. We all knew we were walking into battle.

Lowell sat between Moth and Dodge. He was grim and focused. I knew his mind was on his brother. He did not glance at me, and I tried to keep my attention on other things. The developing bond of friendship between us had been broken, and there was nothing to be done about it.

Mitri dropped a batter-cake onto the plate in front of me, and Moth pushed the honey across the table. I was not overly fond of sweet things, but I was hungry after training, and I knew we had a long journey ahead of us. I took the cinnamon-pot and sprinkled the fine dustings over my meal. When I noticed Lowell staring, I pushed it over to him.

'Cinnamon,' I said. I sounded too brusque, so I went on, trying in vain to alter my tone. 'From Manon. Not too much, or it'll taste foul.'

Lowell spooned the cinnamon onto his own breakfast, and I did my best to ignore him after that. I listened instead to Hemanlok and Moth.

'...don't want you or your lanky fool of a husband to be anywhere near the actual combat,' Hemanlok was saying. Dodge grinned at being referred to as a lanky fool; he knew he was one of the few people in the world Hemanlok was genuinely fond of. 'It'd be a real good way to lose the battle, if either of you were to be captured. You're to hang back. Stay away from the battle until Leldh is dead. You too, brat.'

Hemanlok had called me 'the brat' for years. I did not mind the term itself, but I was troubled by what his words suggested.

'I'm going to be out in the battle myself, Boss,' I said. 'I need to find Leldh.'

'No.' His voice was flat and harsh. 'Not this time. I don't intend to let him get near you.'

I sat back, stunned into silence. Hemanlok did not turn his face towards me. When I looked around the table, no eyes met mine. I set my teeth. I needed to see an end to this. I was not going to cower at the back of the ranks and let others do the work for me.

'This is my fight. I need to do this.'

'You called us all in, girl,' Flicker reminded me. She could never resist having a say, especially when it gave her a chance to trouble me. 'You wanted Boss to help, aye? Well, now he's helping. Give it a rest. Ain't a one of us cares about your glory-quest.'

'This has nothing to do with glory.'

'Could've fooled me.'

'Three years, and the two of you still haven't quit sniping at one another,' Hemanlok growled. 'Put a stopper in it.' He sat up, raised his head. His white eyes glared in the light of the kitchen. 'You'll do as I say.'

Not much had changed. Hemanlok was unused to disobedience. I bit my tongue. When it came to battle, I would do what I had to. So long as Leldh died, it did not matter one way or the other.

When we reached upper world, we were greeted with a bleak and heavy sky. Winter, sweeping in from the north, was always slow to reach Luthan. I had no doubt we would be marching in the rain and sleet, possibly even snow. It would be easier for a while when we swerved away from the coast but I dreaded our passage through the mountains. It was possible we would have to do the unthinkable and travel through the Valley on our way to Caerwyn. I could not consider what such a thing would do to Lowell Sencha, or how much danger it would put us in.

We all took separate tunnels to reach upper Luthan, or staggered our travel. No matter our cause, it was imperative we leave the Debajo guarded and protected. We would be fighting alongside the lawmen and soldiers of Luthan, but it made us temporary allies, not friends.

I went on my own. It was obvious to the others I wanted no company, and I was glad they did not make an issue of it. I brushed my hands along the tunnel walls, savoured the musty scents that always promised the Debajo. As I emerged through O'Shea's, I saw a number of other Rogues. They were getting in a last drink before departure. Some of them winked at me, but we did not exchange words. I was glad of it; I doubted my ability to string together coherent thought. I let them to their drinking, trusting they would join us beyond Luthan's northern wall.

I met with Moth and Dodge in the narrow corridor separating the Primero and the Ultimo. Dodge wore some of Donovan's clothing, more suited to combat if we were surprised. They stood at a height, though Dodge was much skinnier than the muscular Donovan. Moth was clad, as ever, in a simple dress. Not yellow this time, but dark grey. She carried her healing bag, and the smells of herbs and tonics stung my nose.

Men and women filtered out of the Ultimo armed with rusted, dented weapons. If they survived the battle at Caerwyn they would be given pay, possibly enough to feed their families for a month or so. Still, they had to provide their own weapons, and they would be put on the front line of the battle. A woman passed me with a carving knife at her belt and a frying pan slung over her shoulder with some thin, fraying rope. I felt a tug of respect, and sorrow. I knew I had brought this upon them, even if they did not recognise it.

The crowds started to gather as we reached the edge of the city. People bidding farewell to their loved ones, and people there to witness the spectacle of Luthan's army amassed. They were excited; war is a delight when it is far away, and you do not have to reckon with the consequences. I wondered if they had any notion who we were facing, and what resources he had at his hands. He was capable of driving men to fall upon their own swords. We had the Watchers with us this time, yes, but they would only assist our odds; they were no guarantee of a victory. Hemanlok was weak outside Luthan and Moth could defend neither herself, nor others. Melana was...Melana.

I walked out beyond the city walls and winced as I looked over the forces amassing. Kirejo's ineptitude hit me with blistering clarity. A king is of no use if he spends all his reign waging war, but nor is he a true king if he fails to maintain the defence of the city. It was easy to tell the Rogues from the soldiers and civilians, because they were the only ones who appeared battle-ready. The only ones with well-kept weapons and proper armour. I stared around at the soldiers. Many were too young, or too old. Some were fat and ungainly. I admired their courage but lamented their unreadiness. I felt I could see their deaths play out before my eyes.

The army had numbers, at least. The people from the Ultimo shuffled to the front, hunched themselves over just shy of the officers. Civilians from Ciadudan stood behind them, marching close to the trained soldiers. Men and women from the Grinaja, given the chance to fight for their freedom, were heavily guarded. The Rogues fanned out between the ranks. I watched as men ran along the rows, taking names. It was an unspoken rule, acknowledged and obeyed by all soldiers, that the Rogues would not be listed among those gathered for war. As far as official records stated, we did not exist.

'Dodge and I are going to join the healers, dear,' Moth said. She caught my arm and kissed my cheek. 'Keep steady. You know where to find me if you need me. We are here with you, Lycaea. You are not alone this time.'

I doubted my smile was convincing. Dodge gathered me into a crushing hug, then followed Moth towards the healers' cart. They travelled towards the back of the army with the washers and the cooks. Hemanlok, I knew, would be travelling further behind them still. He would not suit the ranks, and would only cause chaos among the officers who tried to command him. As for Melana...she had said she would meet us on the road, which I took to mean just before we reached Caerwyn. She was not the sort to march. She could step through the shadows, travelling miles in just a few moments.

'Seen the souther-waer yet?' Mitri was at my elbow. I shook my head. I should have been able to identify them easily; they would stand higher than anyone in Luthan, except perhaps Hemanlok.

'They're late,' I replied. I swallowed. 'Can you make an estimate of our numbers?'

'Looks like a thousand or so upper-folk, but the runners haven't come back with a list yet. We're looking at about six hundred Rogues.'

Not enough. Daeman's numbers were twice ours, and all trained fighters. I pushed the thought from my mind. It would have to be enough. We did not have time for despair. I shifted the weight of my pack, adjusted my sword at my hip, and made my way to the front of the ranks. I would do as Hemanlok had ordered, but for now I would march with the people of the Ultimo. Of all our army, they were giving the most to gain the least.

It was hours before we set off. I stood with some of the men of the Ultimo, showing them how to clean their weapons after use. Several others, including the woman with the frying pan, looked on. When we were called, the thin wretches snapped to attention quicker than anyone else. I scanned the officers and the cavalry. Kirejo, to no one's surprise, would not be gracing us with his presence. If Queen Ela had been a ruler in her own right I did not doubt she would have ridden with us, but she had to at least pretend to stand with her king on all counts. Instead, we had several officers from the Primero who had paid hearty sums for their command positions. Their armour looked shiny enough, but I doubted it would survive a hackbut or a volley of arrows. They rode about the army on temperamental horses, barking orders. I wondered if they were even aware they commanded Rogues. If not, it was going to be a difficult journey for them.

We marched at midday. This, at least, I was accustomed to. Leldh's army had been trained with brutal precision. I remembered hours of standing in the sun or the snow, weeks of marching endlessly through the dark and the light and the mud. Sleeping through hail. I had been Kaebha at the time, but part of me had still been awake, watching and screaming throughout. My body adapted. I helped the Ultimo-dwellers where I could. They were too emaciated to endure such travel easily, but I reminded myself they would be better fed on the march than they were at home in Luthan.

Sometimes my attention wandered, and I searched for Lowell Sencha. I did not see him on the first day, but on the second night I caught sight of him after we had set up camp. He was taking lessons from Donovan in hand-to-hand combat. Flicker sat by, and even from a distance I could tell she was mocking Lowell. I felt stirrings of anger, and bit back a growl. He was trying. He was involved in something far bigger than he was accustomed to, and he was doing his best. She had no right to belittle him for it.

Nor did I have a right to fight his battles for him. Lowell had made it clear he did not want my company. I kept my distance.

The days bled into one another, and the weather worsened as I had predicted. We passed Coserbest, and gained some three hundred people to help us. It was more than I had expected. They were simple folk, and good ones. The quartermaster who raised me hailed from Coserbest, so even the accent brought familiarity and comfort. They brought durlow oil, a thick soupy substance taken from the great furred monsters of the sea. It was better than whale-oil for lighting fires, and would complement the blast-powder we had from the Wharfers. We had good supplies from the town as well, so our rations were a little less restricted.

The souther-waer were still absent from our ranks. I was starting to worry they would not join us. Their refined senses, fierce courage and superior strength would have served us well, both in finding survivors and combatting the enemy. If they did not arrive in the next few days, I would have to contact Hemanlok and ask him to go back to seek word from them. The thought grated at me. I needed his presence. He gave me courage.

On the open plains between Coserbest and the mountains we had to huddle close to keep warm, and stretch waxed canvas over our heads to protect us from the worst of the elements.

Men and women from the Ciadudan sometimes had tents – the Rogues certainly did – but the people of the Ultimo were lucky if they had even a canvas sheet. Fights started to break out; the provosts were called more than once to deal with the participants. I saw one boy, arrogant and angry, beaten bloody for fighting over food. He could not have been older than fifteen, and his howls put a damp chill over the camp. I was reminded of Kaebha. I folded my fear into myself.

Later, Moth came across to look after the boy's hurts. He spat at her, but she did not flinch. She put a poultice on his back and, as she worked, I knew she poured her power into him. She could not remove the red welts for fear of being uncovered, but she could dull the hurt. Even though the skin had broken and he had bled, he would not get the rot. He was sullen and silent by the time she had finished, and I knew he regretted spitting at her. I could understand it, though; he was tired and frightened, and too young to be going to war. I was reminded of myself at his age, walking into Caerwyn with all the strut of a nobleman.

The next day, I carried the boy's pack. I showed him how to handle a sword when we stopped to camp. He had one of his own, which had belonged to his mother before she lost a hand and was sent to the Grinaja for theft. The blade was in surprisingly good condition, and the boy learned quickly. He hardly spoke a word to me, but he worked hard. Soon I had a group of youths who wanted to learn. The first boy was still the most promising. I resolved to mention him to Hemanlok when this was over. I was sure one of the gangs would be able to find a place for him, if he lived.

If any of us did.

Lowell

Time was I never imagined leaving our Valley. I was the elder Sencha boy, destined to follow the family in shepherding. I had been prepared for a life without movement or adventure; I was content. Now, I was marching with an army. I did not know whether to be elated or bitter. I focused my heart on my little brother. Kemp. Alive, imprisoned somewhere in Caerwyn. If we could save him some part of my old life could be salvaged. I prayed to Felen for his safety, thanked Freybug for the chance to save a member of my family.

The journey was long and harsh. I travelled with the people from the Ciadudan, along with Donovan and Flicker. It was difficult. I was anxious and uncomfortable amongst so many people. Most nights, I could not sleep. During the day, I distracted myself by continuing to study combat. Donovan was a good man, and spent much of his time and energy picking up where Lycaea had left off training me. Flicker, on the other hand, was as hostile as ever. I could do nothing right. She lounged around the camp, laughing at my feeble attempts to spar with Donovan.

When I had time to think, I found myself searching the ranks for Lycaea. I eventually found her at the front, with the people from the Ultimo. Even from a distance, she seemed grim and brittle. I wished she had never told me about Kaebha. I could not think of her without imagining the sour smell of blood.

People joined the army as we continued north, but I knew we were smaller than Lycaea had hoped. The souther-waer seemed to have abandoned us. I was sick with disappointment. I had thought better of them. I had thought they would stand with us, for the sake of all waer. I had not expected their cowardice.

By the time we arrived at the foot of the mountains, tension was rising. That night, Hemanlok's Own gathered. We met to the south of the camp, and stayed awake and quiet while Flicker went to find Hemanlok. Moth and Dodge joined us as we waited, and finally Lycaea, from the Ultimo ranks. She did not, would not, look at me.

'What if the souther-waer don't show?' Mitri asked in a low voice.

'We'll have to change strategy,' Lycaea replied. 'Hit in controlled, quick strikes rather than meeting him in plain battle. It'll be much harder to draw him out that way, though, and harder to penetrate the walls. I don't like our chances. Better if we have one tight force hitting him, and a few smaller parties striking simultaneously. We don't have the power to hold him in a siege.'

'Sieges are a nasty business in any case,' Moth said, surprising me. Sometimes I forgot all the years she had lived. It followed she must have seen all manner of battle as well, even if she had not actively been involved. 'I would not put it past Leldh to keep Caerwyn locked in and escape through some secret means himself, if it comes to a siege.'

'Will he meet us in battle otherwise?' Donovan asked, voicing my sudden alarm.

'He won't be able to resist the chance to humiliate us,' Lycaea said. She crouched by the fire to stir the embers.

'Are we going through the Valley?' Hywe asked. It always startled me when he spoke up, and when I remembered he and I shared a point of origin.

I had not considered the possibility of going through the Valley to reach Caerwyn, though it seemed obvious. I stared at my hands. To go home, and find it in waste and ruin…

'It took some talking, but I managed to convince the commander that the mountain paths are safer for us,' Lycaea said. 'Leldh will be using the Valley as training grounds for his soldiers. It's close enough to Caerwyn, and he's been looking for good forest area for a while. He's always had his eye on the Valley.'

'Won't that take longer?'

She shrugged. 'A little longer, perhaps. But it's a safer route.'

I could not disguise my relief. Dodge put a reassuring hand on my shoulder.

'Still no sign of the souther-waer,' Hemanlok said, his gruff voice breaking through our conversation. 'I went back a day, but couldn't find them.'

Lycaea bit her lip. Moth tugged a hand through her hair.

'Can you go back further, brother?' she asked. 'I feel we will need them before this is through.' Hemanlok growled in irritation, and Moth touched his arm. 'Please, brother. Time eats all bones. The longer we delay, the longer Leldh has to prepare for our attack, and the longer he torments the poor souls in his keeping.'

'I ain't so keen to leave you unprotected,' he said. 'Don't think you'd do them much good with a sword, Derry.' In spite of his rough ways, he always seemed gentle with the little Healer.

'If you don't go, brother, we will have to ask Melana to do so.'

'Please don't make me deal with that woman again,' Lycaea put in.

Hemanlok ground his teeth. 'Fine,' he snapped at length. His shoulders were high and tight, his fists clenched.

'Thank you, brother.' Moth, with her customary tact, did not press him further. Hemanlok turned from us and disappeared into the shadows of the sparse trees protecting the camp from the south. The tension in the group eased.

'He'll find them.' Lycaea sounded convinced, but she did not look it.

We struggled with the mountain-passes. The wind was desperate and rain assaulted us at every point, making the way treacherous and slippery. On the second day in the mountains we lost a man. He fell as the sunlight died. After that, many secured themselves to others with ropes, and we all moved at a slower pace. I tried not to imagine the drop. On the way to Luthan from the Valley I had been too preoccupied with thoughts of my family to be so concerned. Now, with the weather peaking and my head clear of the grieving haze, I was all too aware of the dangers.

And Lycaea. I was aware of Lycaea.

Sometimes I caught a trace of her scent or saw a glimpse of her. Instantly recognisable, even from a distance. Straight-backed and focused. Relentless and unyielding. Confused thoughts of her distracted me from the hard march, and from the threats posed both by the mountains and what lay beyond, in Caerwyn. Half of the time, I saw her as she had been in Luthan; my friend, my ally, difficult and blunt though she was. At other times I saw Kaebha. A torturer. A murderer. Daeman Leldh's loyal servant. The stench of blood and silver threaded its way through my nightmares.

Night fell in a sea of crimson clouds, and I moved along the narrow mountain trail towards Lycaea's part of the camp. The Rogues liked to keep track of our numbers, and Flicker had sent me to gather the muster roll from the soldiers marching with the Ultimo-folk. It was at least an hour from where I had been travelling with the others; the folk of the Ultimo were always pushed far to the front, away from the main camp. Even in an army, the people of the Ultimo were shunned from the rest of Luthan. They were guarded almost like prisoners themselves. As I approached them, I felt stirrings of both pity and disgust. We all stank of sweat and the road, but it was worse where the Ultimo-folk camped. The humans from the Primero and the Ciadudan complained about it; it was much stronger for my waer senses. I breathed through my mouth and tried not to show my revulsion.

The people of the Ultimo bore the marks of exhaustion

and malnutrition. Their clothes were of little use against the elements and they had a shortage of tents and blankets. They crouched in the shadow of the mountains, huddled close and shivering. Although the rest of the army was camped an hour or so to the south, where the trail was wider and less exposed, the people from the Ultimo were on the face of the mountain. The ledge was narrow, in full view. Guards were posted at all times, and there were young runners ready to sprint back in warning in the case of an attack.

Lycaea was awake, as I had expected, and training. She caught my scent and turned before I could say anything. She took a small step back and lowered her staff. Her angular face was hard.

'Has Hemanlok returned?' she asked.

'No.'

'Is something wrong back there?'

'No.'

'Is there something you need?'

'Muster rolls.' The *smell*. The hard, cold scent of silver. Bloodied hands. I saw her killing the soldiers in the Valley, saw her striking Dodge with a sword. I avoided her gaze.

'I collected them an hour ago.' Lycaea pressed the rolls into my grasp.

'Thank you.' I turned to leave, but her hand snapped out and grabbed my elbow.

'Come aside,' she said. She stepped away from the others, heading up the narrow mountain path and behind a crop of rocks. I followed her reluctantly.

Lycaea shifted her weight uneasily, her shoulders tense. Her face had lost some of its harshness. I did not know what to say to her. There was nothing left to say.

'I'm trying, Sencha.' It was a mutter, bitter and short.

'I know.' I found myself leaning away from her, trying to edge closer to the main camp.

I'm trying. As if it could make up for the people she had tortured and killed. What did she expect me to say? Did she seek absolution? It was not mine to give.

The silence ached. My throat was tight. Part of me wanted to bridge the gap, to take her hand and bring her comfort. How could I, after all she had done?

'Lowell.' Her voice was strained now, and full of pain. 'Wolf. I'm not the same person I was. I'm not…' She glanced around to ensure no one was close enough to hear. 'I'm not Kaebha anymore, Wolf.'

Our eyes met. She must have read my hesitation. Her face tightened.

'I have to go, Lycaea,' I told her. 'There are things to be done back at the camp, and Flicker wants the muster rolls.'

'Let me try to show you. Give me a chance, Wolf.'

The pain in her voice gave me pause. Lycaea was proud. It was not in her nature to beg like this. I turned back to her and waited.

Her expression flickered. Fear. Desperation. Resolve. Then her shoulders hunched, and a strange ripple passed through her arms. Quiet, quick clicks sounded from her bones and tendons. Her skin flushed and her hands spasmed. She lowered her head, shuddering.

'Lycaea?' Alarm hastened my pulse. 'Lycaea, stop. What are you doing?'

But I did not need to ask. I knew what a Shift looked like.

She pitched forward – tried to catch herself with her hands and missed entirely, her weight falling on her elbows. Her back arched and she collapsed the rest of the way to the ground. I dropped to my knees beside her. She breathed in struggling gasps. I could hear air rattling through her chest.

'Lycaea.'

Sweat rolled down her brow. 'Help me,' she choked. 'Help me do this.'

She clawed at my hands and I laced my fingers with hers. She was already in the Shift. There was no backing out now. Fur was starting to spear through her skin. I kept hold of her hands. It was not her first Shift, but it was still going to hurt.

'Lycaea,' I said. 'Hold a moment more. Remove your clothes, so they do not tear.'

She almost ripped them anyway in her haste to be free of them. I helped unlace her shirt and pull it over her head. Whimpers twitched through her body.

I placed my hand flat on her back. 'Good,' I said to her. 'Good, Lycaea. Try to relax. Keep your breathing steady.'

She lurched forward, pressed her brow against my shoulder. I could feel the muscles and bones of her back as they realigned. A strangled sob jolted her frame.

'Hurts.'

'I know. Just a little further now.'

I almost fell back from the rush that came with her Shift. She rolled away from me and lay in the dirt, panting.

Her fur was silvery-white. She was lithe and elegant, a wintry wolf with vivid green eyes. I touched her shoulder. The fur was soft and new. She did not move or respond. I scooted closer and gathered her onto my lap, wrapping my arms about her.

She was Lycaea. Not Kaebha. Kaebha could never have done such a thing, she would not have had the courage. Guilt enveloped me. We had come far enough together, Lycaea and I. I should have trusted her.

I stroked a hand over her head, lowered my brow until it touched the back of her neck. 'Hunt with me?' I whispered.

She raised weary green eyes and looked at me. Then she picked herself up, slow and shaking. I had to help her the first few steps. I stripped my clothes, folded them and set them aside with Lycaea's. I Shifted, feeling air and life rush through me. I could no longer smell silver and blood. All I could smell was another wolf, another waer. Lycaea stumbled into step beside me, bumping her side against mine. My wolf instincts surged to the fore. It had been so many months since I had hunted with one of my own kind. She and I were *pack*. I felt as if I could hear her heartbeat. My own was flying. I nudged her, then sprang away. She was too drained by the Shift to play, but her tail waved back and forth slowly.

I jumped in and out of the rocks. I wanted her with me. She leaned against a low-growing tree, watching, slow to read the ways a wolf talks, but attentive. I stayed close to her, nudging her, pawing gently at her shoulder. Her energy gathered as we wandered, steps growing lighter and more confident. I sprang at her heels in play, darted away again as she almost tripped into a stiff mountain bush. She growled at me, but her eyes were bright and her tail was still moving.

We were moving further and further from the camp, but I could not focus on that. I could smell goats and mountain-hares, and small scavengers attracted by horse-feed. Lycaea jumped as a rat shot across her path. She lunged after it, then reined herself back. Looked at me for reassurance. I yipped at her and she took off. She was as clumsy as Kemp, charging around with just as much enthusiasm now the pain of the Shift had faded. I ran with her as she lunged after a fat mouse, then a couple of rats, catching nothing.

Unused to the shape, Lycaea did not know how to be quiet with it. Her paws scrabbled on rocks, sending pebbles skittering, and she could not seem to restrain the growls and yips that bubbled in her chest. The rodents were well ahead of us but the rush of the hunt made the effort worthwhile. If we had caught anything I think I might even have eaten it raw, just to have more time with Lycaea before we returned to the camp.

Eventually she gave up. She trotted back to me, sniffing at my face and bumping her nose against my neck. She was gentle, gentler than in her human form. I breathed in her scent and licked at her face. She flicked her ears, uncertain. Pressed her nose to my jaw with a quiet whine.

Then suddenly we both seemed to remember there was a battle to be fought. We turned reluctantly back towards the camp, Lycaea pressed against my side as we padded back to where our clothes were. I Shifted back first to guide her through, but she did not need my help. The Shift was still slow and painful, but her body knew how to adjust this time, more accustomed to the human form. We pulled on our clothes in silence. She was shaking and sweating, but her eyes were bright.

'Pack,' she said, surprising me. I had not known if she

felt it the same way. She caught my expression, and her lips twisted into a smile.

'Pack,' I agreed. 'How are you?'

'Sore. We didn't catch anything.'

'Not this time. Tomorrow night we will.' I stood and offered her my hand. She surprised me again by taking it. I pulled her to her feet. She stepped in close and kissed the corner of my mouth.

'Don't go back to the other camp tonight,' she said. 'Stay here, Wolf.'

At that moment, I would have stayed with her even if the mountains were falling out from under our feet.

I followed her back to the camp. No one had noticed our absence and no one commented on our return. Lycaea found an extra sleeping-roll for me and I set it alongside hers. When we bedded down to sleep I carefully put one arm about Lycaea, ready to move away if she was uncomfortable. Instead, she leaned against me and closed her eyes.

Flicker could wait until the morning for the muster.

Lycaea

I eased into sleep. My dreams were not of Kaebha, or Cooper, or Daeman Leldh. There was no fire. No Caerwyn. No darkness of the cells, or screaming. For the first time in years, I dreamed of the ocean. The lurch of a ship, and the call of a gull. The ocean turned green and melded with the rolling hills of the Valley. Part of me braced for violence and fear, but it never came. Wolves called, and I answered them. Lowell Sencha did not hate me.

He slept beside me that night, warm and close. I slept with my head against his shoulder, my arms about him. My breath matched his. He had looked tired when he approached me, and I doubted he had been sleeping. Perhaps his nightmares had matched my own – though that night, by his side, my dreams were only of wolves and gentle winters.

I woke just before dawn, watched it roll in on the clouds. Rain began to drizzle. I turned over and pulled my blanket up over my collar. The ground was unforgiving, and I was sore from the hunt; it had taken the best of me to Shift, and perhaps a little more than that to make amends with Lowell. My muscles were tight and painful and when I opened my eyes they stung with tiredness. I wanted nothing more than to stay as I was, in the grey world between sleep and wakefulness.

'Lycaea.'

Lowell's voice was low and quiet, but it made me jump and tense. I pulled myself up and stared at him. His face was pale, dark eyes alert.

'What?' I whispered. It was still a good half-hour before we were due to be roused, but Lowell, it seemed, had woken to conduct the ritual of worship for his goddess Freybug.

'Do you smell that?'

'Smell what?' I lifted my head and sniffed. The cold wind. Rain. The stench of an army. Food. Horses. I shook my head, frowning at him. Nothing out of the ordinary. He did not relax, so I tried again. Rain, rock, moss, mountain-goats. Metal. Oil. Sweat. Unfamiliar bodies. Silver.

All I could hear, suddenly, was the sound of my own breath, rasping in and out of my lungs. My stomach clenched, then dropped. Too soon. It was too soon, and we were unprepared. We were on a *mountain ledge*. The pull to Shift was immediate and violent, spurred by an instinctive urgency.

Lowell caught my arm. His voice, shaking, brought me back to the moment. 'Lycaea. We cannot Shift. We need to communicate with the Ultimo-folk. We have to move.'

I set my teeth, forced my wolf back down. 'Get everyone up. Send a boy back to the other groups. Quick.' It would be like the Valley all over again. If we had a chance, it was only slight. We had set guards, but none of them had the same keen sense of smell Lowell and I possessed. I struggled to my feet and went through our part of the camp. I thanked gods I did not believe in for the quickness of the Ultimo-folk. They were awake in moments, boys running back to alert the others.

'What is the commotion?' An officer, abrasive and far too loud.

'Enemy,' I hissed. 'Keep quiet. It's possible we can slip around them.'

'Do not presume to give me orders.' His voice was like a trumpet.

The scents were getting stronger. I was almost mad with fear. '*Quiet!*'

He opened his mouth to respond, but the words never made it from his lips. An arrow sprouted from his neck. Fletched red and black. Blood spat at me, covered me. I could not move. More arrows. Our officers shouted orders, but they lacked authority and the Ultimo-folk lacked discipline or experience. They panicked. Lowell grabbed my arm and pulled me closer to the wall. Impossible to see where the volley was coming from. We were exposed, there on the face of the mountain. Rain washed the blood from my face.

'Get low!' I shouted. 'Keep close to the wall and move!'

Someone fell and I had to step over her. A man wailed, clutching his arm. We pressed forward. Too late, I realised how far we were from the rest of the camp. We rounded the bend and stopped. Men in black and red faced us. They were not surprised. They were ready for us. They had known we were coming. Had they been watching us? Did they have waer amongst them?

'Retreat!'

Panic behind me as our people tried to retreat, and bunched on the narrow mountain ledge. People slipped and fell, screaming, over the edge. I drew my sword.

'Surrender your arms.' I did not recognise the man who spoke to me. Not Cooper. At least it was not Cooper. I kept my sword high, ready to fight. Thick whirs and squelches behind me as more arrows found their marks. Finally, our own archers rallied. Blood and screams. I turned and tried to order the others on the ledge, as our archers shot past me at Leldh's soldiers. We pushed through, only to find more men scaling the mountain on our other side, hemming us in. Someone died at my feet, and I stumbled on the body. A man dropped to the ledge we were on and drew his sword. I hit the face of the mountain, trying to back away from him. He grinned, then jerked, stiffened, and fell limp. The Ultimo-woman with the frying pan gave me a curt nod and stabbed another man with her knife.

I pushed away from the rock-face and used the hilt of my sword to knock a man out. If I could get to the front of the group, I might be able to prevent the soldiers from gaining ground, at least until the rest of our army came to help us. An arrow zipped past. I dropped to the ground, found myself lying on a corpse. Hands gripped my elbows, and Lowell pulled me over.

'Where are the others?' The boy Moth had healed screamed the words at us. '*Why aren't they helping?*'

'They are on their way!' Lowell shouted back.

Even as he said the words, I had a moment of clarity. As far as the officers were concerned, we were just the Ultimo.

It was not the Rogues who commanded the army of Luthan, but people from the Primero. The Ultimo-folk were there as a buffer. There to be shot down. We were a distraction, and they would let us die so they could escape the ambush.

A man grabbed Lowell from behind, raised an axe to strike him. I swung my sword into the man's side. He screamed and dropped his weapon as his flesh split. Lowell pulled away. I gripped his arm and turned him around so we could fight back-to-back. He had a sword, but he was of little use with it. We could not Shift here, though; energy released by the Shift would send people flying off the ledge. Neither of us could risk it yet.

Something slammed into my shoulder. I felt impact before I felt pain. I slumped against Lowell. He whirled around and dropped his sword in his attempts to support me. I tried to keep a grip on my own, but it slid from my useless hand. An arrow-shaft protruded from my shoulder. Pain found me then; I screamed against it. I heard a dull thud and Lowell fell away from me. A hand wrapped about my shirt. Hauled me up. I stared into a pair of blue eyes. Met the familiar face. As ever, he was spotless, immaculate, untouched by the chaos. His lips curled into a languid smile.

'Why, Kaebha,' Cooper said. My vision swam, and he slapped me across the face. 'No, no,' he said. 'I want you awake for a little while longer.' He showed all his teeth. 'It is nice to see you again. Back where you belong. Our master has missed you so. He has hardly been the same since you left.'

'Wolf.' I craned. '*Wolf.*'

Alive. Hurt, but alive. He stared at me with dull, dazed eyes.

Cooper stuck a thumb in my wound. I screamed until my

voice snapped. Then I kept screaming, but could make no sound of it.

'Do I have your attention?' Cooper sounded amused. 'Not very polite of you, Kaebha.'

I struggled, but I was losing blood, and pain made me weak. Cooper flicked his eyes away from me. Bored. Disdainful. I followed his gaze. The people of the Ultimo were on their knees. It was a fight they could not have won, though they'd fought so bravely.

'Kill them all,' Cooper said. I howled. Cooper held up a hand as someone grabbed Lowell's hair. 'Except that one,' he said. 'Bring him. We'll have some fun with him later.'

'No. *No!*'

Cooper wrapped his long fingers about the arrow shaft and ripped it from my flesh.

Kaebha tucked the papers into her satchel and slung it over her shoulder. She had already been at the camp too long, and she had enough information for the Watchers to act upon. It was time to leave. She did not think Leldh was suspicious, but there was no real way of telling. Cooper certainly thought something was amiss. They had disliked one another on sight, and that had grown into outright hatred over the weeks Kaebha had spent with them in the forest at the foot of the mountains.

Kaebha discarded her cloak and left the tent. She was dressed entirely in black now. The darkness of the forest beyond the camp gave her some ease. Once she was out of the perimeter, she would be safe. After that, it would be a matter of days before she met with Hemanlok, and only a few weeks before she was home.

Picking her way around the tents, Kaebha reached the low wall that had been erected about the camp. It was semi-permanent, there for four months whilst they saw mercenary companies and bought slaves. Kaebha wished she could do something to help the unfortunates that were brought there, but she had to trust Ashe would do his best on their behalf. That much was out of her hands; she had been there to observe, not to intervene.

'And where might you be going, Kaebha?'

Kaebha's stomach lurched. Her face felt hot and cold at the same time. She looked over her shoulder at Cooper.

'Out on patrol,' she said.

'With such a full satchel? Without your cloak?' He smiled and stepped closer to her. He was a handsome man, but the smirk on his face made him cold and ugly.

Kaebha held her ground and shrugged. 'It's not that cold.'

'Empty your satchel.' He snatched the bag from her shoulder and upended it on the ground. 'Hm. I wonder what a soldier wants with so many papers.' He stooped to take them up.

Kaebha bolted.

Cooper did not shout or curse. He laughed. Kaebha flung herself past the wall. The camp behind her was suddenly alive with fire and torches. She tripped and stumbled across the ground before her eyes adjusted to the darkness. Her legs ached and grew heavy. Branches slapped her in the face. She could feel blood on her forehead from where the skin had split. Her feet skidded in the treacherous ground as she reached for a tree, trying to drag herself forwards.

'It has been years since anyone tried to infiltrate my forces.' Leldh strolled past her. 'I must commend you. It was a full week before we realised what you were doing. Whoever forged your papers was quite an artist.'

Kaebha could not move. It felt like someone was standing on her back. She could scarcely breathe, and her pulse felt sluggish as it beat in her ears. She stared mutely at Daeman Leldh.

'Your mistake, of course, was getting your information from the slaves.' The look he gave her was pitying. 'Half-breeds, changelings, elementals. They will do anything to save themselves, and they did not hesitate to turn you in. I am afraid you will not have a chance to do better next time. Cooper.'

The Pellish man stepped forward, smiling.

'As I said,' Leldh went on kindly, 'you will not have another chance. You will not be returning home to Luthan, Kaebha. But you have some time left, and if you tell me what I want to know then I will ensure that time is not spent entirely in torment.'

The pressure alleviated at least enough for Kaebha to get some words out. 'What do you want to know?'

'Who sent you?'

'I work alone.'

Their eyes met and locked. Kaebha's heart wrenched at his golden stare, noting a look she knew well but had not seen there before.

He was mad.

'Cooper, take her back to the camp.' Leldh's grip on her limbs faded, but there were soldiers surrounding her before she could take advantage of it. 'Have her chained well and post a six-man guard. Burn the papers she took and see to it the slaves are questioned further.'

'When will you see her, lord?'

'At dawn. Keep her awake until then.'

'Any other orders, lord?'

Leldh looked back at Kaebha. She stared past the soldiers at him, her heart as quick as a rabbit's.

'You know what to do,' he said.

*

They took us down the mountain paths, to the Valley. Lowell was unconscious. I was bound, carried by Cooper's horse as the way broadened and we reached the Gwydhan. The movement of the horse gave me constant pain. They had bound my shoulder roughly; not to give me comfort, but to keep me from dying before Leldh could have his fun. The smell of blood overwhelmed me.

Cooper, behind me, whispered poison in my ear as we went. If I tried to move or speak he jabbed his fingers into my shoulder.

I let my head drop forward and remained still. I could not let myself revert to Kaebha, nor lose myself to pain and fear. There would be chances to escape. If not for me, then for Lowell. Unconscious though he was, he did not seem badly hurt. If I could keep them distracted they might not even pursue him.

He was slung carelessly across the front of someone's saddle. Limp. Pale. Blood stood out against his white face, stemming from a blow lost in his dark hair. Every so often, his unfocused eyes would open, and fear clenched my throat. Then he would slip away from awareness again. It was for the best. If he was unconscious, they could not torment him. And I knew they planned to.

The rain beat down on us as we followed the river. The Valley unfolded before us, grey and mourning. The trees ached with the tragedies they had seen. Even now, months later, there were traces of what had happened. Shreds of clothing. Decomposed bodies, half hidden by the undergrowth.

As if the ground wanted to hide the evidence of the horror. As if the earth itself was trying to shelter and bury its own.

The horses struggled through the mud of the river-bank, their hooves sinking in deep. Leldh's men whipped the poor beasts until they bled. The lurching of Cooper's mount made me retch. Vomit spattered across his shining black boots, and he swore. He pushed me from the horse. I rolled to lessen the impact on my wound, but it did not help. I groaned, lay in the mud. Cooper dismounted and grabbed my hair. Hauled me onto the grass, into a sheltered hollow.

'We make camp here,' he said. He dropped me again. I saw a man drag Lowell from the horse. They slung him to the ground, and he rolled until he was beside me. I found his hand and held it tight. So cold in mine, but when I slid my fingers to his wrist, I found a faint pulse. Alive, still. All I had to do was keep us alive until the others came for us. Until Hemanlok caught up with us. He would come, this time. I forced myself to believe it.

Cooper's smell drew closer. I raised my eyes. Tall, blond, elegant. He squatted beside me as the other soldiers built a small smoky fire. The wood was damp, but they managed to get a flame going.

'He will kill you this time, you know.' Cooper's voice was soft. He grabbed my chin, held it in his smooth fingers. 'He cannot afford to let you live again, even for his own amusement. Sends a message, you know. To the soldiers, and to the filthy half-breeds. He was fascinated by you, but it has finally come to an end. I must say, I will be relieved when we are at last rid of you. Life has been good since you left. It will improve further when you are dead, and Lord Leldh can focus on better things.'

My wolf gave me strength and courage. I spat at Cooper's face.

'How does it feel, Cooper?' I asked. 'Bested by a half-breed. Even when I'm gone, there'll be others. You're just not good enough. You'll never be good enough. You're a foot-licker, always have been. He won't give you your own command, because you don't have the stomach to *take* command.'

Fury twisted his handsome features as the spit slid down his cheek. He wiped it away and released my chin.

'Play the Rogue all you want, Kaebha,' he said. 'You and I both know who you really are. And so do your companions. No one will come for you, or your flea-bitten companion. Just like last time.' His face contorted into a smile. 'You will die, like your precious little half-army. One woman tried to fight our soldiers off with a *frying-pan*.' He laughed. 'For her cheek we killed her slower than the others.'

He stood and moved from me. He dealt Lowell a solid kick to the chest. I heard bones crack, and a muffled yelp. Cooper smirked and went about posting guards for the small camp. Once he was far enough from me, I wriggled closer to Lowell.

'Wolf,' I whispered. Lowell groaned and opened his eyes.

'Lycaea?' he croaked.

'We're in the Valley,' I whispered. 'Lie still. Don't draw attention to yourself. They're taking us to Caerwyn.'

'Home.' He closed his eyes, and a pained smile curved his lips. 'I am home.'

'Wolf. Listen. They're taking us to Caerwyn.'

'Home.'

'Wolf. Listen to me.'

'Home,' he said again, and I let him have the moment. It would be fleeting.

Lowell

I awoke to the sound of water, and the touch of sweet wet grass. Trees stretched above me, long and loving. They ached and creaked with the fresh wind, leaves sighing. My head throbbed and my side shot sharp pain through the rest of my body, but I could smell sheep and rabbits, and oncoming rain. For the first time since the beginning of winter, I was home. I breathed deep, ignoring my ribs. Home, in the Gwydhan Valley. There was even a golden moon to greet us, ripened almost to fullness. I kept my eyes skyward. I knew Leldh's soldiers surrounded us. I knew the Valley was no longer a place of peace. Looking at the moon, though, half-hidden by the trees, I could almost forget.

I could hear Lycaea breathing beside me. With difficulty and pain, I rolled over to face her. Her lips were blue with cold, and her shoulder was bound with a rag. She reeked of blood and sweat. Her green eyes met and held my gaze. Why had she not Shifted? It would heal her wound over. I moved my tied hands over the mud and took hers. I had vague memories of waking before now, but nothing my mind could grasp. Our fingers were cold. Hollow haunted our every moment.

'They're taking us to Caerwyn,' she whispered.

'The others will come for us, Lycaea.' I searched her face, waiting for confirmation. She said nothing. 'Hemanlok will come for us,' I tried again. She nodded, but seemed unconvinced. No one had rescued her last time. We lay in silence. I watched emotions play out on her face. Fear. Despair. Potent anger. The last stayed, and relief coiled in my stomach. She knew how to use anger.

'I'm going to get you free,' she said.

'Both of us.'

'If I can. If not, you need to meet with the others. Find Hemanlok, and Melana.'

'I go nowhere without you. Can Melana help us now?'

'Hard to say.'

'Up. Get up!'

A horse-whip snapped on my back. I choked and struggled to my feet. My hands, bound by thick, coarse rope, gave me little aid. Standing was agony. Lycaea supported me but she was injured herself, and there was only so much she could do. My head swam and throbbed, and I had to lean on her to stay upright. The soldiers jeered at us. I dropped my gaze and clenched my fists. They called Lycaea names that broke my heart. Anger roused the wolf in me, and it was all I could do to fight it back. For once, it would do us no good.

They dropped rope coils about our necks and tied the other ends to saddles. We had to thrust our bound hands through the loops to keep from being strangled, and even then there was so much pressure it was hard to breathe as we were half-dragged behind the horses. I stumbled to keep up. We walked uphill, pulled forward sharply by the horses. Fear kindled my anger, kept it hot in my belly. I imagined them dealing such treatment to Kemp, and could not see beyond the red haze of my eyes. The only way to clear it was to think of Lycaea, and of what the Valley had been before the attack.

As we neared the village, I recognised buildings and farms. Some were burnt and in ruin. Others stood as if nothing had happened. I saw people move in and out of what had been the baker's house and realised with a shock that soldiers and their families had moved into our homes. I saw a pregnant woman kissing a man in the uniform of Leldh's men.

'How could they?' I muttered.

'We're waer. To them, we're not people.' Lycaea spoke through gritted teeth. Perspiration gave her skin an unhealthy sheen. 'Far as they're concerned, they're just happy to have a house for their families. Spoils of war.' Her eyes flicked in my direction. 'Your house, beyond the village? Who knows what they've done with it.'

The rider in front of her, the blond man who had caught her in the mountains, looked over his shoulder at us. *Cooper,* I reminded myself. The other soldiers called him Cooper. A Pellish name. We lowered our heads and fell into silence. I had thought about my own home, of course. Our little house on top of the hill, surrounded by gentle hills and the relief of the forest. I longed for it, and dreaded seeing it again. My last glimpse had seen the house shrouded in smoke and flame.

We passed through the village, paraded along the dirt street. I saw that some of the buildings had been turned into bawd-houses and taverns. My horror mounted when I recognised some of the women working there. Valley women. Waer. Girls I had been friends with, women I had known from the market. Pity eclipsed any disgust or anger I might have felt. They did not look at me. They were cowed and thin, dressed in rags that showed too much flesh. I could see bruises.

Oh, my people.

The place stank. I had never been at ease there but still, it had been a place of worth and community. My family had come here to trade goods and gossip. We had gone to worship-house on the outskirts, but I could see even from the middle of the village it had been razed. The beautiful spire, of which we had all been so proud, was gone.

We spent the night locked in a cellar. It was a strange relief, with the guards on the other side of the door and no longer as watchful. I propped myself against the wall. They had given us water and tough bread. Lycaea and I ate without a word. Nausea rose in my belly with each bite, but I knew I would need the strength and be thankful for it before long.

'You should Shift.' I broke the silence.

She let out a pained breath of laughter. 'Doesn't matter much,' she said. 'They're not going to let me die unless it's by Leldh's hands.'

She removed her clothes all the same, and Shifted. It was agonisingly slow, but by the time she was in her wolf shape again, the shoulder-wound had stopped bleeding and was starting to close over. I stripped and followed suit. Energy flew out from me as I did, then powered through my body.

The regeneration sealed my head wound. It was still there, and still painful. But no longer a threat.

I paced the cellar until Lycaea's eyes closed, unable to settle. When she was still, I forced myself to calm and lay beside her. My intention was to warm her and perhaps protect her if I could. She moved closer to me, resting her head on my back. I did not stir, and I did not sleep. I found myself praying; seeking hope from Freybug. Seeking strength from Hollow. Seeking luck from Felen. Just for that night, I was a waer of the Valley, and I remembered the faith I had followed for so many years. The faith of my family, and of my people.

I waited for dawn, and dreaded it.

The new day brought rain, sweeping down from the mountains and pelting the earth. We reclaimed our human shapes and pulled our clothes on before the guards could open the cellar. They bound us again and half-dragged us up the stairs. Cooper was standing outside. He bared his teeth into something that could have passed for a smile.

'My lady Kaebha,' he mocked. 'I trust you slept well.'

She met his gaze, unfaltering, and his smile slowly died into a sneer as he shoved her forwards. The soldiers tied her to the horse's saddle again, this time by her hands, then did the same to me. I stood quietly and allowed it. We could do nothing in the heart of the village, I reasoned. Our chance would come when we were closer to my home. Near the forest, and the caves. The rain would cover us, help us to run and to hide. And there was always the chance aid would come.

I could smell home before we even crested the hill on the other side. I knew the grass, and the sheep, and the earth beneath my feet. Lycaea kept her eyes on me, as best she could. She had to crane her neck and pull against the rope to catch my gaze. I wanted to Shift. I wanted to be wolf, in my own home, with my family. My teeth ground. I could not focus. My heart was irregular, pulsing too slow and then too fast. I stumbled along behind the horse, trying to keep my attention on putting one foot in front of another. Lycaea had told me not to look at the hill, to avoid seeing what had become of my home. I tried to keep my eyes on the mud. But something drew my head up, and I stopped where I stood.

Our house had been cleared away. Blackened posts remained, but there was no house. Our garden was gone. The building was gone. It had been replaced by gallows.

Gallows.

Swinging with bodies. I recognised the blue uniforms of the three lawkeepers. Men who had worked so hard to keep our Valley peaceful.

'Of course, we found out where you stayed,' Cooper said. He was talking to Lycaea. I meant nothing to him. 'Seems a pity the family inside were already dead. We could have had fun with them. Regardless, we decided to make an example of this place. To remind the locals of the price of defiance. I think it has a nice aesthetic, do you not? At the top of the hill. Picturesque, really.'

Gallows.

I swayed, then dropped to my knees. The soldier in front of me snarled and grabbed the rope, yanking on it. I jerked forwards, fell to my elbows in the mud.

'Get him up,' Cooper snapped.

The soldier swore and swung from his saddle. He stormed

towards me. I waited. Anger squirmed through my body, twitched my muscles and bones towards a Shift. The soldier reached for my neck. I slammed my bound hands into his face. He reeled back. His sword was at his belt. I gripped it, just, slid it out a few bare inches. I looped my binding around it and pulled until the rope snapped. The soldier rallied and swung at me. I ducked. Drove my elbow into his gut. Cooper screamed an order. My hands were free.

'*Go!*' Lycaea bellowed. 'Wolf, *go!*'

I Shifted, and it sent the soldiers around me back a few inches. I fell upon the soldier who had been riding before me, and I killed him. There was no rein or control of my wolf. There was no guilt. I was teeth, I was fur, I was snarling and a desperate need for blood.

'Stay back from him!' Cooper was off his horse. He held Lycaea close, held his sword to her throat. 'He will infect you.'

Lycaea was frozen at the edge of the blade. I stopped. Crouched. Waited. Muscles tense, coiled. Panting raggedly. Covered in blood. They kept a loose circle around me. I read fear in Cooper's face for the first time. He dragged Lycaea a step back. A thin line of blood slid down her throat where the sword bit her skin.

I was not going to leave her.

I stepped closer to Cooper. He could not afford to kill her. He had to bring her back to Leldh. He dragged Lycaea a step back, pointed his sword towards me.

'Not a pace closer,' he hissed.

The moment the sword was gone from her neck, Lycaea acted. Slammed her head back into his face. Drove her elbow into his gut. Cooper bent and wheezed. Blood spurted from his nose. Lycaea sprinted forwards, half-Shifting as she went. I barrelled ahead of her. The Shift knocked Lycaea to her knees; she was not quick enough. I leapt on a soldier as he started towards her. Blood. Teeth.

Something hit my back.

I was blind.

I collapsed. My body was wrapped in wires of pain. I was neither man nor wolf. I could not Shift. Strange sounds tore from my throat, filled the air. I could smell my own flesh as it burned.

Silver, I thought, and everything slipped away.

Lowell

'Lowell. Wolf. Wake up.'

My mouth was dry. My muscles ached. Everything stank of blood. And the voice beside my head was like a rock scraping my temple.

A hand settled on my shoulder and I growled. The voice sounded again, this time stern. I recoiled. Unfamiliar scents flooded me. It was cold.

'Wolf. Easy. Easy, Sencha.' Lycaea. My body eased, and the rest of the world slipped into my consciousness. It took a few moments for my eyes to adjust.

We were in a cell. The walls were built high about us. There was a heavy wooden door to one side; a barred window allowed a small amount of light to seep into the room.

'Good.' Lycaea sat back. Her face was pale in contrast to the darkness about us, and her hands clenched and unclenched in her lap as she regarded me. 'Can you Shift?'

I pushed my shoulders back and Shifted, shuddering as pain rolled down my spine. I could feel the burns from the silver. Shifting could not alleviate those wounds. Lycaea's hand sought mine and she squeezed it. She handed me a pile of ragged clothes.

'These rags were on the ground when we arrived.' I did not want to think where they had come from. 'You were lucky,' she added. 'The silver was barely on you for a few moments. You have some bad burns there, though.' Lycaea hesitated. 'Wolf, there are waer captive here. I can smell it. The scents are faint, and I cannot tell if they come from the Valley.'

'When did we arrive?'

'Late last night. They brought us on the horses. Every time you looked as if you would recover, they covered your muzzle with a soaked cloth and you went under again. I thought they were killing you. I was conscious the whole way.' She stopped, and her hand shook. She found her voice again. 'Cooper made certain of that,' she went on. 'He wanted me to see it.'

'Are you hurt?'

'Not badly.' She pushed her hair back from her face. 'They haven't taken me to Leldh yet. Soon, though.' Accusation filled her voice. 'You should have run, Wolf. You had a chance. You could have made it. You could have gone to the others. Don't you understand? So long as Leldh dies, it doesn't matter. I don't care.'

'You went into Caerwyn alone last time,' I told her. 'I wasn't going to let it happen again.'

She dropped her face into her hands, shuddering. 'Lowell, what if I –'

'You will not.' I pressed my brow against hers. 'I trust you.'

The weight of that trust pressed her lips together.

'How delightful.'

A pair of cold blue eyes stared at us, amused. Long fingers wrapped about the bars and Lycaea leapt to her feet, crossing to the door in a few long strides. She punched the man's fingers, and he tugged them away with a grimace. Lycaea's face twisted into a satisfied smirk.

'Still too slow, *Cooper,*' she snarled.

'Not as slow as you are, Kaebha,' he retorted. 'Back in a cell, just like old times. Not alone this time, though.'

His face split in an unpleasant leer. He addressed me. 'You should have chosen your friends more wisely. She will be the death of you.'

Lycaea lunged through the bars again, but Cooper was ready for her this time. He drew out a rod of silver and pressed it against her arm. Lycaea called out in pain and staggered back into me. Cooper watched without expression.

'If you hurt him,' Lycaea choked. 'If you touch him, I will kill you, Cooper. I will *kill* you!'

Half a dozen soldiers appeared behind Cooper as he opened the door. Three of them entered the cell. I grabbed Lycaea's arm, and she swung around to grip me. She held me tight, arms about my shoulders. I could feel her heart beating against my chest.

It was futile. They almost broke her arm to pull her away. I shouted for her to Shift, but when she tried they burned her with silver. I lunged after her, found myself knocked back with a sickening blow to the head. Sinking to my knees, all I could do was watch in stunned silence as they dragged her out of the cell and closed the door behind them. The last I saw of Lycaea was her hand, fingers splayed as she reached for me. Then she was gone.

Cooper's voice echoed down the hallway, cutting through her curses and shouts. 'Come, Lady Kaebha,' he mocked. 'The Lord Leldh wishes to see you.'

She did not return for hours. When she did, she would not speak. The silence stretched out between us like a shroud.

Lycaea's eyes burned and sparked as she paced back and forth. Her hands trembled and her entire frame was tensed and suffused with anger. When she glanced back at me, I saw a silver-burn on one cheek. The other was swollen from where someone had struck her. Her clothes were torn, and there were purple marks on her neck, her arms. When she moved, the collar of her shirt fell, and I saw more bruises. I wanted desperately to go to her, but she turned from me, still pacing.

I opened my mouth to speak, but faltered at the last moment. I did not know how to reach her.

Lycaea moved without tiring, her form shuddering as she covered the ground between the walls of the cell. Every so often, she cast her eyes at the roof above us. There was no escape, and no way to hide from the cold. Lycaea's pain was killing me.

'You should keep moving.' Her voice cut through my thoughts. I stood and followed her pacing. She went on. 'It's too cold to be still.' She took my hand and started rubbing my fingers. We continued to walk, and after a while, once some feeling had returned, I took my turn in rubbing hers.

'Thank you.' Her voice was still as cold as the stone about us. But as I met her gaze, it was less harsh, her lips no longer drawn into their tight line. I stopped rubbing her fingers and she wrapped them around my hand. Neither of us spoke for a long moment.

'You should try to Shift,' I tried.

She wrenched her grip from around my arm. I stepped back, startled. Levelling her finger towards me, she spat out strained words, fuelled by fear.

'You should never have come here!' Her voice cracked and she flung her arms out to the side. 'I knew this would happen, I knew they would use you against me! I should have left you behind, better for you to have *died in the Valley* than this!' There was a sickening thud as she slammed a clenched fist against the stone. Though I heard a quick hiss of pain, she gave no other sound, pressing her brow to the cold bricks of the wall and breathing steadily.

Her words sickened me, but I could not bring myself to blame her for them. He had hurt her, and it had shattered her fragile confidence. My mind flitted back to our journey, to our arguments and slowly building friendship and to her current fear and pain. It was tearing us apart.

Lycaea

The chamber was almost empty. Leldh liked things sparse and neat. There was a rack of gleaming instruments on the wall, and a slab in the middle of the room. Leldh relaxed on a chair at the far end of the chamber. I saw him as soon as the door swung open. Deep in my mind, Kaebha took a knee and bowed her head. I fought the compulsion. I was Lycaea. Not Kaebha. Never Kaebha, never again.

'Kaebha.' Leldh stood to greet me. His golden eyes gleamed in the light of the torches. 'It has been too long.'

I could say nothing in reply. Cooper held my neck. Everything hurt. Lowell. Lowell. My mind rattled with disjointed thoughts. Kaebha, torture, silver, Luthan, Lowell. Hemanlok. Hemanlok, please. *I was so afraid. Leldh smiled. He caught my face in his hands. They were gentle. Soft.*

'Cooper, where are your manners?' Leldh demanded. 'Find our Kaebha a seat. She is weary, and we have much to discuss.'

Cooper hooked a chair with his foot and dragged it over. He pushed me into it and bound my hands behind my back again. Fear slowed to a dull pulse in my head. They were going to hurt me. I closed my eyes. Pictured the streets of Luthan, the lush green of the Valley. Lowell Sencha's quiet brown eyes. Hemanlok's smirk. Moth's gentle smile, and Dodge's steady warmth. I could not fail them. I would say nothing. And I would not revert to Kaebha. Not this time.

Silver pressed against my cheek. Searing flesh. Agony.

'Lycaea.'

I did not face Lowell; afraid if I did, he would see the pain in my face. Bowing my head against the wall, I controlled my stance, breathing with difficulty. I flinched away as Lowell placed a hand on my shoulder. I would not let myself feel for him. He meant nothing. *Nothing.*

'Lycaea.'

And yet I wanted to turn around. I wanted his smile, his grave faith, his trust and his compassion. I wanted to know his mind. He had stripped me of my defences as surely and painfully as Daeman had. I was vulnerable now, as vulnerable as I had been to the Daeman's will.

'Lycaea. Turn around.'

I maintained my resolve, gritting my teeth. I wanted to seep into the stone wall. To be nothing, as I had once been with Kaebha. She had done terrible things, but she had never been forced to feel the repercussions of them. She had been able to go without that guilt and now I felt every needle of it.

Kaebha could not help me.

'Lycaea. *Please.*'

At the last word, my resolve broke. I turned and Lowell was there in an instant, catching my hands. His brown eyes were bright and focused, his face set.

'We came this far. We have to finish it.' His fingers locked with mine. 'I am not ready to die. Not here, in a cold cell. We need to make it out of here, together. We need to trust one another, and survive.' He lowered his head, so his brow almost touched mine. 'You have my heart, Lycaea. I would give you my soul.'

I pulled away from him. My heart slowed, the blood flowing sluggishly through my veins. A soul-bond. He was offering to show me his darkest secrets, the deep and shadowy workings of the mind beneath his consciousness, of the innate centre that made him who he was.

And all he wanted in exchange was trust.

Trust.

Was it too much to ask?

'Give me your hand.' The voice came from so far away it took me an age to realise it was mine. Lowell stretched out his hand and I took it, clasping my fingers around his. I faltered. There was a chasm between us, and he stood on the far side, trying to reach me. He could not clear it alone. I had to meet him halfway.

I opened my soul to Lowell Sencha. My mind flew, connected with a blaze of light and power. I did not flinch. The chill of the cell gave way to heat. Our souls met, moving back and forth and blending in an inexplicable dance. His deep, rich brown met my forest green, combining and humming as we explored the new sensation. In an instant, I could feel everything he did. The terror of seeing the inside of a cell for the first time. The longing for my lost family, the feeling of belonging somewhere smaller, but stepping out for a cause.

I was thrumming and stinging with the pain of words past and the guilt of deeds undone. Victories that could never be savoured, so bitter their cost. I was terrified of the torment I knew was coming from Leldh. I was in pain every time my love was in pain.

After what seemed like an age, I could no longer tell the difference between our two minds. The basic, raw emotions were the same, regardless of the cause. My guilt for Kaebha's actions, his guilt for surviving while his family perished. For leaving Kemp to unknown torments. Love for one another, foreign and faltering. My grief. His grief.

We were not alone.

There was a pressure against my lips, so faint that for a while I could not understand what it was. Memory shuddered through me. Lowell's mouth touched mine, gentle but insistent, and I tensed. There was only Daeman in my mind then, and Lowell sensed it; he made as if to pull back. Then the darkness slipped away and I stumbled into him. The worn cloth of his shirt creased in my hands and I drew him closer to me.

We released each other only when we ran out of breath, and I pressed against the stone wall, its chill a reminder of reality, bringing me back from the extremes of emotions that the binding of the two souls had brought us. I was conscious of Lowell's presence, his every movement vivid in my mind's eye.

For a short while, everything was warm, and right, and good.

*

At midday, we heard them coming up the hall. Lowell and I waited. I kept my head down, fighting the anger that brimmed inside as they came nearer, their weaponry clanking, their footsteps loud.

The lock clicked and the door groaned open. Nine guards, armed in case one of us broke loose. It took a lot for humans to control the waer and Daeman would not risk me breaking free again. One stepped forwards, his lips curling into a lazy, cruel smile. My eyes snapped towards him and I drew a sharp breath. Cooper.

'Two dogs,' he murmured, his tone amused. 'The bitch and her wolf.' He leaned back against the wall, rubbing his chin with one hand. Lowell and I climbed to our feet. A soldier moved forwards, a rod of silver clasped in one hand. There was a hiss and Lowell shouted in pain, releasing me. I cursed and clutched his arm, holding fast.

Cooper stepped forwards. He grabbed Lowell's hair, wrenching him backward, and chuckled. 'Your turn now, Wolf.'

I snarled and lunged. A soldier grabbed me and forced me against the wall, holding a silver knife to my throat. Lowell was dragged against the opposite wall and slammed into it. His head snapped back. There was a crack, and a smear of blood on the stone as he slumped. I shouted and started to move, but the knife at my throat pressed against my skin, burning as it made contact. I pulled back again. The soldiers began to drag Lowell away.

'Wolf!' I shouted, trying to grab the hand of the man with the knife. 'Wolf, wait, don't…' A blow was dealt to my head. I stumbled backwards until I hit the wall, stunned. The door swung closed behind them, leaving Cooper and myself alone in the cell. Cooper smiled.

'You know what we are going to do to your wolf?' he asked. He chuckled. 'We'll reduce him to nothing.' His blue eyes showed a flicker of pleasure, of perverse joy. 'And you're going to help us.'

'I will not.' I drove no energy behind the words. Cooper smirked, shaking his blond head.

'Torture him or let us kill him,' he commented. 'It is your choice. You could keep him alive.'

I stared at him, thoughts buzzing through my mind. Dead or mad. Wolf, dead or broken. Kaebha, or Lycaea. And I had to choose. I drew a shaking breath, trying to think. Lowell would rather die. He would rather die than be tortured, and see me return to Kaebha. I would rather have died than endured the torture I did. If someone had been willing to intercede for me on that account, I would have been grateful. I knew I should let it end. Lowell would want me to.

But I needed him.

'Not so arrogant now, are you, Kaebha?' Cooper mocked. I closed my eyes.

Then, there was nothing but coolness in the back of my mind. There had never really been a decision in the matter, for me. I knew what to do.

Kaebha stirred.

'Kill him.' My voice was calm, cold. Barely my own. I set my jaw and straightened my shoulders, not removing my gaze from Cooper's surprised face. 'Go ahead and kill him.' *Forgive me*. 'He is nothing.'

I clenched my fists. I had come so far, and lost so much.

Cooper turned on his heel without a word, storming out of the cell. He despised being caught unawares. If he did not kill Lowell now, his bluff would be called and he would be weakened. If he finished my Wolf, he lost his leverage and power over me.

The cell door ground shut. The bolt slid across. Cooper's footsteps echoed down the stone corridor for a few moments before I was left alone. I sank to the ground. The feeling I had gained through our soul-bond seeped away with agonising slowness, leaving my digits stiff and immobile. Kaebha shot through my veins like poison, hissing her malice. She knew the easiest option. Just allow Daeman to have his satisfaction. It was the less painful way. I could let my feelings sweep away; forget what I had recovered and rejoin Daeman Leldh and his people. I could be part of his triumph, witness his victory. It could be so easy for me. I had done it once before.

A sudden whiplash of emotion. Anger, pain, grief, humiliation. Before, but never again. I was not Kaebha. I was Lycaea. A waer. Bound to Lowell Sencha, even as he was to me.

I turned in the cell. Searched for anything I could use as a weapon. I would not lie down and die. I would not let them kill Lowell. Lowell Sencha, my Wolf, who had saved me from the river and brought me back from Kaebha.

I started to chant my mother's name. I needed her now, more than I ever had. I could forgive her the years of neglect, and cruelty, and madness. I just wanted one deal from her. My voice rose in the silence of the cell, thrown back at me from the stone walls. The guards mocked me from the other side of the door. I ignored them.

'Melana. *Melana!* Mother, I need you!'

My voice tore. A sob snarled in my chest, left me breathless. The silence robbed me of hope. With dull eyes, I stared at the shadows.

They started to move.

Lowell

I knew they were going to kill me.

I was strapped to a flat slab of stone, stripped to the waist. For a while I could not raise my pounding head; then when I managed it I wished I had not. The room about me was large and dim, lit by a few sparse candles. Gleaming weapons caught the lights and threw them back at me. The place reeked of blood and silver. I turned my head to one side, trying not to gag.

A man stood on each side of the slab. Cooper's flawless skin glowed in the light as he sharpened a knife, blue eyes fixed on his work, clean and precise. An elegant man with a rotting heart. I wondered if he had ever been like Lycaea, torn between a normal life and these horrors. Whether he had ever doubted, or tried to break away. His blue eyes slid towards me, and my stomach clenched. It did not matter, I realised. He had no doubts now.

The man on my other side was more relaxed. He was not in uniform, but wore instead a casual shirt and breeches. He lounged against the edge of the slab, whistling as he flipped a knife and caught it. I knew him instantly for who he was and what he had done. He had ordered the deaths of hundreds of innocents. He had invaded a place of peace and murdered my people. He had nearly destroyed Lycaea.

Daeman Leldh smiled at me, and I found I could not smell him beneath the reek of silver.

I turned my eyes to the ceiling. If they were going to kill me, I would not give them the satisfaction of my despair. I took a slow breath. Lycaea lingered in the back of my mind, a pillar of strength in a world where everything was crashing down.

'Kaebha told us to kill you,' Cooper said in a low voice.

My voice was shockingly clear to my ears. 'You're going to kill me anyway.'

Leldh smiled. 'Your name is Sencha, am I correct?'

He took my silence as confirmation.

'I studied the waer for a long time, Sencha. I had good reason to. They rose up against the just rule of my people. Traitors, vagabonds. Mongrels.' His voice remained pleasant, calm. 'I have wanted to settle the odds for a long time now. This is just the beginning. My research unearthed several interesting facts. For example, the waer blood can be diluted by the ingestion of aconite. Much like silver, it prevents you from Shifting; unlike silver, it is permanent. I have learned the effects of silver on the waer, and how much individuals of various types can withstand. Yours is a fascinating race. But what I have found most intriguing is the soul-bond.'

He knew.

Cooper laughed aloud, moving at a nod from Leldh. He went over to the rack of weapons and withdrew one before pivoting to face his master.

'Lord, may I?' he asked. His voice almost cracked with anticipation. Daeman nodded, smiling, and Cooper strode out to the door. Daeman shot a fleeting look in my direction before returning to flipping the blade.

'I am sure you know how it is with a soul-bond,' he murmured. 'How much we can hurt her by killing you. You give too much of yourself with it. I feel Kaebha should be here to witness your demise. After that, well. She will be at my disposal. And that can go so many interesting ways.'

If they killed me, she would be left in torment. And if she were made into Kaebha again... I gagged, choking for a moment as hot bile stung my throat. Daeman smiled.

He moved quickly. The knife was made of steel, not silver, but it was enough. I screamed. My legs kicked and jerked. Leldh drew the blade out and stabbed it into my shoulder. He was working his way across to my heart.

I believe he would have struck the fatal blow then and there, had not Cooper slammed into the room. His breathing was ragged, his face drained of colour.

'She's out,' he gasped.

Leldh lowered his weapon. His golden eyes gleamed. 'How?'

Cooper hesitated, unable to answer.

A terrible smile crossed Leldh's features.

'Oh, yes,' he said. 'Our Kaebha, and her beloved Watchers.' He had forgotten me. He dropped the knife and went to the door. Cooper followed him. The door slammed behind them. My muscles eased and I tilted my head back on the stone. Not their Kaebha. My Lycaea.

'For now. If she survives.'

The woman stood in the shadows of the room, one hand lifting her dark locks. Her rosy lips curled upwards, her skin white in the dim light of the candles. She was tall and beautiful, and she walked like a cat. I did not suffer a moment of doubt. In spite of the cunning beauty and the cruel smile, something in her sharp eyes reminded me of Lycaea. I knew, without question, that this was her mother. Melana. The Dealer.

As she leaned over me on the slab, one hand came to stroke my neck.

'Poor boy,' she crooned. I flinched at her touch. She moved her hand to where I was chained, whispering a quiet word. The chains dissolved in her hands, falling to sand on the floor. For a while I did not move, not wanting to risk it.

I found my voice. 'Help *her*.'

She clicked her tongue against her teeth and took my arm. Her grip was surprisingly strong as she pulled me upright. Her fingers dug into my shoulders as she held them tight.

'I already have,' she replied, voice sharp. 'Come. We need Hemanlok.' She extended an imperious hand towards me. 'Take it,' she ordered, and for a moment I saw Lycaea in her expression. I accepted her hand, ignoring the pain in my arm. She threw her head back, her dark curls flowing away from her face as light surrounded us. I was unprepared for the jolt that accompanied this. Tingling sensations spread through my limbs and torso, a feeling as if I were being split in two. Then I hit the ground, hard.

For a moment my muscles were too tense to function; then I rolled over, my eyes still closed. The early morning sun warmed my skin and when I opened my eyes and sat up, it blinded me. It did not matter. I could hear everything. And my nose told me more than enough. I was out of Caerwyn.

'Lowell!'

Moth wrapped her arms about me. I could smell her tears. I gasped for air. She rubbed my back, and rocked me. Dodge crouched on my other side, laughing.

'I canna believe you're alive!' he exclaimed. 'Luck of the Bonny Gods, lad!'

I looked around. We were outside of Caerwyn. She had taken me out of Caerwyn. I shuddered, fought the urge to vomit. Melana herself seemed unaffected by the travel. She stood a few feet away from us, talking to Hemanlok. The rest of the Own were gathered around us. We were in a rocky copse, surrounded and protected by stone ridges. I could smell the army. They were somewhere close. Mitri, Hywe, and Salvi were there with us.

'What did they do to you?' Moth whispered. Her hand was on my bloodied arm and shoulder.

I ignored her question. 'Lycaea is gone from her cell, but it is only a matter of time before they find her.' I jerked around to face Melana. 'Why didn't you bring her here?'

'She only dealt to get you out,' she drawled. 'We needed a distraction, and she volunteered for the role.'

I twitched as Moth put her hand over my wound. She breathed a soft word, and sparks ran along her hands. The injuries flared, then went cold, then numbed. I looked away, not wanting to see her power weave my skin back together.

'We need to attack now, then,' Mitri said. 'Boss, are we ready?'

'Oh aye,' Hemanlok replied. 'We're ready.' He started to walk towards the edge of the copse, but Melana caught his shirt. She turned him to face her.

'Lycaea kills Leldh,' she said. 'That was my deal with her. Not you. Not me. Lycaea kills him. Do you hear me, Hemanlok? I'll not be thwarted in this. His blood, by her hand.'

He reached up to her neck and turned her head so as to whisper into her ear. She remained still as Hemanlok said something to her in low tones. When he drew back, she nodded sharply. He gave a wolfish grin and gripped her hand. Sparks flew about their fingers, sealing whatever bargain they had made.

'Tell them to meet me on the rooftops,' he said. Then he swept a hand about, to catch the attention of the Own. 'You lot get ready, get armed. I'll bring her back here first. As soon as we're here, the army needs to start marching, so get to the officers and tell them to ready their troops now. And you, Melana…'

Melana flipped her hair over her shoulder. 'What?' she demanded.

Hemanlok smirked at her. 'Wait until I come back with the brat. Then meet us at the gates. You got that?'

'Indeed.' She made as if to turn, but Hemanlok stopped her again.

'Lana.'

'*What?*'

Hemanlok's white teeth flashed into a sudden, unexpected grin.

'Raise hell,' he told her.

A smile spread over Melana's face and she nodded. 'I can do that.'

Lycaea

Melana's intervention bought me time, and Lowell's freedom. Soldiers clattered behind me. The corridors of Caerwyn were narrow and winding, but I had spent three years there. I knew the fortress well enough. I skidded around corners, knocked into walls. My mouth was dry. It was hard to swallow, hard to breathe. Everything hurt, but I knew Lowell was alive. It charged my legs, pushed me on.

I slid into a hallway, found myself facing a guard. Melana had killed the ones outside my cell. The man facing me drew his sword and lunged. I stepped to the side, grabbed his arm and snapped it backwards. He screamed. The sword clattered to the ground and I snatched it and ran him through. Blood splashed onto the flagstones. I pulled the sword out. Forced myself forward.

The east side of the fortress was the best point of exit. If the army had made it through the mountain-pass they would be waiting there. It was my best chance of getting reinforcements, walking into battle rather than dying first. I had never run so fast. I swung into alcoves to avoid soldiers. Sweat coursed down my face, ran over my back and pasted my clothes to my body. Twice I slipped, fell on my elbows and knees, almost gutted myself with the sword I had stolen. Both times, I had to drag myself up and hide. The first time behind a tapestry. The second time in the shadow of a door.

When I made it into the open, light blinded me. I did not have time to let my eyes adjust. The courtyard was too exposed. Walls ran along either side, and buildings beside them. At the top was a ridged walkway. Too far from the roofs to cross, but the ridges would give me more protection. A straight route to the eastern wall. I took the stairs two at a time. Behind me, soldiers clattered out of the narrow halls. I could smell Leldh, knew he was with them. At the top of the stairs I turned, unable to help myself. Stopped. Sweating. I could see him, standing with his soldiers. My hatred seethed. I wanted him dead.

But not now. I had to get out first. Get to the army.

Leldh's eyes met mine, and his lips curled into a smirk. Bowmen halted just behind him. The wall would give me scant protection from their arrows. Daeman gave the orders and the bowmen lifted their weapons.

An arrow was released. The aim was high. It *missed*. I dodged to the side and my feet slipped, I sucked in air and fell and for a dread moment there was nothing but me and the air.

And then a jolt. I stared at the ground beneath me with wide eyes, taking in a sharp gasp. Arrows zipped past me and I could feel their deadly hum as they cleft the air.

Something was holding me by the scruff of my neck, the grip firm. I barely swung as I was lifted back onto the ledge. Perhaps I was already dead.

Taking a shuddering breath, I risked looking up. My heart almost stopped. I dangled limp as Hemanlok steadied me. He had none of my uncertainty with the height and narrow ledge, was as balanced as if he had been on level ground.

I choked out something inarticulate. Above the ringing in my ears I could make out Daeman's shouts. And the pounding of my heart had never been such a welcome sound.

Hemanlok hauled me over the edge of the wall, keeping a good grip as he swung over. There was a large gap between us and the next building: too much for me, and a wide distance even for the big Watcher. Hemanlok did not baulk. He adjusted his grip on me and leapt from the wall to the roof, as I had seen him do so many times in Luthan. Once there, he set me down on a flat section of roof. I sank onto it, curling up. My breathing was too fast. I thought my lungs would explode.

Once Hemanlok was beside me he picked me up like a child. I grabbed the front of his jacket. He moved to the edge of the roof. In a single great stride, he cleared the distance from one building to another. To Hemanlok, every rooftop was the same, and his blindness made no difference at all.

We descended, crossing from the highest rooftops to the lower ones. We were almost at the ground by the time Leldh's men had made it to the highest roof. Hemanlok chuckled as we reached the last roof. I turned in time to see Melana's Shadows descending on the soldiers, moving like spiders. The masked, cloaked figures were merciless; intent on their prey. I could not tear my eyes from them. Soldiers were flung from the rooftop. Cracked and splattered on the ground below. One of the Shadows grabbed a man, hauled him close. Dark tentacles wormed from beneath the Shadow's mask. Tore the soldier's throat open. Sucked at the gaping hole in his neck. I gagged.

Hemanlok spun me to face the edge of the roof. He threw us off. We hit the ground hard but he broke my fall. The wind was knocked from my lungs but I had no time to recover. I rolled away from Hemanlok and stumbled to my feet, trying to keep track of the ground and work out where we were.

To the north-east, where the rocks were craggy and sharp and Caerwyn was raised. Not so steep as the west side, which framed the river. A floor of rock ended abruptly at a small cliff a few yards away. Not wanting to risk stumbling over, I steadied myself on a boulder.

'Move, brat,' Hemanlok ordered. He started to drag me towards the edge of the cliff. I dug my feet into a dip in the rock, setting my jaw as new suspicion dawned in my mind. I had been fooled before with images of my gang. I would not be fooled again. He was in a perfect position to throw me over the cliff. After being moved from that cell, I would not be killed just when I was so close to freedom.

The Watcher growled. 'A bit late to be wise, brat.'

He came to face me, setting his large, gloved hands on my shoulders. Every inch of my body ached and strained, and I knew I was a mess. In the face of his collected, unruffled aura, I felt as I had when I first joined his gang: small, inadequate and inexperienced.

'You've been Leldh's creature for three years. He made you torture people. He made you kill people. He took everything from you.' His grip on my shoulders tightened. 'And now it's time to take everything back. You got that, Lycaea? You got me?'

I gaped at him, stricken mute.

'Mayhap you got me mistaken.' His voice took an edge. 'That weren't encouragement, brat. That was an order. C'mon. We're going. Unless you'd like to go back into that cell?'

I followed him to the edge of the cliff. He began to descend, and I watched him for a moment. My hands were still stiff and numb with the cold. There was no way I would make it to the bottom.

'You'll never make it t'the bottom,' Flicker scoffed. 'It's too far for a brat like you. You'll fall and break your neck. And the boss'll have my hide.'

'Go and boil your head in horse piss,' I retorted. I started down the side of the building. My hands burned. Flicker let out a low cry of exasperation, coming to the edge of the roof.

'You'll die!' she called down. 'Come back here before you fall!'

'Fall?' I asked. 'Not likely!' I sped up and forgot the pain in my hands, swinging from one windowsill to the other, finding footholds with bare hands and feet.

I cleared my head. Take everything back, Hemanlok had said.

I clenched my teeth and started to scale the small cliff.

It was difficult to grip the stone for a while. My fingers slipped and my feet fumbled to find the right holds. It was like I was sixteen all over again, trying to make my way down a Luthanese wall. I risked a smile. Trying to keep up with Flicker and Mitri. There was a rhythm to the climb. Breathe in, find a hold. Breathe out, lower yourself. The muscles adjusted to it. They knew the rhythm. It was like scaling rigging, like climbing a tree. The whole world was Luthan. Just bigger.

Breathe in, find a hold. Breathe out, lower yourself.

My blood pounded, steady and regular.

At one point I slipped. Stones rained down from my footholds and my hands dragged along the rock, searching for something to grip. I slid until I was level with Hemanlok. I caught a rock that jutted out and looked to him, my heart racing. He snorted, face turned away.

'That's one way of getting down,' he remarked wryly as he went on. 'Just miss all your grips until you either kill yourself or reach the bottom. Novel approach, brat. Might wanna try it out some other time, though. We got other things to think about.'

I said nothing for the rest of the descent, but I felt warm to my core. As far as Hemanlok was concerned I was as Rogue as I had ever been.

We reached the ground some time later, Hemanlok unruffled as ever, me sweating and flushed in the face. We hiked around the rock, heading south. The day was growing warm in spite of the snow, and the sun was high. I rubbed my aching eyes. Hemanlok stopped in the shadow of an escarpment. I looked at him expectantly.

'What now?'

'We regroup and plan,' Hemanlok said.

'Regroup with whom? What about Wolf? Melana?'

'Trust me,' he said. The conversation had ended. His lips curled into a smirk. I settled my hands on my hips, feigning indifference as I leaned with him against the rock. It was our old game of pretend. I knew we were waiting for something. It would come, and it would come soon. I just had to trust.

It was only a few moments before a familiar scent drew near. I pushed off from the wall, staring at Hemanlok. His teeth flashed into one of his rare smiles and he nodded. I took a few hesitant steps forward, looking over the expanse of cliffs and mountains about us. The scent was drawing closer, mingling with sweat and dust. Behind one of those ridges, someone was searching for us.

Then Lowell darted out from behind a ridge, flung his arms about me. My arms locked about his shoulders. We were both talking at the same time over one another; half-broken, disjointed phrases that said nothing and everything.

I reached out to wipe the tears from his cheeks just as he did the same to mine.

Hemanlok, never one for emotional display, cut through what Lowell was about to say.

'No time, brats. Much as I love hearing how wonderful it is to be alive, we gotta get a move on.'

'Where are the others?' I asked, but he was already on the move, striding along the rocky ground as if it were the tunnel leading to the Den.

'Getting together the army,' he said. 'We march *now.* You and Wolf are to go in and find the prisoners. Get the weak and wounded out. Bring the rest in to fight.'

We followed our boss along pathways, winding about tall rock faces. Caerwyn loomed over us. For so long, I had borne that shadow upon my shoulders.

We halted by a corner, peering around. The entrance to Caerwyn stood in plain view; surrounded by pillars and stone workings. Ten guards paced the edges, clad in their red and black. Across from us, about a corner on the other side, I could make out a shadowy figure.

'Melana,' Hemanlok muttered. I drew in a sharp breath. It *was* my mother, hips swaying as she moved over to the guards. I watched, transfixed. The guards raised their weapons at her, but she spread her hands wide, showing she was unarmed. Her voice was low when she spoke, and did not carry far. Hemanlok must have heard what she said, however, for his eyebrows shot up and his lip curled.

'Hell,' he muttered.

'What is it?' Lowell asked. 'What is she doing?'

'What Melana does best,' Hemanlok responded. 'Manipulating and seducing. This won't take long.'

We watched as Melana reached the soldiers. She said something else to them and after a moment they both laughed. I had seen this game played out many times. She could have achieved the whole thing with just a word, but like a cat she enjoyed the play. The physical contact, which she craved.

She pressed her lips to one man's neck. He stiffened, then went slack in her embrace. She turned to the other and repeated the gesture. The man sank to his knees and fell on his face.

The remaining guards started towards her, but Hemanlok was already there. Fast. Lethal. Moving with impossible speed for a man of his size. The soldiers he killed did not have time to draw a breath before they were on the ground. We stayed back. I watched in silence as the Assassin worked. Lowell lowered his eyes. Muttered a prayer. Hemanlok turned back to us and sheathed his blades. His face was fixed in a rare grin. I had forgotten the pure pleasure he took from killing.

Melana, one hand resting on her hip, beckoned to us. We hurried forward and the rest of the Own came from the other side, rushing to the door, where Melana handed Lowell a knife. I came last, eyeing my mother. She handed me two daggers for myself. Before I could move on, she caught my shoulder and pushed my staff into my hand. Grudging gratitude swept over me as I gripped my weapon, though I did not know how she got hold of it. I nodded to her, and her words stopped me before I could proceed.

'It is good.'

'What is?' I lifted my chin, surprised to find her mirroring the action.

'That you are alive.' She paused, then nodded. 'Yes. It is... good.'

'I am glad you feel that way.' A respectful silence settled between us before I released her from it. 'Come on. We have to go.'

'As do I.' She stepped away from me. 'I have my people to prepare.' She wriggled her shoulders, tipped her head back, and smiled as darkness crept from the walls. It wrapped about her body, hugging her for a moment before sucking her into the darkness. I shuddered and turned away. Had to trust her to return when we needed her.

We congregated in an alcove, coming together to hear Hemanlok's low commands. 'Brat, Wolf, you need to go through and find survivors. Bring anyone you can. Meet at the courtyard within the hour. If you can be there sooner, do what you want, but stay out of sight. Wait for the signal before you come into the courtyard for combat.'

'What's the signal, boss?'

'When things start blowing up,' Hemanlok grinned.

'Are the souther-waer coming?' Lowell demanded.

'On their way,' Hemanlok said. 'They found more recruits. We can't wait for them, though. Things are already moving, and Leldh knows it. We can't give him a chance to reinforce his position. By now, he'll know of the army. He'll be amassing his own people.' He drew himself upright. 'Go. Now. We're counting on you.'

I could hear, in the distance, the sound of drumming feet and orders being shouted down the ranks. Ours or Leldh's, I could not tell. There could be no delay. I had made the deal with Melana. I had to be the one to kill Leldh. And with the Ultimo-folk slain – *My fault!* my mind screamed – we needed the prisoners to help us.

I took Lowell's hand, and we left Hemanlok. We slipped through the gate and past the courtyard, into the halls of Caerwyn itself. The stairs coiled about the building like a serpent, long and narrow. The way was lit with candles, less frequent as we approached the cells. If there was a breakout, Daeman did not want the prisoners to be able to see where they were going. Lowell stayed close. His scent kept me grounded, kept me from forgetting who I was. Held Kaebha at bay.

This time, we met no one in the corridors. Leldh's soldiers had all been called onto the walls. I knew they would be readying vats of oil and siege-weapons. I tried not to think on it. I tried not to imagine the people of Luthan being burnt and bombarded.

We stopped by the cells, the stink, I could tell, hitting Lowell with physical force. I worked the lock on the door that led to the row of cells. It was a simple mechanism; Cooper had once shown me how to get around it. Clicks echoed down the hall as locks snapped open and I gave a grim smile. Something good could come of me yet. I pushed the door open, stepped onto the row. A simple pathway between the lives of the damned and the destroyed.

The prisoners cowered back. Sometimes, as many as two score people were crammed into each of the small, squalid cells. It was as easy to die of suffocation as anything else.

I was suddenly mute. How could I speak to these people? These people. I had helped to imprison some of them; I had tortured some of them.

Lowell stepped forward, calm and steady. Level when my own mind was in turmoil.

'We are here to help you,' he said, 'but there is a battle still to be won, and we cannot do it alone. If you are able to fight, please come to the front of the cell.'

For a while, there was no movement. Then some of them started shuffling to the front of their cells. Most of them were disabled in some fashion; missing fingers or limbs. But they were willing to fight.

Lowell rested a hand on my shoulder. 'Go,' he said. 'I will find the other waer, and meet you out there.'

I kissed him. 'Be safe,' I said as I left him.

Lowell

I will never forget the children we pulled from those cells. Skinny mites with large eyes and pale faces. Three of them had been born in the cells and had never been outside. There were nine children in total. They gathered against the back wall, eyeing me. In spite of my coaxing, they would not move.

The adults clumped together and watched me with haunted eyes. I tried to speak calmly, with authority.

'We need someone who is able to take the children away from here, to safety.'

An old woman stepped from amongst them, raising a wrinkled hand. From the way the young ones rushed to her, it was evident she had been taking care of them. Eight of the children flocked about her. For a while, the last escaped my attention. He was a small, dark child and he lingered in the shadows. When I noticed him, he shrank away from the light. But I could see there was a set to his face. A familiar nose and pointed chin. Under the smell of grime and mould, there was a trace of family there; of nights by the hearth and days spent in the long, fresh grass.

I stared at the boy in shock. Before I could prevent it, a hoarse choke ripped itself from my mouth. The boy spun. Our gazes met and I took a step backwards. His face, previously obscured by the shadows, was a mess of scars. Burns. Some were still angry with an infection that had left one of his eyes cloudy with blindness. When he stretched a hand out, several of the fingers were missing, the rest of the hand malformed due to more burns still.

He was my little brother; a baby, and yet a child no more.

I came to crouch before him. There was no recognition there. When I reached out a hand he flinched back with a growl. The old woman spoke.

'Dragged him outta a burning house, they did,' she said in rough accents. She was not from the Valley, but sounded like she was one of the chipre-folk. 'Barely got him out alive, poor mite. He's turned in the head though. Never does naught but growls at people, he does. When they moved the others of his kind they left him behind by accident.'

I ran a hand over my face. My little brother. Our Kemp. And he was alive. My mind almost refused to comprehend it. For months, I had thought him perished. There had been almost no chance of getting him out of that house. My eyes were suddenly burning. It was hard to see through a blur of tears. I stretched my hands out to my brother. He snapped at me, trying to bite, but I pulled him into a gentle embrace before he could take off one of my fingers. He was rigid in my arms. Then he began to squirm.

'You said "his kind",' I managed. 'Where did they go?'

'Dunno.'

I did not want to let him go, but he would not be safe with me. I had to send him away. I released him, and he hobbled away from me, hid behind the elderly woman.

'Someone go with them,' I said hoarsely. 'Keep them safe.'

The old woman gathered the children close and led them down the hallway, flanked on either side by other adult prisoners. Kemp trailed a few feet behind them. He did not look back. My throat constricted. Kemp.

I forced myself to turn my attention away. There was a battle still to be fought. I would reclaim him after, and try to recover what had been lost.

The children and the old woman were followed by the many who were sick or injured, or had no fighting skill. They left us with almost two-score of people who were able to fight. There was no way of telling if the souther-waer would reach us in time, or if Luthan's army would succeed unaided.

I gritted my teeth. We needed more. We needed my people.

'Is there anyone else?' I asked. 'Anyone from the Gwydhan Valley? People with the dark hair and pale skin? And brown eyes?' The people stared at me, mystified. Some shook their heads.

'When they feed us, they take more food in there.' A scraggly boy of perhaps seventeen spoke up. He pointed to a door. It led to a narrow, dark tunnel.

The tunnel was so thin we had to walk in single file with our elbows tucked in to our sides. I had to stoop; the ceiling was low, too low for an adult to walk through comfortably.

We came out into the open; another row of cells. It took

some time for my eyes to adjust to the light. I stood blinking in the middle of the path between the tunnels. Then, as my eyes adjusted, a welcome sight greeted me.

Women, men and children gathered in the cells. Pale-skinned and dark-haired. Slender and small, with the scent of the waer. Kinsmen and women. Wolves. I was looking upon the remnants of my old life; and tattered and shredded though they were, they lived still. I ran to the locks and started to explain our situation. An excited buzz filled the cells. They had been hurt and frightened, but these were not the cowed prisoners we had seen in the other cells.

The first door opened and my people rushed out. They crowded about us, speaking in the familiar accents I had so missed. I saw childhood playmates, old teachers and elders, respected members of our community.

We were a pack. It was something the Own had been able to imitate, but not to replicate. Nothing could capture the sense of a pack like the Valley waer could.

'Two groups. Get into two groups. Those able to fight, and those who cannot.'

Lord Alwyn pushed his way to the front. He was beaten and battered, but there was strength in him still. I stood taller, and he reached a hand to clasp mine.

'Well-met, Master Sencha,' he said.

'My lord.'

I addressed the two groups. 'If you are unable to fight, go through the tunnels and take the stairs. Stay as quiet as you can. There are still soldiers throughout Caerwyn, though it is our hope that Luthan's army has drawn them to the east side of the Keep. Lord Alwyn, I ask for you to choose five others and escort them safely out of Caerwyn. And then, when they are safe, return to fight.'

I outlined the rest of the route and we ascended through the tunnel. I was unaccustomed to my people being so unruly. They demanded answers from other prisoners, spoke with excitement of the battle, and pain at what they had loved and lost. The old decorum remained, but was charged by anger. It was a cry for justice, and to put ghosts to rest.

We raced down the stairs. By the time we were in the main section of the fortress, fallen soldiers marked the path. There was a dull sound that grew into a roar. The ground shook. I stumbled. Black, acrid clouds rose from beyond the wall. Blast-powder. I bared my teeth. *Hemanlok.* The walls had fallen. Our people were in.

Rubble was scattered across the floor and the dust made it difficult to breathe or see clearly. Some men screamed, trapped under large stones. We picked around those who implored us for aid. I forced myself to recall what they had done to us. I looked back to the waerwolves we had freed. They walked close together, shoulders high. One woman had Shifted already and her hackles rose with each step.

I focused on Lycaea. She was close, or her thoughts would not have been interleaved so strongly with mine. I tried to scent her out over the dust, but it was impossible. We increased our pace. Sounds of battle grew louder, and after a while the courtyard came into view. We shrank against the wall, hidden from view by the rise in the land and a set of barracks. Beyond the wall, battle raged. We could smell the dead and the dying. I peered around the corner. Almost turned to run. Men and woman struggled through the crush of combat. Blood.

Screams. Someone fell and was trampled. Leldh's soldiers tore through the ranks of the Luthanese, cutting them down.

Behind me, someone Shifted, and the blast of energy released stirred the air, lifting the hair on the back of my neck. I launched forward. The Shift was effortless. A snarl ripped from my throat, and the ground rushed past me. My paws were nearly skinned with the pace. My people joined me. Death was on the wind, in our voice, in our soul.

Blood. Sweat. Earth. The howl, the hunt. The waer plunged into the forces of the soldiers, an unstoppable river of fur and fang. There was an answering roar from the fighters in the courtyard. Waer formed a guard, charging forward in a pincer movement to cut into a row of soldiers. Steel shone in the sun and clashed. The attack was ferocious, the retaliation no less so.

I dived through the fray, desperate to find Lycaea. My nose was useless in detecting her, for the smells of battle pervaded every other scent. I relied instead on our soul-bond. In my Form, I was aware of the people clustering around me; my mind probed at each, skimming over them. I recognised some. Hywe, Donovan, neighbours from the Valley. Then, like a burst of light, a green, tightly controlled mind grazed against mine. I raced towards Lycaea, ducking between a waer and a soldier locked in combat. The soldier fell back, expecting me to join in attacking him, and the waer gained ground. I did not look back to see the outcome.

Lycaea was pitted against Cooper. I skidded to a stop, not wanting to distract her. Keeping close to the ground, I slunk around to crouch by a pillar, ready to intervene. She worked with precise, hard movements, her staff a blur as it thudded against the flat of Cooper's blade. She was filthy, stained with sweat and blood and dust. It was a stark contrast to Cooper. He was clean, his uniform in order and his sword buzzing like a hornet.

A growl ripped from my throat. Lycaea did not turn, but her mind locked with mine. I edged closer, feeling each breath, each heartbeat. They were both skilled. Daeman's best. But Cooper was not tired or injured. And he was wearing Lycaea down. Her exhaustion seeped through me. My blood was sluggish, my limbs heavy and sore. Even if Cooper was dead, there was still Daeman to best if the battle was to be won, and however many more soldiers besides. There was no end to the striking limbs, the blood in the dirt, the bodies.

I pulled myself from her mind as a man drove a spear into the ground by my stomach. I rolled and snarled at him, ready to jump. Flicker took him out with her whip, the metal star at the end of one tail lashing at his eye. Blood and fluid spurted to the ground. He screamed. I turned away. Lycaea was tiring too quickly.

'Shift, Lycaea!' I screamed above the sound of battle. My mind locked with hers, pressing the thought at her. '*Shift!*'

Her limbs contorted, her body adapting to the Shift. Energy split from her, blasting the ground. The dust rose and stones flew out, hitting my flank. I winced, but the mild pain was shunted aside with the rush her Shift gave me. The soul-bond charged us both.

Cooper had more to deal with than stones. He had been unprepared for the Shift, and stumbled backwards. His sword, mid-strike, flew from his hand and spun a few feet away. With new life, Lycaea sprang at him, carrying him to the ground.

Cooper shouted, and the shout became a scream as Lycaea clawed at him, opened her jaws upon his neck and bit down. His shriek died into a gurgle. Lycaea stumbled back, her steely fur stained crimson. She had no time to dwell on the victory. People were already filling the space their combat had taken place in, stepping over or on Cooper's body with no heed for it. I reached her side, taking her scruff between my teeth and pulling her into a clear space where she could breathe. She panted. Blood soaked her muzzle and her front, flecking her body down to the tail.

Luthan's army was deteriorating. We were too few. The waer, ferocious in their initial attacks, were starting to wane. Deprivation and months of mistreatment weakened them. I saw a group of soldiers fall upon Hywe, and I knew he was dead before they came away. Donovan and Flicker fought back-to-back, surrounded by armed men. Donovan was bleeding, holding his side with one hand as the other vainly swung his sword. Mitri was on the ground, motionless, defended by Shard and Salvi.

I was at Lycaea's side. She Shifted back, painfully. She had not had the time to remove her clothes before, and they had ripped and torn with the Shift. They hung from her in rags now. The wound in her shoulder, half-healed by her last Shift, had fully closed over. She was shaken and breathless, but her eyes were wild with a fierce joy. She grabbed her staff from where it had fallen on the ground.

The ground shook. A clap, then a roar, and walls about us fell in a smothering of dust. Snap-sticks and durlow oil. Blastpowder. The smells were acrid, poisonous, but they swelled my heart. *Hemanlok*.

I could not see Hemanlok himself, but I could see people slammed back as he walked by. Melana joined him. I saw her, briefly. Her arms reached skyward and shadows poured from her fingertips, whipped about her head. Her people fanned out behind her, slipping into dim corners of the courtyard and dragging soldiers into their embrace. I watched dark tendrils crawl about a man's neck, then snap it. Another man vomited an inky-black substance, then twitched on the ground until he died. The Shadows descended on him. They consumed him.

A howl followed the sound of a heavy explosion. I jerked around. It was like no howl I had heard before. Deeper, throatier, born of sand and rock. I stared, motionless, as the souther-waer hit us like a hammer through glass.

Lycaea

Blood and fur. Howls. The souther-waer swept through the ranks and fell upon their prey. We had contacted only the Greypaws and the Rustfurs, but half the desert came to our aid. I knew now why they had taken so long. They had been recruiting. I found my voice lifting with theirs, inarticulate and triumphant. Leldh's soldiers started to fall back.

We needed to find Leldh.

The rush of the Shift was still on me. I gripped Lowell's fur, not needing to speak to communicate with him. We broke into a run. Headed for Hemanlok, because around him we would be out of danger while we searched for Leldh. There was no point trying to sniff the Kudhienn out. The battle was a rage of stench, and there was no picking one from another. My staff swung, knocking someone away as they lunged at Lowell. Lowell ducked between two combatants. Something whirred over my head and hit a man standing on the wall. People from within Caerwyn's battlements fired their hackbuts and arrows, but they were no match for us. A wall exploded. Waer and Luthanese poured in.

We reached Hemanlok. He was all brute force and darkness. Melana skipped and laughed behind him. Black vines shot from her hands. One pierced a man's chest and I watched him die in a burst of blood and blackness. Lowell started back and growled. I kept my hand on his back. His fur was warm and sweat-damp. Hemanlok rounded to face us.

'Leldh,' I shouted to him. 'Boss, help us find him!'

'Melana!' he snapped back. My mother turned and tossed her head back. Her eyes flooded, became black. Her hand shot to the east.

'Derry,' she slurred.

'Derry's safe,' Hemanlok snapped. 'She's back at the camp with Dodge and the other healers.'

'Derry.' Melana's eyes flickered back to blue and her voice rose into a scream. '*The Healer!*'

I broke into a run before Hemanlok could move. Lowell was with me. Melana lunged behind us, grabbed us. Shadows sucked us in. They filled my lungs. I screamed, and my voice cracked as we came out the other side, by the eastern wall. In the shadow of Caerwyn, on the edge of the battle. We hit the ground. I dragged myself to my feet. My bones felt waterlogged. Shadow-logged. Lowell whined, struggling to stand. A familiar scent rushed into my nose. My muscles tensed. I stared at Leldh.

And Moth.

The Healer stood stiff and quiet, her chin high. Leldh held her tight. One hand across her stomach, the other gripping a knife. She was already injured. Her lip was split. Bruises flowered on her neck and face. Her dress was spattered crimson. *Dodge,* I thought, but could not form words. The storyteller was prone in the dirt, a dark pool of blood gathering about his body. He twitched horribly.

'Well, now,' Leldh said. 'Here we are.'

'Let her go,' Melana hissed.

'Step back, Wytch,' he replied. 'Your time is done. I want Kaebha. Come here, Kaebha. You and your dog.'

I walked forwards. Moth met my gaze. Her grey eyes were dull. Lowell kept pace with me.

'It has been amusing enough,' Leldh said. 'You did not disappoint. But I grow bored now, and I want my Kaebha back. It is over. Come to heel, and I will let the little Healer go.'

'*He lies.*' Lowell, tense and still, whispered into my mind.

'*I know.*'

'Come to *heel,* Kaebha.'

I could not breathe. At the end of all things, as I had dreaded, it came down to Kaebha and Leldh. It always had.

Leldh smiled. I could count every tooth. I cleared the distance between us and let the defences about my mind drop away. Leldh pushed Moth away from him. Melana stepped through a passing shadow. She stepped out with her arms around Moth, then hauled her back. Moth choked as black tendrils curled about her, and then they both disappeared.

I closed my eyes.

Just us now. Lowell. Daeman Leldh. And me.

Kaebha opened my eyes.

*

Kaebha kept her eyes fixed on Leldh. She saw everything differently from these eyes; the eyes she had shunned for so long. Leldh had always told her wolves were feral, that the more she rejected that side of her, the better she would be. But his words had been spider webs. Thin, and wrought of silver. For the first time, he had no sway over her.

The black wolf pressed close to her side, offering his wordless support. His mind settled against hers. He was a welcome passenger in the carriage of her thoughts, brown eyes guiding her through the confusion to a set, clear understanding. She had only ever been breathing for this moment.

They faced Daeman Leldh as woman and wolf. Her back was straight and her green eyes locked with his golden gaze. One hand rested on the black wolf's back, loose and relaxed.

Daeman smiled. 'You heed commands so well,' he congratulated her. 'Is it because you think your precious Watchers can save you? They have no power here. The Healer lacks the strength, the Dealer lacks the focus and the other…' His lip curled in distaste, but she saw fear flicker in his eyes. 'The other is busy trying to save his little Rogues.' He stepped closer. 'They cannot help you.' He drew a blade from his scabbard, a coldness settling over his lips and turning the edges down. Kaebha spun the staff in her hand, her free palm still resting on the black wolf's fur.

'I will not be yours again. You've lost, Daeman. No matter what happens here, you've lost.'

Daeman's sword lashed out and caught her arm. The skin tore and blood spat at the ground. Kaebha caught her breath. Her staff spun again, knocking the blade to push it away. The wolf at her side snarled and moved one paw closer to Daeman, growling. Kaebha was relaxed. She set her feet apart and bent at the knees to secure her balance. Daeman's sword hissed through the air again only this time she was ready. She deflected it with her staff and they began to move in a silent dance, locked in steps each knew too well. She remembered her lessons from him. She knew how he worked. Years ago, when he took her for the first time, he had the element of surprise. Now there was nothing but the old steps they had waltzed together for three years.

He broke their routine first, jumping backwards and pulling something from where it hung at his belt. Silver. She could feel the hissing heat of it. She and the wolf snarled together, dropping away. It was difficult to see the object he held in the sword-free hand. The wolf recognised it first, and fed the information through to Kaebha. A clamp. A silver clamp. Kaebha stepped in front of the wolf, protecting him. If she was injured, she could fight on. If he was, she was not so sure.

Kaebha drove her staff at Daeman's knees. His sword bit at her hand and she almost lost her grip on the staff. She caught it with her free hand and rammed the side into Daeman's shoulder. With sharp, hard movements, he twisted so his weight pressed the staff down, his sword coming across to hit her side. Kaebha's knees buckled. Daeman threw his hand out, and the clamp disappeared. The wolf snarled. Perhaps he felt it before even she did. All she registered at first was the sound. A hiss, like a snake. Then the faint smell that rose, like burnt meat. And then the pain, spitting through her leg.

Kaebha blinked. Suddenly she was on the ground. Daeman tossed out a nonchalant hand and flung Kaebha's growling companion to the side. The Kudhienn man crouched beside Kaebha and dug his fingers into her shoulders. He wrenched her upwards until they were bare inches apart. He was whispering something, but Kaebha could not tell what he was saying. It was intended as a threat, but all she could hear was the pounding of her blood as it sped to her leg, the rasping of her own breath in her ears. The black wolf was somewhere nearby. He was stunned, too dazed to return to her.

He could do nothing to shield her mind. And neither could she.

Daeman wrapped his thoughts about hers. She baulked. The black wolf's mind stumbled against hers. There was a single moment, a breath of time in which all three minds were linked in a triangle of wills, conflicting and merging. Pain, loss and grief echoed within them all, and were indistinguishable.

Daeman was the first to break free, a mental breath before he dived back into Kaebha's mind once more. He attacked savagely and quickly, thinking to crush her, to destroy her mind and leave her body as a shell. But Kaebha had anticipated the move. As his mind surged forth, she relaxed, letting Daeman's consciousness seep into the corners of her own. She let him feel the warmth there. The soul-bond between herself and the wolf. Expecting resistance, he fell into her without a lifeline. He could not draw back. She embraced him like a tender lover, and he was too shocked to struggle. She felt him vulnerable and young for the briefest of moments, and it was all she needed. Keeping him locked with her, she wrapped Lowell's thoughts around her own.

Lowell's memories, almost completely empty of Daeman, suffused with her own, swirling in unison until Daeman's mind was diminished. His mad, desperate hatred, displaced in Lowell and Lycaea's bond, struggled to break free. But Lycaea's mind still entwined about his, pulling it in, sucking it through the darkness of her own thoughts. Murder, torture, anger, bitterness. And deeper into the soul-bond. Into the depths of trust, redemption, understanding and vulnerability. His wholeness writhed and twitched beneath the onslaught of this unfamiliar power. Then he was gone, smothered by their embrace.

A hand pulled at Kaebha, and her fingers unlocked from the back of Daeman's neck. A knife fell through the air. There was a short, sharp sound, then nothing.

Kaebha watched as people ran over and around her. A face appeared over hers and a hand pressed against her palm. If someone spoke, she did not understand the words. She rested in blood and dirt, and waited for shadows to carry her away. The man beside her took on the Form of a wolf once more, circling her to prevent anyone from crushing them, trampling them in the panic of flight.

The snap-sticks ringing the walls of the courtyard were set alight as the battle started to dwindle, a final burst of defiance to end the fighting. Hemanlok moved the Rogues out of danger, while the souther-waer scrambled to evade falling stones. The waer abandoned their various battles, escaping through any route possible. Only the black wolf stayed, his ears down and his tail low as he stood over Kaebha. He placed his paws on her chest and settled himself across her as stones rained around them.

When they were pulled clear of the rubble, neither wolf nor woman was moving.

'Hold her still. Hold her still, dear, I can't work when she thrashes.'

'He fades fast, Moth. We need you over here.'

'*You will not let my daughter die!*'

We hovered between life and death, strangely aware of both. Dust and rock, blood and sweat, vomit and tears. Moth pressed on my wounds, stemming the flow of blood. Donovan forced something between my teeth. My limbs moved of their own accord, jerking and flailing as pain thrummed through my core. I heard Wolf retch.

Darkness.

'Make sure it is clean. The last thing they need now is the rot.'

Water. My eyes opened to glaring light. My breath was so

loud in my ears that it hurt. I tried to speak, and gentle hands smoothed my hair from my face.

'Don't talk. Rest. We're going home, dear. We're taking you home, it's over now.'

A surge of pain pushed me upwards and I grasped someone's arms. My body tried to Shift, clicked between human and wolf. The pain was unbearable.

'Leldh…' I choked on the name.

'It's over. He's gone. Donovan, come here, I need your help.'

Pushed down again, the smell of herbs creeping into me. I turned my head to the side and found Wolf's face in the haze rising across my vision. His face was grey with pain.

'Lycaea.'

Darkness.

Leather. Salt. Oil. Spice. My mouth was ash. I could not feel my left leg.

I opened my eyes to a dim room. Sunlight struggled at the curtains, which were thick and drawn to keep the room cool. I set my teeth against the throbbing in my head. Luthan, but not the Debajo.

'I love you.' Barely more than a whisper. I am not sure whether I said it or Lowell did. A hand found mine and I felt a kiss upon my knuckles.

'I can't see your face.' I wondered if he could piece together the words from the dry crackle of my voice.

'Just as well.' Lowell lifted my hand and traced it across the swellings on his jaw and temple. My eyes slowly adjusted to the gloom. He was propped up with pillows, on a chair. We were silent, finding our way slowly back to the world.

The door opened. A boy, at first silhouetted by the bright glare, shuffled in. When he drew near I saw that his face was twisted and curled by burns, but I knew he was a Sencha. I looked at Lowell.

'Kemp,' he told me. 'My brother.'

Lowell touched Kemp's head. The boy jerked away and came around to investigate me. He pushed his nose into my hand and sniffed eagerly. I turned my hand over and stroked his head. The left side of his skull was mostly bald, hairless where the burns were most severe. His mouth was pulled down on the same side, showing his teeth. He was missing some. Pity wrapped my lungs. I forced myself to look at Lowell, to ask the terrible, necessary questions.

'Did the Own lose anyone?'

'They lost Hywe and Salvi,' Lowell replied. 'Salvi took a blow intended for Mitri. Hywe was trampled. We almost lost Mitri too, but he's recovering now.'

Grief. Guilt. I could not think of Hywe being crushed, or Salvi bleeding on the ground. The boy, Kemp, climbed onto the bed beside me and rested his chin on my shoulder.

'Dodge?' I asked. Dreaded the answer.

'Alive. Alive, Lycaea. Moth healed him. It was close, but he made it. Leldh was in a hurry. Didn't take the time to finish him off properly.'

I knew the answer to the next question, but I had to ask all the same. Had to be sure.

'Leldh's dead?'

'Dead.' Lowell leaned forwards and pressed his brow against mine. 'It's over, Lycaea. It's done.'

'Stay with me,' I whispered, and he did.

Epilogue

Lycaea never expected there to be a life after Daeman Leldh. For a long time, their fates were so interlocked that she could not imagine an existence without him. But still, after his death she breathed, and her pulse beat strong. A few weeks onward she was able to sit up and talk.

For some time, Lycaea was a shadow of herself. Moth was stretched thin after the battle, healing her husband and as many of the injured as she could. She brought us from the brink of death, but even Watchers have their limits, and finally she could do no more to help us. Even as she could not restore Kemp's sight or his lost fingers, Moth could not fully heal the silver-wound in Lycaea's leg. Those marks of Leldh's cruelty will always be with us.

When Lycaea could walk – albeit hindered by her wound – we took Kemp and followed Moth and Dodge to Tadhg. Further than any Valley waer has travelled, according to our lore. Dodge was slower than usual, his own wounds troubling him at points throughout the journey. Still, his spirits were as hearty as ever in his home city. Surrounded by other storytellers, it seemed only natural for him to turn to us and demand that we tell our tale. He wanted everyone to know what we had fought for, and lost, and loved.

The idea took within me, and at every opportunity during our travels I committed quill to parchment. I gave as much of an account as I could, but without Lycaea's words it was empty. Our story began and finished with Lycaea, and without her it could never truly be complete.

She was reluctant, and I had to argue with her the whole journey from Tadhg back to Luthan, but she gave in. We stopped in Luthan for a while and let her write out the bulk of it. Too many times, I found her hunched over crumpled pages, sobbing uncontrollably. Leldh and Kaebha were gone, but shadows remained. Sometimes, still, she and Kemp woke in sweats, or screaming. Dark nights.

Eventually we decided to make one more journey before we left the past to rest. We did not discuss it; we simply woke one morning, packed our belongings, gathered Kemp and left Luthan.

We came here, to the Valley.

After the battle at Caerwyn, Alwyn brought the survivors back to the Valley. The souther-waer helped to drive out the remaining soldiers and their families. They lingered a few months to help rebuild. We will stay here awhile, in the old bakery, to assist with the restoration of the worship-house and the village. Lycaea has taken some of the women under her wing; those who were left here when the others were taken to Caerwyn. She is teaching them to fight. They are frightened and angry, but I think they will heal in time, as much as any of us can. Lycaea is hoping they will come south with us, to Luthan.

Kemp follows Lycaea everywhere, these days. He remains a wolf in his mind; we are slowly teaching him words: how to speak, and how to be with people again. Lycaea pretends to find him a nuisance, but she spends every spare minute with him and will not hear anyone speak a word against him. Sometimes it is difficult; I remember the young boy he was, and the future he would have had here in the Valley. But I remind myself that he is young, and he has our love to help him mend.

We will not settle here. Lycaea grows restless even now, and I cannot stay where the scars of what happened are still so raw. There is also much to be done in Luthan, for there are changes to be made for the people in the Ultimo. Many lives were lost in the mountains because of the divide in Luthan, and it cannot be allowed to continue. We will do what we can, and then we will return to our travels. Although Lycaea and I work for the Own still, we are not tied to the city. Anyway, Hemanlok is expanding his reach.

For a while, he talked about sending us to Caerwyn to keep track of Melana. It is hard to tell whether she claimed the bastion for sanctuary and peace, or whether she has a longer game in mind. Lycaea and I discussed at length the possibility of going, but eventually we refused. We see the wisdom in being aware of Melana, but our work in Caerwyn is over. We will leave the Watcher business to the Watchers.

Kemp and Lycaea sit on the floor just a few paces from

me. She is using smooth white stones to teach him how to count again. He watches her with his one good eye, solemn and attentive. Usually, slight scents and sounds distract him, but Lycaea always has his complete focus. She is more patient with him than I have ever seen her.

Soon, Kemp and I will observe the Grey Worship, and then we three will go for a walk before the rain starts to fall. I can smell it on the air. The sky will turn crimson tonight, and then black, and then the Valley will be alive with the smells and sounds I used to know so well. It seems fitting to end our tale here, by the swollen river and the wild sheep. We can never restore what was taken from us, but we can remember it, and pay honour to those we lost.

After that, we go where the gods take us.

Acknowledgments

I can't thank everyone enough for the patience, good humour, and support they have shown in the last ten years. Consider this my best attempt:

To Mum and Dad, who encouraged my thirst for stories and who read every draft of my own.

To my brothers Ben, Danny, and Joe, who never complained when I made tea and burnt toast at 3am.

To the team at Text Publishing, especially Editor Extraordinaire Mandy Brett, YA Goddess Steph Speight, Map Master Simon Barnard, and the glorious Imogen Stubbs.

To Juliet Marillier, the wisest person I know, who showed me how to take my book beyond the first draft and who has helped and inspired me ever since.

To the Katharine Susannah Prichard Writers' Centre (KSP) and the Society for Children's Book Writers and Illustrators (SCBWI West) who welcomed me with open arms, and who provide such a haven for writers in Western Australia.

To Jess Caddy, for lending a pair of fresh eyes to later drafts and helping me work out the geography of Oster (and for buckets of herbal tea, countless book chats, and hundreds of entertaining emails).

To Kristin Lane, whose cries of 'I believe in you!' and 'Do the do!' pushed me through long nights of editing – and to Gemma Goepel and Beverly Twomey for their love, enthusiasm, and fantasy know-how.

To Rebecca Warnes, who spent hours brainstorming with me and who helped me celebrate every milestone.

Last (but never least) to Jenn Godfrey (and The Cat) who started me (and Lycaea) out on this journey ten years ago.